Long Road, Many Turnings

Second Edition.

Best wishes,
Mary

MARY McCLAREY

To all my family, with much love and thanks for your warm and generous support, always.

Map of Family Journey.

Carr Family (West Cork)

Maeve (b.1850) *m* Tomas (b.1843)

Seamus (b.1877)   Ruari (b.1879)   Roisin (b.1882)

Collins Family (West Cork)

Hannah Collins (b. 1848) *m* Joseph Collins (b.1840)

Deirdre Riley (b.1875) *m* Michael Collins (b.1870)   Joe Collins (b.1868) *m* Fiona Owens (b.1874)

Michael Og (b.1896) *m* Gina   Dan (b.1897)   Hannah(b.1900)   Kitty (b.1902)   Agnes (b.1907)

Finbarr (b.1916) Eamon (b.1919)

West Family (London & Wales)

Arthur West (b.1869) *m* Doris Williams (b.1870)

William West (b.1894) *m* Kitty Collins (b.1902)   Eve (b.1897)   Elana (b.1898)

Ellen (b.1927)   Daisy (b.1931)   Billy (b.1935)

McCann Family (Northern Ireland)

Margaret Mullins (b.1891) *m* Jimmy McCann (b.1887)

James (b.1919) Maureen (b.1920) Eddie (b.1921) Maisie (b.1923) Annie.(b.1925 d.1935)

Eddie McCann *m* 1947 Ellen West (b.1927)

Toby (b.1948)   Teresa (b.1950)

Contents

Chapter 1. 7

Chapter 2 32

Chapter 3 54

Chapter 4 94

Chapter 5 156

Chapter 6 190

Chapter 7 197

Chapter 8 208

Chapter 9 225

Epilogue 231

Chapter 1.

Roisin. Drimoleague, West Cork, Ireland 1907

'Go now, scholars. Go straight home and stay together,' urged Roisin Carr, as she did every afternoon. Her back aching, her feet sore from standing on the hard, cold floor and her mind elsewhere. A cloudy afternoon, with fitful showers throughout the day, rattled the windowpanes and caused an eye-stinging smoke to blow out of the open peat fire.

Roisin was a keen and dedicated teacher and, although young to be the sole schoolmistress, she could hold the class well enough during lessons. Now she found it impossible to make her voice heard above the hubbub of eleven children ready for release.

With harsh scraping of corner stools on flagstones, swinging of legs recklessly over the rows of wooden benches which provided most of the seating and noisily gathering slates and chalks to bring up to the teacher's high desk, the boys and girls aged between six and twelve, were headed towards the open door.

These children would not dawdle; the day was too cold and damp, and the light was already fading.

Many had around two miles to travel and Roisin often stood at the school doorway watching them, their heads down, crossing the bleak and windswept fields before reaching their homes.

At this time of year, the hawthorn bushes were barren, late autumn was drawing to a close and a whistling wind warned of irritable weather ahead. From the schoolhouse door, Roisin could just discern the outlines of small groupings of cottages and outbuildings across the surrounding open farmland, where families often lived close together, fields divided up for sons.

Today the children were noisy and urgent as they left the schoolroom. Roisin folded her arms and leaned against the wall letting them squeeze out the door as a single entity, like a shoal of fish, wriggling over each other in an attempt to get out. She knew they would soon disperse across the fields and lanes, breaking off into family groups the closer they got to home.

The habit of the mothers was to light a candle and place it in the window. Once the twilight faded it would guide their children home. Roisin wondered whether she would ever light one for her own children and watch them run home, attracted to the candle, like moths.

She closed her eyes for a moment and let herself dream. The older child would see the light first, he would be hungry and would urge the younger children, 'Run faster, hurry up, see, Mammy has the tea on.'

They would splinter from the main group and although the younger ones would be reluctant to part company from their friends they would also be scared to be left behind.

She imagined the younger ones jogging along after their older siblings, stumbling on the rough ground but not stopping.

They would not be like the poorer children in her class who carried their shoes strung around their necks for safekeeping. No, her children would be properly shod, and she would be the best mother, a great help with their homework too.

Roisin opened her eyes and shook her head, her great mane of auburn curly hair drifting out from the bun she had secured that morning. 'I'm well enough in looks,' she told herself, 'and certainly a good worker, any man would see that, but there aren't many looking for a wife with independence and education around here, so it's unlikely, but twenty-five isn't too far gone now is it?'

A tall, solid young woman, with green eyes enhanced by long dark eyelashes and a fair, freckled complexion, she was an only daughter, and standing up to her two boisterous older brothers had made her ambitious and determined.

Smoothing her heavy tweed skirt over her hips she leaned forward one last time to warm her legs against the heat of the peat fire, before reluctantly moving across the room, righting the stools and picking up abandoned items, wondering at the ability of these boys and girls to so readily drop and forget their few possessions.

Would her children do that too, she wondered, feeling keenly the position she occupied in the community. Although she was the teacher, her identity was as a single woman, a situation referred to as, 'Ah, sure she has no family.' She was outspoken and always ready with a quick retort, 'Wild goose never laid a tame egg', she would tell Barry Og, when his hair grew at several angles across his head, just like his father's. Or, 'Every old crow has a young white as snow,' her response to the O'Brian girls boast that Mammy and Dada had praised their progress. She tried to fit in and most of the time it was easy. She had a few friends and her brothers kept in touch. She lived with her mother in the schoolmaster's house, owned by the church.

Her thoughts, as always, returned to the pupils while she tidied the slates and chalk, rubbing her dry dusty hands over the back of her skirt. One child, Kitty Collins, meant more to her than the others. She was a precious goddaughter and Kitty's mother, Deirdre, was her best friend.

Roisin knew Deirdre was having a difficult time coming to terms with her recent loss - a long thin little daughter fully formed with skin like the membrane of an egg. She had arrived cold, still and much too early. Roisin had been there when Deirdre and Michael wrapped and buried the tiny body in the small corner plot at the outer edge of the graveyard.

'That bloody priest, Father Daley,' she muttered. 'He's looked up to and goes unchallenged, but he's no father to this parish. Ha! So, he offers a blessing, but he won't say the Mass for a dead baby.' She shook her head at the memory of the priest and his influence over the parish. Her position at the school provided some security but she knew where the power lay, and she knew to be careful around him.

Damping down the embers of the peat fire she pulled the shawl her mother had woven over her head and across her chest, giving her coat an extra layer of protection against the gathering chill, before taking a great stride out the door and into the schoolyard.

She secured the door with a bar to keep the rising wind from catching, no need for locking she had long ago decided. Stepping carefully around some muddy puddles, she walked towards the house where she knew her mother would be ready with the tea, bunching up her skirts impatiently against her thighs, trying to avoid the gorse bushes which shuddered in the wind, appearing to reach out and snag her.

She wondered what it would be like to walk home in a place where she could wear clothes designed to flatter rather than protect. Dublin, maybe?

She wondered why she had never been there. Or the North? Deciding it would have been better than the countryside at providing her with a longed-for social life she reckoned that she didn't really want to leave now; anyway, Mam would hate to see her go.

Within a minute, she had covered the few hundred yards to her home. She was wrestling with an irritant in her teaching programme. Father Daley wanted more catechism and less history. The families, many of whom were descendants of famine victims wanted history. The children wanted heroic and fantastic stories. 'Boer War, Brian Boru the Irish Giant, the Famine, IRA rebellion, Catechism, reading and writing, a bit of mathematics, Holy God, what do they think should come first?' she asked the empty ground ahead as she strode quickly on. Approaching the house, still muttering to herself about the impossibility of keeping the children's education balanced, she saw in the gathering twilight the outline of Father Daley's horse and cart.

'Ah now, what would he be wanting here? First Communion soon, he's maybe planning a lovely visit to the school to get the children ready for their First Confessions.'
With the oil lamp glowing through the front window it was clear that her mother had brought the priest into the parlour. No doubt he was at this very moment taking tea.

Walking to the rear of the house, she let herself in quietly before hanging her coat on the peg and, taking a deep breath, turning into the best room.

There she was, Mam. Maeve to the women, Mrs Carr to the men, looking like an older version of Roisin. Same thick head of red hair now heavily streaked with grey, tied back tightly in a bun.

Her shoulders broad and strong and wearing her best fine ankle-length skirt, which suggested she might be a woman who spent her time indoors awaiting visitors.

Roisin smiled at the thought, knowing her mother was a busy woman; gardening, growing vegetables, keeping chickens, and always helping the neighbours too. That fine woollen skirt would be hitched up in a trice, tucked into her apron, and on would go the boots at every opportunity. And now her mother was entertaining this uncompromising man, this priest, arrived only last year to the parish, sent unexpectedly by the Bishop of Cork to replace the ailing Father McCarthy.

She reckoned Father Daley was aged not more than forty, a good ten years her mother's junior, his weak blue eyes seemed lacking in any emotion and his pale clean-shaven face might never have seen the sun and wind, so delicate and unlined was his complexion. He was carefully balancing his teacup over the table to ensure no drip would land on his freshly laundered suit, his impossibly white tab collar contrasting starkly with his smart black clerical shirt. Maeve, leaning forward slightly, her hearing was not so good, appeared to be respectfully listening to his views but Roisin expected the conversation would be meandering through liturgical topics of which she knew her mother really had no interest.

She leaned back against the wall, listening a moment, thinking it would never do to interrupt the man. Tea was laid out on the table, best china, freshly baked fruit-bread, and butter.

'All the best, of course, for himself,' noted Roisin. 'Why should a man who has renounced all earthly goods only ever be served tea from the daintiest rose-painted cups?' She resented his assumption that it was always all right for him to have the treats, no sins of the flesh there now, and she wondered what else he liked to treat himself to.

Maeve had looked up sharply as Roisin closed the door gently behind her and now, not liking the look on her mother's face, she braced herself for bad news. 'Good evening, Father, hello Mam.' Roisin stooped to kiss her mother.

'I'll come straight to the point,' announced Father Daley, 'There's been a letter from the bishop asking me to find a teaching placement for a family man who has been employed in Skibreen. The school there has closed, and he needs a job... and a home. I'm sure you understand Roisin, no need for me to spell it out now. This grand house just for yourself and your mother, while a man needs a roof over his head. We'd be lucky to get him and his fine young Catholic family.'

'Why are you telling me this Father?' asked Roisin, frightened by what she had just heard. She was deliberately refusing to believe the implication and determined not to make this easy.

'We will be appointing Schoolmaster O'Reilly to the school after the Christmas break, Roisin. That will give you a few months to find another post and a house for yourself and Mrs Carr here. God willing you will obtain a situation within the parish without too much trouble.

'I myself will give you a grand reference and you're well known across these parts for the fine woman you are. God bless you Roisin, it's His will we must obey, you must trust His holy ways now.'

Roisin, conscious of the sound of her blood pulsing in her ears, felt the solid floor rock beneath her as she moved to reach for her chair.

She had a sense of time standing still. In that moment between entering the room and drawing her chair to the table her understanding of her whole life had changed. Body numb, she was unable to speak, or unwilling to do so, until the priest had left, gulping down his tea, and raising a hand in blessing over the two women.

'Now Roisin, we'll put away the tea and I've here some bacon for your supper,' said her mother returning from seeing the priest out and attempting to sound positive.

Roisin had a pain in her throat, she could hardly swallow and rubbing her hands anxiously up and down her arms, she felt prickles of sweat break out in her armpits. Cold and shaking with the shock, she found it difficult to make her tongue and teeth behave.

'Mam, it's so unfair, I'm a good teacher, so I am, and he has no right to do that, And I love those children, they're mine to bring on, so they are.' Swiping angrily at her face, which now had tears coursing down her cheeks, she felt her eyes stinging more than they had ever done by the smoke from the school peat bricks.

'Now, girl,' her mother's face was turned away, she was pouring tea, afraid to see her daughter's pain. 'You know the church has to make difficult decisions in these times, and you would expect a working man to have the right to a job over a woman. Maybe you should have found yourself a good man and spent your days raising a family, but no, you wanted another life. Well this is how it is, and you have been very fortunate to have had the fine teaching job now for five years, so we will pray tonight for guidance and maybe start a Novena together - you know St Joseph never lets us down. And will you write to your brothers Ruari and Seamus now and ask them what should we do?'

When Roisin's mother finally turned around, she realised her daughter had stormed out of the house minutes earlier and was now angrily kicking the empty milk churn in the back yard, shouting 'Bloody priests, bloody men! Damn the lot of them.'

It was only when Roisin broke the skin on her toes that she stopped kicking. The wind was getting up, mild rain wetting her head and face and the hot angry tears running down to her neck were giving no relief.

She believed she had worked so hard for this job, a diligent pupil at school, then away to college in Cork for two years before returning home, knowing this would be her life now and accepting all that went with it.

No man to herself at night, no children. Since Dada died it was just her and Mam, and the boys of course, when they came home.

Roisin and her mother passed the meal in silence. Pushing food around her plate and refusing to engage further with her mother's plans for prayer, 'I'm not staying in tonight Mam, I'm taking the horse. Don't wait up for me'.

Roisin pulled on her coat, wrapped her woollen shawl around her shoulders and went out through the half door at the back of the house before her mother could object. She knew well that the older woman would lie awake if her daughter was out riding late across the open countryside alone, but tonight she didn't care. Mounting her horse bareback, she cantered across the fields in the direction of town.

Drimoleague, had been a small, although still picturesque, village, until developed into a town when the railway from Dunmanway to Skibbereen opened some thirty years earlier. Since then the town had grown quickly. Roisin had taught the children that two hundred people now lived in Drimoleague with the shops and public houses built over those years changing the town, making Main Street into a main street.

It was a popular, attractive, colourful town and Roisin was always at pains to make sure her pupils appreciated their homeland and were aware of its history.

She rode easily into the edge of the town, tying her horse up to the post by the side of the town's best hotel and moved quickly, with more confidence than she felt, through the front door of O'Sullivan's Bar. She was hit by a wave of warm air, smoke, and beer fumes.

The room was noisy with male voices and smelt of damp from tweed jackets. She shrugged off her shawl while she scanned the floor for the familiar face of her friend.

It was easy to spot Patrick, as most heads had turned to the door when it swung open and, embarrassed by the sudden rush of attention; she smoothed her hair and licked her lips, tasting salt from the earlier angry tears.

Roisin had met Patrick Halligan a year ago after being introduced during a social gathering at the Collins's, before Deirdre had lost her baby. She found him to be an easy companion. He was a bit of an outsider, an Ulsterman, a Northerner, which made her feel safer spending time with him than with other men in the parish and Roisin knew she couldn't afford to start any gossip.

He was an attractive man with a good head of dark curly hair, although too thin for his long frame. He had introduced himself as an agricultural salesman, from Belfast, staying at O'Sullivan's on monthly visits. He'd been enthusiastic in his descriptions of the ways that he supplied horse medicine - worm powder, liniments, and hoof oil across the county. He made the most of his visits by giving himself a bit of a break, he said; walking and generally enjoying the area before heading back up north. That was all she knew. She could tell that he was lonely, seeming to enjoy having an unattached woman to talk to and she asked no questions about his home life or family.

Patrick, like the others, looked up as she came in, a flash of recognition crossing his face as he nodded briefly, not exposing their friendship. Slipping quietly from his seat at the bar at the same time as she made her well-practiced move into a dimly lit snug at the back of the room, he asked,
'Would you take a port and lemon for yourself, now Roisin? I'll get the drinks, so I will.'

Roisin's eyes gradually became accustomed to the change in the light and looking around she, observed, not for the first time, how the place could do with improving. The paint was yellow with nicotine stains and the once cream walls were now a dull brown.

It was impossible to tell where the original colour ended and there were shades ranging from caramel caused by the men's pipes to chocolate patches closer to the open peat fire. The whole place was still lit by oil lamps and candles, although Roisin, knowing that electricity was being used in public buildings in Cork city, hoped it would not be too many years more before the power lines would reach Drimoleague.

O'Sullivan's was a traditional hotel but, whilst most public houses in Ireland had signs on the door saying, "No Women", or, in smarter city areas, had dedicated lounges where women could "take their ease" alongside the men, the owners here had never followed that route. They liked to open the doors to whoever could pay and if that meant accepting women into the bar then the O'Sullivans felt it was not too high a price.

Putting the drinks down on the table between them, Patrick waited for Roisin to begin.

'I'm to lose my job, my teaching job.'

She found she couldn't continue. Having said it out loud made it true, and she didn't know what would follow. She took a swallow of the port and lemon, but only a small one, she wanted it to last her the evening.

'Ach, away, that's terrible bad news Roisin, what's the reason for it?'

'A family man is to come from Skibbereen and take my job and they will take our house too.'

Patrick's clear blue eyes met hers, so different from Father Daley's she thought. No spark in the priest's eyes at all. Patrick responded to her anxious look with a questioning glance. He took a mouthful of stout, placed his glass back on the table wiping his mouth with the back of his hand, 'Will ye get another job, or go away, or what? There's plenty of work in other parts for a grand wee girl like yourself.'

He was trying to sound relaxed and knowledgeable whereas in truth he had no idea. He certainly didn't think that asking his wife Oonagh to help a good-looking young woman friend would be an option.

He liked Roisin, enjoyed her company and was attracted to her looks; particularly her striking red hair and lovely eyes, but he thought he wouldn't want to generate any problems to interfere with his current comfortable existence.

'Sure, I have plenty of choices, Patrick', stressed Roisin, already suspecting she heard a strain of pity in Patrick's voice, and that was an emotion she never could tolerate. 'I might open a school for girls in Drimoleague itself, the...' She stopped, realising that Patrick wasn't listening anymore, and anyway that didn't matter because she wanted to ask him for something else tonight.

'Patrick, I wonder are you travelling back up to the north anytime soon? It would be great to have a bit of time together, maybe even find a nice and private room where we could get to know each other better and chat a while without being overheard?'

Patrick looked surprised, as though he had misunderstood, but when Roisin put her hand over his on the table and raised her eyebrows, it gave him a clear message, one which he would be unlikely to ignore.

Roisin could hardly believe what she was doing, but her inner turmoil was telling her to get back at them. The men, the priests, and the ones who had the power she could never enjoy.

'Not the north, no, Roisin', panic rising at the thought of Oonagh's reaction should she ever see him with Roisin. 'But Dublin now, the middle of December, I could be there, and it would give me time to arrange things, so.'

Patrick's voice stumbled; his face flushed. 'You could take the train to Dublin yourself, an' I'd meet you there, I can arrange a wee bit of business, you can look around at the schools and the like and we will stay at the Castle Hotel. It's a grand place, you'll love it. Need to change in Cork of course, but it could be done. The hotel is right near to Amien Street Station, on Rutland Square itself. Great for the Exhibition too, if you wanted to go whilst I was working. Ye deserve a treat, Roisin, it'll be our Christmas celebration, just the two of us.'

Roisin twisted the stem of her glass back and forth between her palms whilst considering the wisdom of what she was about to do. She felt like a bird of prey, hovering for a moment before swooping. Like the bird she could see where this was leading but she wasn't a predator, she did not need to do this to survive.

She wondered whether this the most reckless, ill-considered decision she could make but before leaving O'Sullivan's it had been agreed.

Stepping outside, she saw that it was still raining, but softly now, with a pale moon slowly appearing and disappearing behind clouds giving just enough light to see the outline of her horse, tied to the post.

A soft whinny of recognition as Roisin untied him caused her to wonder who might have seen him here, but too late now to worry about gossip. No need for a saddle, she had been riding bareback, like all the children did, since she was eight years old.

'It's done now,' she muttered aloud. 'They couldn't stop me going off and doing what I wanted then, and they still can't.' Not being entirely clear who she was referring to, but feeling gratified at having taken action, she turned her horse to face home, giving him a kick with her heels, directing him away from the road and across the fields.

As the weeks passed, Father Daley visited the school regularly. Roisin hadn't known how much she despised him. The vanity he displayed in his impeccable dress irritated her, but it was his smirking as he told the children they would have a new teacher next term which upset her the most.

'We'll find you another place for sure, Miss Carr,' he said one day, looking her up and down carefully until she wondered whether she was for sale.

Quite often she felt the tenuous link of control she was holding onto snap. Her self-esteem shrivelled like a small grey cobweb. She brushed it away and tried to go about her teaching as usual. But all was not as usual. There was a cold frightened place just below her rib cage, which was never there before.

Day after day she wondered what to do. The priest had offered another smaller house in the town and the opportunity to take up a post in a newly opened girls' sewing school. She'd heard of the like in other places, sewing schools, skilling girls in needlework and knitting. She rejected that offer straight away, insulted because he had not offered her a professional teaching post, only that of an assistant.

Time passed. She still hadn't made a decision and there was no news from Patrick either. She decided that her best choice might be to emigrate, as her brothers had done. Ruari and Seamus had left for England after school, finding work as labourers in the building trade.

Roisin wrote, asking if there was any opportunity for digs, and over time she tried to balance moving away from Drimoleague against reluctantly working as an assistant teacher, albeit on a temporary basis.

Leaving home one morning a few weeks before Christmas, her mother called, 'Letters from the boys came yesterday, Roisin, and there was one in here for yourself, I'd forgot to tell ye.'

She passed a sealed envelope over to Roisin, the set of her shoulders showing her reluctance.

Already half out the door, Rosin took the letter and shoved it in the pocket of her tweed skirt, waiting behind until the last child left the classroom at the end of the day before drawing her chair up to the fire and opening the letter. She recognised the handwriting as Ruari's.

'Dear Roisin,
I'm sending this letter sealed as I don't know how much Mam knows about your plans. We have found a good address in Kilburn where you can stay. It's quite near us now, there's plenty of Irish living here, in fact they are calling it County Kilburn. You need to be careful to get in somewhere that they don't tolerate alcohol, there is more of it taken here and you never know how the drink will do away with people. There's signs in the windows in some places, "No Irish", but this part is grand. Plenty of Jews here, but we don't meet the Jews, they keep to themselves.

Sure, we are not afraid to work hard and many of the lads here need help with the reading, writing, and understanding of numbers, so you would have plenty of requests in the evenings, maybe meet some nice fella yourself too. The money's not great now, but it's enough and there's good socials and dances and the like.

We've not met the girls of our dreams yet now, Roisin, and we will still be able to send the money home to Mam, but you will need to get on to your own two feet. Let us know if we should keep the place for you now, girl, we will be home ourselves at Christmas so we could all go back together.
God bless you.
Your loving brother,
Ruari.'

Crumpling the letter back into her pocket Roisin felt grim. She knew she needed to make plans, but felt lonely and scared, not her usual optimistic self. Pulling the heavy schoolroom door closed behind her and dropping the heavy latch she felt drained of any hope for her future.

'Roisin, here girl, have you not a word of welcome for your old friend now?' Peering through the drizzly evening mist she saw, silhouetted against the greying light, the instantly recognisable profile of Patrick.

'What are ye doing here, so?' she asked, a little scared, but pleased. She had neither seen nor heard from him since their encounter in O'Sullivan's Bar.

'Sure, I'm back for a few days now and I thought we might arrange that Christmas treat we promised ourselves.'

As Patrick walked towards her, moving to put his arm around her shoulders, Roisin's spirits lifted. This was the first time he had publicly shown any sign of their having a physical connection and she wondered whether he would call her his woman. Would it really give her a chance for a future after all?

'Well,' she told him, with a wry smile, 'I'm sure I don't have anything else to keep me here once the school finishes. I'll meet you, so.'

Patrick's smile suggested he was quietly satisfied, as he walked Roisin back towards her schoolhouse home. Although he couldn't know where this was going, he wouldn't have been the first man to take up an opportunity with a good-looking woman and he'd have known to be careful.

Roisin meanwhile knew exactly where 'this' was going and realised she needed some advice from her married friend, Deirdre. Whilst she and Deirdre had different opinions on the importance of educating girls, she knew she could rely on her friend for the intimate information she needed.

Roisin rode her horse over to see Deirdre the following Saturday morning, there were still a few weeks to go before the planned trip to Dublin, and no date had yet been finalised. Knowing the children would all be outdoors, for a while at least, and that Michael worked long hours in his few fields, she expected to have Deirdre to herself.

Deirdre was wringing washing from a metal clothes bucket and draping it over a line above the fire when Roisin arrived.

'This is a treat Roisin! Come on over to the fire and we'll get some tea in a minute.' As Roisin knelt to join Deirdre on the rough floor of the cottage, she pulled her thick skirt beneath her as a cushion. Whilst helping her friend wring out the sodden clothes, Roisin told her about the trip to Dublin before broaching the intimate request.

'I'm not very sure what I must expect when we are in the room together. Alone, y'know.'

Deirdre smiled wryly, 'You have used the very words I asked once too, Roisin. Before we married, I asked Michael what would be expected but he was so embarrassed I think he deliberately misunderstood.

D'ye know he said, "We'll be just grand now, you'll see. You can have your own bit of independence; a few shillings to call your own. How about taking on the chickens? Now that would be a great help and a good way to earn a bit just for yourself". Chickens! Really that was not at all helpful. Not the advice you are looking for, Roisin! So, then I asked some of the recently married women at my work instead. An' what they told me was just as useless.

"You bleed the first time, but after that it doesn't hurt", and "I always says a prayer to Our Blessed Lady when Eamon starts, it helps take my mind off it."

'But in spite of all that good advice, our wedding night was just great. Michael was gentle and careful and when I told him "Well now, that was not half as bad as I was expecting", he dedicated the following few days to improving that expectation.'

Deirdre smiled at her friend, remembering how, before the week was out, his hand on her leg had awakened nerve endings she never knew about. Before this last baby, such thoughts used to cause a warm deep melt in her belly. Nothing seemed to work as it used to anymore.

'So, what should I do, Deirdre, to make it easier on myself? An' I wouldn't want there to be any "consequences".'

'No 'deed, that ye would not want. I hear Eileen Callahan is in trouble, her an' some young fella from out the road. Nice girl Eileen, I worked with her a bit at Ramore House. Don't know him at all now, but I don't think he has anything to offer the poor girl.'

'Ah, I'm so sorry to hear that Deirdre. I knew Eileen well, she was one of my best pupils, halfway through her schooling when I came here, lovely girl. Very protective of her little brother Timmy too, as I recall.'

'Well there won't be much for her here now, best pupil or not. She's not been too clever around the boys I'd say.'

'Oh, I can only wait to hear Father Daly at that one, he's so holy but has no love or charity in him at all.'

'So, get back to the subject Deirdre, and here let me help you hang these clothes above the fire now. Tell me what will help, prevent…, you know.'

'The girls, my work friends you know, were after tellin' me about the best chance not to get caught. There's days in the month when ye won't fall and there's days when ye might. Set your visit to the days when you have just finished or near about to start, that's the safest. It worked for me. Although Michael wasn't too happy. But sure, I got a three-year gap between Dan and Hannah. Two years after Hannah came Kitty.'

'An' the rest of it, Deirdre? Must I just wait and see?'

'It's a bit, private like, Roisin. Ye'll learn to take it slow and ye'll be conscious to be quiet too, any fear o' bein' overheard now, sure that would be awful altogether.'

Deirdre smiled as she recalled how, newly returned from honeymoon, she'd enjoyed the heat of his strong body on, in, and around her and how she had learned to move without making the bed creak and so wake his mother.

'Sure it never took me long to fall, and never took me long to birth them either.' She reminded Roisin with pride. 'Mind the breastfeeding didn't make any difference at all to preventin' and with my second I heard myself described as having 'one under the coat and one on it.'
'An, wee Kitty, she has had the best attention and care from the whole family; she was the baby and so clever! Sure, she walked, talked, dressed herself at an earlier age than any of the others. An' of course she's our baby again now.' Deirdre sighed, looking up at Roisin who was busying herself with straightening the clothes rack, from which drips were falling onto the hearth and avoiding her friend's eye.

'No sad thoughts or "what-might-have-beens" now, Deirdre. Ye'd not been needed at Ramore House today so I'll try a bit of your soda bread here, and ye' can tell me how it's done.'
Deirdre smiled, pleased for the opportunity to share with her friend.
'Sure aren't we grand, so,' she said. 'We've never known a shortage of food. I know many do have memories of the great potato famine, but it ended over fifty years ago.'

'Well, it did take many lives in the area now, and sure the terrible effects of the famine are still alive in the minds of the older generation. I know that, Deirdre, I know many families have a real deep fear of hunger. An' I'm sure 'tis that fear, and the memory of fear, is what keeps us focussed on food. D'ye think Father Daley fears a famine, he's a fine appetite for sure'

'Appetite for what Roisin? I've no doubt the man is holy, he's ordained by the bishop so he must be a good man, but I cried sore when he denied us a burial place for baby Anna. I've certainly no appetite for him!'

'Ah well, what's done is done now Deirdre, your baby, my job, I know they don't compare but we were both wrecked by him, so we are.'

Roisin put her hand on Deirdre's, 'Would you just stop for a minute, you're cutting up onions, throwing them in with the mutton, an' putting those few cups of water in. I know you will keep busy Deirdre, but can we just have five minutes?'

Sitting close together, the two women continued speaking quietly, comforting each other and understanding that each was grieving.

'Anyhow Deirdre, I'm goin' to get out there now and find a bit of living for myself. He's a fine man, Patrick an' not from round here so there won't be any trouble. I don't see any wrong in it an' you can be sure I'll not be one to look sideways at the likes of young Eileen Callahan.'

'No indeed Roisin, but be careful none around here sees ye' for God's sake. They'll build a story quick as look at ye' and have your reputation ruined. There'll be no school mistressing for ye then, I'd say.'

Promising her friend she'd be careful, she gave her a hug and left her to her chores. She knew Deirdre needed to keep busy, she hoped it took her mind off the loss of her baby, but now she had preparations of her own to see to.

When the time came, Roisin had no difficulty in evading her mother's questions regarding her visit to Dublin, and she walked through the town and down to the station alone, her head held high, not caring who should see her.

The Cork train meant she had to change for the long journey to the capital, but she never doubted the wisdom of what she was about to do. She'd listened to Deirdre's advice, adjusted the timing of the trip to suit her own monthly cycle and she was looking forward to the weekend ahead.

Roisin saw Patrick straight away, waiting for her on the platform at Amien Street Station and she confidently took his arm as they walked the short distance through the busy Dublin streets to the imposing entrance of the Castle Hotel.

Checking in as Mr and Mrs Carr, Roisin thought Patrick seemed embarrassed as he fumbled with the key and made small talk at the hotel reception desk.

Detaching herself from the conversation she stared straight ahead into the oversized hall mirror above the desk She considered her reflection, this tall country woman with the good green eyes, her thick curling auburn hair slipping out from the hairpins she had so carefully arranged that morning.

Wearing her best red coat with her grey shawl wrapped over her shoulders now, not covering her head as she wore it in Drimoleague. 'Am I asking more from life than I have a right to?' she wondered. 'Well, time for me to take whatever I want, not much more to lose once my school and my children are gone.'

Climbing the wide carved staircase, she looked down onto the reception area warmed by a great log fire. Crimson velvet covered the wing-backed armchairs which seemed to stand guard on either side of the ornate, gilt fireplace. She expected it would feel glorious and decadent to sit by the fire, order a tray of tea, and people-watch. The fashions and the style, no shawls here, not even on shoulders, all good woollen coats. But she was mostly impressed by the freedom to come and go without being noticed. The noise and the busyness of the Dublin streets outside contrasting with the muted and refined air of the inside. She'd made two changes on the trains from Drimoleague and although it had been a long tiring journey, Roisin felt it was worth it to be here. She thought it truly resembled another country.

She marvelled at the way the reception staff and the porters treated the customers as though it was the most natural thing in the world for a woman, or even a strong fit man, to be unable to carry their own luggage a few feet to the stairs or the lift. It amused Roisin to think that probably these rarefied creatures were perfectly used to lugging briefcases full of important papers or, in the women's cases, heaving shopping, children, and bicycles around. 'But not here,' she turned towards Patrick, although he wasn't near enough to hear her. 'Oh no, soon as they step through the door it's all changed. I'll enjoy this for a couple of nights so I will and remember all the details to tell Deirdre.'

'Let's get you upstairs now, girly', Patrick's voice interrupted her thoughts. 'I've to go out to a meeting this afternoon but I'll be back in time for a bit of dinner. Maybe you would like a wee lie down first?' Opening the door and showing her where their cases had already been deposited in the room, he gently pulled her inside. 'Ah, come here my lovely girly, I've waited a long time for this.'

Later, but not much later, Roisin, having dozed off, awoke to an empty bed. She felt sore, rumpled, and disappointed. They had been rushed in their lovemaking and although Roisin had never expected romance, Patrick's indifference to her needs and the almost operational speed with which he thrust and groaned had not been what Deirdre had led her to hope for.

'It's not as though I am a complete virgin,' she muttered, recalling the boyfriend she had had in her student days in Cork but hadn't thought worth mentioning to Deirdre, she really didn't want to be judged. 'Well, the worst part about that was the risk, a risk for not a lot, and worry for the next month whether there would be "consequences". Holy God, that was awful all right. An' all that trouble I went to to fix around the dates like Deirdre said! I needn't have bothered. Patrick's rubbers, French letters he calls them, were all ready. I wonder does he always keep them handy?'

Later they had the 'bit of dinner', Patrick had promised, in the hotel's main restaurant. He talked, in far too much detail, Roisin thought, about that afternoon's sales meeting; and although impressed with both the food and the dining room, she felt her appetite diminish with each passing minute.

'Patrick, I really don't need to be educated by you,' she told him after a particularly lengthy description of how horse liniment worked. 'I don't mind discovering a few facts, but not all of them all at once now.' I must be lonely, she decided, to have to listen to this all evening.

The first light seeping through the curtains the following morning woke Roisin early. Reaching out to stroke the soft curls on the back of Patrick's head, she pulled back, fearing this familiar gesture might imply something more than he wanted. Shifting herself nearer without touching his sleeping form, she moved her head forward, breathing in deeply, to savour him more closely.

Her nostrils were filled with a rich aroma, a mixture of sweat and a hint of horse liniment overlaid by the strong clean smell of soap or shaving foam. Roisin shivered at the premonition of what that particular mixture would remind her of, whatever the future held.

Patrick would be out all day and Roisin sensed that the intimacy of breakfast might not be comfortable, so she slipped quietly out of bed, using the water in the china washstand to freshen herself.

Pulling her dress and linen undergarment on quickly, shivering in the chilly unfamiliar room, she made her way downstairs. She'd already planned that treat, basking in the anonymity of the hotel, shielded by reading a paper by the fire perhaps, ordering some tea and then later she would explore the city, quite alone.

She imagined herself a regular customer as she descended the stairs. 'I am gracious,' she reassured herself. 'I am here in one of the best hotels in Dublin, good as anybody.'

Taking a seat in one of the wing-backed armchairs by the open fire; she ordered tea and picked up a complimentary copy of the Irish Independent.

She was still scanning the front page, scrutinising the adverts for the Great Exhibition and planning her day, screened by the large newspaper pages. 'Independent and Irish myself, this change might be just what I need,' when a familiar voice rang out across the foyer.

'Careful with that luggage now boy, straight up to the room with you.'

Roisin's heart stopped, 'Father Daley?' she whispered, 'Surely it cannot be. This is more than bad luck, this is disaster.' She could see it all unfolding - scandal-adultery-mortal sin-no reference. Her inevitable flight to London in disgrace and her mother's heart broken. Unsure whether to hide behind the newspaper or try to make her escape before she was seen, she prayed that Patrick would not come down the stairs looking for her.

'It's Mr & Mrs. Casey,' said the voice. 'We have a reservation for our usual room please. That's correct, same as last month, double room overlooking the square.'

At this Roisin dared raise her head. It was Father Daley, without a doubt, playing every inch the part of a well-dressed husband. He put his arm protectively around the shoulders of a young, pretty woman who looked up at him in admiration.

Blood pounded in Roisin's ears as she stood up. The Irish Independent dropped onto the floor with a sigh, causing Father Daley to look up, straight into the mirror over the receptionist's desk.

He saw reflected the person he wanted to be - a handsome man, smartly dressed, respected, admired, successful, married.

He also saw the colour drain from his already pale face when Roisin moved towards him.

Stunned for a moment he felt it could not be happening, this time he would get no second chance with the bishop, no discreet change of parish as before, just scandal-adultery-mortal sin-no reference. Frozen to the spot, he couldn't look away from Roisin's eyes in the mirror.

'Good morning, Mr. Casey, I don't believe I've met your wife, have I now?' she asked calmly although her mouth was dry, holding out a shaking hand to the woman at his side, she introduced herself.

'I'm Roisin Carr, schoolmistress of the children's school, just outside Drimoleague. We had a bit of a misunderstanding recently, Mr. Casey and myself, regarding my post; but I think we will have to change that now, don't you agree Mr. Casey? It will suit us both very well.'

Chapter 2.

Deirdre. Drimoleague, West Cork, Ireland 1907

It had been a windy day. Squally showers prevented the pale sunshine from quite breaking through and soon the daylight would fade. The short day meant that Deirdre Collins had to work quickly in order to finish her chores before the evening set in. A farmer's wife, the mother of four children and a woman who had recently buried her stillborn baby girl. Desperately unhappy, she was trying to cope with her loss.

As their farm in Carrigmor was only a mile from the school, she expected her children home before the twilight gave way to night. She also knew they'd be wet and muddy from their run across the moorland and they'd be hungry, demanding, and full of chatter.

Thinking of the school, her mind turned to her friend Roisin, who had recently returned from her visit to Dublin with her male friend. She'd seemed very happy and told Deirdre that she had changed Father Daley's mind about her relinquishing the schoolmistress role although she had been a bit evasive as to the reason.

Deirdre considered her friend's life without envy.

She enjoyed Roisin's company, she liked the way she would push the boundaries of acceptability whilst never quite going too far and she always looked for her good opinion.

But she did think that Roisin's being unmarried and having no children was too high a price to pay for financial independence.

'Well, sure, and I have my own work, too. Maybe less now since the children came along, but still I love it. They are a grand English family, the Radleys, over at Ramore House. They think I'm educated enough, and I think I've showed that, so I have. Working my apprenticeship as still-room maid. My God, that pantry was cold. Then who would have thought it, all the way up to assistant cook, no less.

They all said they loved my pastry and I get brought in - it has to be me - for the shoots, for the pies. Oh yes, education or not, I did alright. Now at home, they're happy to eat away at the leftovers - the vanilla slices, the jam puffs, and all the fancies that are never seen outside the big house.'

Deirdre was a slenderly built, fine-featured woman, brown-eyed with dark, wavy hair. Her looks were not untypical of West Cork. Many local anecdotes had suggested that it was a Mediterranean colouring, coming from the intermingling of genes between the Irish of West Cork and the survivors of the Spanish Armada - wrecked off the coast of Ireland in 1588. Deirdre liked the story and hung onto the idea of having Spanish blood; it compensated for her never having left Ireland.

'But I was a city girl, once, a Cork girl,' she told whoever asked. 'I only moved to Drimoleague for the chance of a job at the big house. I wouldn't go back to the city, it's all changed anyhow, and I love these wide-open spaces, to say nothing of my good fortune at having captured Michael Collins on my way home from Mass. He wasn't thinking about my education, that's for sure.'

Michael owned a small farm, and when they met, he was sharing the single-storey homestead with his mother. His younger brother Joe had married two years earlier and moved into a nearby farm in Derryduff.

'So, your Da,' she often told the children, 'was so impressed with this city girl and her fancy ways, that he moved her into this house, married, within a year of courting. Your mother wasn't too pleased though, was she, Mickey?' The children would listen to these stories, and others, about how their mother had lost contact with her own mother and sisters in Cork and how Drimoleague became her home.

She had been alone with her thoughts all day and had managed to keep busy, but it seemed a long time since dawn when Michael left the house, calling up the stairs, 'I'm away out now to the early milking at Ramore, I'll be back for my dinner at midday.'
' 'Deed would you ever drop in at your Joe's for your dinner, Mike? Fiona is due and ye can tell me how she is keeping.' Deirdre thought that if Michael called in there to eat at midday he could see if there was any help needed.

Deirdre always wanted to look out for the children. She considered that her sister-in-law, a somewhat self-centred woman to Deirdre's mind, was not overly capable.
'Maybe I am getting better, sure I didn't think about my poor baby when I opened my eyes, I thought about Fiona's baby, so is that a good sign?'

That morning she had given herself a few minutes until she'd heard the clunk of the latch as Michael left; then rising and kneeling by the bed to say a few 'Hail Marys', prayers for the safety of the family, she'd quickly dressed in her working clothes - a long woollen skirt and thick woollen stockings. First thing that morning she'd changed the cold boiled cabbage leaves which served as soothers to her hot heavy breasts and then wrapped her shawl tightly across and over a rough linen shirt, knowing it would be stained and wondering how long it would be before her milk dried.

'Straighten up now, Deirdre', she had told herself. 'It's lucky you are to have the great children the Good Lord has sent you, be lookin' after them now.'

Later in the day, leaning out the small, deep-set windows which overlooked the open moorland she felt her happiness fading. The open scenery used always to give her spirits a lift, and she'd often chide her neighbours, 'Sure ye don't know you're born, living here in this beautiful place, ye only have to look out the window to know you're blessed.' Now it looked as bleak and empty outside as she felt inside. She knew the baby was gone; she expected she could have more and to lose a pregnancy was not so uncommon, in fact she knew there were even a few for whom it was a welcome loss.

During the afternoon Deirdre'd tackled a job she'd known she couldn't ignore any longer. Dragging her trunk from under the bed, she carefully picked through the folded piles of linens. With every child she made a few new garments and she had been completing the last of these tiny robes when the too early cramps came, eventually overwhelming her and her baby. Finding the task difficult, she managed to put aside a small pile - inner petticoats, carefully stitched and a couple of heavier outer garments simply embroidered. The petticoats she decided to give to Fiona, telling herself that she'd keep just one in her little girl's memory and knowing there would be plenty of hand-me-downs at Derryduff.

'As for this fine table linen "only used for best," not anymore, you're dead now, Mrs Collins.' She had raised her eyes heavenward as she always did when speaking to, or of, Michael's mother; never doubting she was being watched. 'So, I can use what linens I like. I think I'll bring these out on Sundays now, it's the most likely day for guests and if we don't have any, sure the girls will learn how to set a good table.'

Sorting out the trunk had filled the afternoon and now she picked up a bucket, moved out to the rainwater barrel by the back door and, dipping the bucket into the black murky barrel, filled it halfway, carelessly letting some slosh over her feet.

Although they had a good well and a pump in the yard, Deirdre always used the soft rainwater for washing hair and faces. Heaving the overfilled bucket indoors, she dipped a bowlful into the blue china washbasin in front of the fire. A brief wash served to tighten her face and pulling her hair into a neat bun at the base of her neck made her feel a little better and fresher as she left the rest of the water aside for the children's muddy return.

The day's silver sky was turning to grey as Deirdre reached for a new candle from the high shelf above the fireplace. Placing it in the window for the children, it comforted her to have it signal the beginning of the end of her day. She used to cherish a day alone, working quickly to have all her chores done before the change of tempo which came with the arrival of the children. Now she craved the distraction of their company.

Through the sound of the rising wind outside she heard her neighbour's voice, although discerning the words was difficult. She waited until the flicker of the candlewick steadied before opening the back door.

'Deirdre, would you ever come with me to Fiona's, she's getting the pains now and we need to gather.'

Through the twilight she could just make out the bulky frame of one of her neighbours, Maud Blaney, who was, in Deirdre's opinion, a bit of a know-all. She was in her pony cart, and appeared to be impatiently waiting, jiggling the pony's reins, in the middle of the road.

Pulling her coat on, Deirdre quickly looked around to make sure all was in order for when the children came in from school, before stepping quickly out the door and over to the cart.

She'd been expecting this call. Having safely delivered her own four children, Deirdre was often asked to help other women in labour. And of course, Fiona was family.

Shivering, she quickly wrapped an outer shawl over her coat. It was a good quality woollen shawl, a deep red weave, chosen to compliment her dark colouring and recently purchased in Cork City.

It was a special, unexpected, and, she guessed, compensation gift from Michael. Stepping into the pony cart alongside her sturdy older neighbour, she felt her breasts tingle with milk and realised her body was also thinking of Fiona's baby.

'We'll see how she is, now Deirdre,' shouted Maud, unnecessarily. 'It's her sixth, but she has been particularly large and very tired. I don't think there will be any problems, do you now?' her words were only half heard above the rising wind, but Deirdre wasn't really listening; she knew what to expect.

There would always be matters which required additional effort, if not exactly problems. Children and men were to be kept fed and at a safe distance until the labour was over, and then there would be personal cleaning, and bed linen to be changed, and hopefully, and God willing, a new baby to be warmed and clothed.

Deirdre appreciated the importance of this ritual in her community; ensuring childbirth turned an everyday occurrence, which had within it a peppering of anxiety, into an opportunity for the women to take control and preside.
It was solely with childbirth that the women were in control, where there was no need for negotiation or compromise.

The whole community, men and women alike, revered and strictly observed the women's role and it was a relief to both that each kept to their own purpose here; not only at the time of the birth but for many weeks afterwards.

The journey from Carrigmor to her in-law's farm was only one mile, but the motion of the cart, bouncing across unmade tracks and skirting neatly around the Big Rock, once the site of the Big Fair but now just an obstacle, was an uncomfortable experience.

Maud was encouraging the young brown pony to trot through the rough prickly stems and tough gorse bushes with their scant yellow pea-like blossoms and as he trotted Deirdre was tossed about on the bench seat, making conversation difficult.

'Youngsters not home yet, Missus?' shouted Maud from the front of the cart, turning her head halfway – which was all she could manage whilst keeping her hands tightly on the reins of the pony, 'Will ye stay with it for a bit up at Derryduff, 'til we see how it goes?'

Then she moved, not waiting for an answer, to the main topic of conversation; hoping for a snippet to add to her store of gossip. 'Did ye hear the news from Skibreen? They say the teacher man who was supposed to take up the schoolmaster's post, well he's been let down. D'ye think Miss Carr will be stayin' after all?'

'I'd never doubted it, Maud,' Deirdre sniffed with displeasure at having to discuss Roisin's affairs with a gossip.

'Roisin Carr is a fine teacher and will be with us until she retires, I'd say. She's a bit ahead of herself in thinking the girls can do as well as their brothers but it comes from her never been married herself, nor never will now I think.'

'Look ye, here's Tommy Mac's boy running home from school.'

How Maud could spot him in the fading light was a surprise to Deirdre, but she thought maybe Maud's curiosity gave her the eyes of an owl.

'Hey, Tommy, how was the teacher today, any news or craic around the school for us?'

Tommy, a skinny lad, dressed in one of his father's worn-out sweaters and carrying his mother's boots by the laces over one shoulder, was reluctant to stop but feared a lash from his father if word got back that he had been disrespectful to the women.

'Not a word, Mrs. Blaney. We had our lessons an' all, as usual, an' Miss Carr telled Michael to recite the tale of poor Finbarr Gearings, as we seen him in town last Saturday. Michael had to say the poem 'I rose from the dead in the year '48, when a grave in the Abbey had near been my fate.'

'Aye, well, good enough for him too, poor Finbarr as was buried alive in a famine pit deserves all the reminisces ye can get him.'

Not interested in the details from the schoolroom, Maud left Tommy with a curt nod of her head and jerked the reins abruptly, pulling the pony to turn a corner as Joe Collins's dwelling came into view. It was a fine longhouse, thatched as they all were, with an adjoining farm building, which housed pigs, hay, stored potatoes, and let the chickens run in and out; keeping them safe from foxes.

The two women arrived at the Collin's house to find the doctor already in command. Joe Collins was well regarded as a reliable payer and thus expected, and got, prompt attention when he asked for it. However, Dr McGuire's services and time were considered a precious commodity, and Joe expected the women of the family to take over as much of the child birthing duties as possible; there would be no need for a midwife.

The women preferred it that way, not wanting a man to undertake any of the more intimate duties, and were keen to support one another through an event which could be as threatening as it could be joyful.

As soon as they stepped through the door into the crowded bedroom it was clear that Fiona was nearing delivery. 'Hmmmm,' muffled Fiona, red in the face and biting down on a twisted cloth, for fear of making too much noise as the children were expected home.

'Dear God, please let this baby be my last,' she prayed, hoping she would survive this and never have to do it again. Six pregnancies in eight years was not an unusual tally but it appeared that Fiona had not grasped the connection between fertility and timing and now feared she may well go on to have six more.

Dr McGuire, avoiding eye contact with anyone, abruptly grasped Fiona's wrist, as though it gave him a distraction. His stance beside Fiona's bed was formal, and his upright posture and grave expression convinced those watching that he was not going to engage in conversation. All the women watched him, aware that clues as to Fiona's progress were to be found through the reading of his face and the set of his shoulders.

He was the same doctor who had delivered all Fiona's children and Deirdre's also. Even if he had known that Fiona did not welcome the frequent pregnancies he would never presume to advise her on how to space her family, any more than Fiona would have considered asking him.

What Dr McGuire lacked in conversation and reassurance was more than compensated for by his being a local man; committed to continuing his medical support for the parish, often going beyond what was required and above all else, he was trusted. Today though he was under pressure, having just left a family with a very sick child. He couldn't be sure, but the rash looked like scarlet fever, and now he was torn between the needs of both families.

Fiona's 'Hmmm' was absorbed into the rhythmical hum of women's voices quietly reciting the rosary. 'Holy Mary, Mother of God, pray for us sinners now and at the hour of our death, Amen.'

Dropping Fiona's wrist, she was pulling too hard on the cloth tied to the bedpost for him to reliably feel her pulse, Dr McGuire motioned the rosary-reciting women aside by an impatient shaking hand movement, as though he was flicking aside a stray insect.

As the women had expected, he opened his black bag, and removed forceps, scissors and curved needles, made from thick shiny steel. Then, as he called for a bowl of hot water, an anxious challenge rang out.
'Ah now Doctor, maybe they won't all be needed?'

It was Sarah Hegerty, an older woman, standing at the other side of the bed. Fiona's hand was so tightly gripping hers that she had lost all feeling in her fingers.

A grandmother herself she felt that gave her the right to question the doctor, whom she had known since he was a child.

'We'll see, we'll see now, Mrs Hegerty. You and I both know there is sometimes a need ...' replied Dr McGuire, feeling very uncomfortable at having to engage in a dialogue, particularly when there was an audience. There was a ripple of movement across the room, as instinctively each woman thought of 'the need' and wanted to protect their most delicate and private area in the face of the laid-out forceps, scissors, and especially the curved needles.

Dr McGuire's instruments particularly terrified one young woman, Caitlin McGrath. She was six months pregnant with her first child and made sure she was near the door in case she needed a quick exit.

Deirdre knew that Fiona always kept a relic of St. Anne, the patron saint of childbirth, pinned to her gown when in labour. Deirdre herself preferred St. Teresa's powders and she was about to offer some when there was one agonised groan from Fiona, a couple of pushes and as she spread her legs the back of a small dark head could just be seen.

The baby's head turned, a wide set of shoulders began to emerge and, hooking one finger under a baby armpit, Dr McGuire eased out first one then the second shoulder. A blood-stained, slippery baby followed rapidly. Fists clenched, eyes tightly shut, he was ready to give the world his first bawled greeting.
'Ah, thanks be to God and his holy mother.'
'Fine boy, God bless him.'

Having cut the cord and a few minutes later delivered the afterbirth, the doctor's work was done.

Fiona felt a rush of maternal emotion; love, relief, protectiveness, and wonder as she waited for her baby, who was being wrapped in warm cloths, eyes wiped, and cord bound around his middle with a torn linen strip. But Dr McGuire lingered over Fiona's abdomen, prodding and listening with his horn-shaped stethoscope. His normally expressionless brow furrowed. He was unsure what he should do next. It was the not uncommon doctor's dilemma; should he to go back to the sick patient he had just left or take care of the patient before him. He didn't have much time, and he had to make a quick decision.

Rolling down his sleeves and washing his hands in the basin, he moved across the room. He saw Maud busy with the newborn, Sarah preparing to give Fiona a wash, and young Caitlin pale and leaning on the doorframe, as though for support. Deirdre was the best choice, he reckoned. She was also trusted by the women - reliable, experienced, and a good mother.

He bent over and spoke closely into her ear, not wanting to be overheard. He then bade the women good evening; 'Sure you have a grand son there, Mrs Collins, I'll see myself out.' Swiftly gathering his bags he prepared to leave the room, taking a quick moment at the doorway to give Catlin's shoulder a kindly squeeze and giving a nod at her swollen belly, with a brief smile as though to say 'it'll be alright when your time comes, I'll be there …'

Maud meanwhile had reluctantly passed the baby to Fiona, who was possessively cradling her sixth child, crying silent tears of joy and relief. She expected the women to call Joe in to see his son. No call was made. After a couple of minutes, she raised her head from the pillow, becoming aware of the disquiet and unease in the room.   'What is it now?'

'The doctor,' said Deirdre.

'What?'

'The doctor said, 'Stay with that woman'.'

'Why?'

''Call me if you need me back.' he said. He's gone on an urgent visit.'

'For God's sake, why?'

42

'Because there's another one in there.'

'Ah Holy Mother, no, not now, you're having me on. Get Joe in here now to see his son before I die.'

'What do we do now?' asked Caitlin, her reassurance vanishing at this unexpected turn.

'Take the baby out to Joe, Caitlin, and tell him we are not finished yet.' Deirdre's decisive voice helped to calm the frightened atmosphere in the room. Most of the women were hoping Dr McGuire would walk back in the door and some thought prayer was the only action they could take to hasten his return. On their knees now, more of the rosary was recited, followed by a special prayer to St Anne.

Deirdre and Sarah Hegarty, meanwhile, being less convinced than many of the others of the power of prayer, kept a watchful eye on Fiona; regularly checking beneath the blanket for any increase in bleeding which, they had decided, would give them the right to send for Dr McGuire immediately, regardless of cost or the needs of his other patient.

Fiona let out a protracted groan as the contractions began again. It was not a long process. A few more followed by a gush of water, before the back of a small head emerged. Pulling back the blanket, regardless of who might be peering in the window, Mrs Hegarty fixed Fiona's heel firmly to her own hip, calling Deirdre to do the same on the other side and, watching Fiona, red faced and angry, give one more push, wrapped a clean cloth around her hands just in time to support the head of the second baby as it squirmed and slithered, almost gratefully, into her waiting hands.

'A little girl, Fiona, you have a pigeon pair! Do you want to hold her?'

'I want my little laddie. Who has him? How can I love two babies at once? Or feed them both? How can it be ... who will help me?' Fiona sobbed, exhausted and drained. 'Where is Joe, ask him what should we do.'

No one noticed Deirdre, taking the baby from Sarah and holding her close.

43

She was torn between the anger she felt towards Fiona, who had rejected what she herself so desperately wanted and the wave of possessiveness and hope which was sweeping over her as she held the warm, tiny body. She recklessly wondered whether she would run before realising that of course she wouldn't. The room blurred, she hardly heard the discussions, the persuasions taking place or Joe's worried face. He realised that his wife was not going to take this child to her breast. Their son was already there.

Deirdre looked down at the small crumpled face, into a pair of wide-open eyes, which seemed to be asking to be loved and, as she stroked the back of the baby's smooth soft hand, the tiny fingers opened like a starfish. It seemed almost deliberate, Deirdre thought, the way the little fingers clamped around one of her own and she felt sure that they had both come to a decision.

'I'll take her, Fiona, just for now. I have milk and I've seen them do it in the Big House. Wet nursing, it's very common really, and she is my niece after all.' What Deirdre didn't say was that she had found something she had lost and that she would not be letting it go again.

A few hours earlier, running through the fading light, Kitty Collins had her head down and her eyes on her sister Hannah.

She saw ahead of her a pair of mud-splattered legs, and, nearer her own short legs, she heard a rhythmic slurping noise coming from the mud as her small feet sprinted across the moorland.

Eight-year-old Hannah, two years ahead of Kitty, always led the way and Kitty expected to be looked after. She was a sallow-skinned child, with a dark head of curls and strong brown eyes which suggested she had a deep strength of will and determination, much of which she had inherited from her mother. And her place in the family as the youngest had led her to expect first call on her mother's attention.

As the two girls arrived panting and cold, at the back door of the empty house, Kitty felt that her world had stopped.

The lit candle stood in the window, as silent recognition that her mother had remembered her, but why was there no kettle on the fire?

'Where is Mammy?', she demanded of Hannah, suspecting her of having some information which had not been shared. The boys, who'd arrived minutes earlier, barged in the door bringing with them some extra twigs for kindling to bolster the peat fire, which was always left banked until teatime. They were pleased the house was empty. It meant there would be some freedom to forget their chores, at least for now; but they were also hungry and, ignoring the mutton slowly stewing over the fire, made straight for the cupboard to look for food. Hannah added the twigs, coaxing the fire awake and she hooked the kettle on to boil for tea. Michael, meanwhile, reached into the cupboard and found not only the fresh bread but also a fruit cake wrapped in linen and pushed to the back.

Delighted with the bounty, the cake was unwrapped and between setting the cake on the floor and finding a knife to cut it with, the children composed a makeshift meal which suited them better than mutton stew. Sitting as close as they could get to the fire they ate from their hands, not bothering to get plates or set the table, 'Sure Mammy wouldn't want us to get all that stuff out, she'll be back soon and tell us what to do.'

Three of the four children, sharing the cake and waiting for the hot tea, were enjoying the impromptu meal and congratulating each other.

'Sure, this is the best, Michael.'
'You're a wonder, so you are.'
'Is the tea ready yet, Hannah?'
'Give over, you'll hog the lot.'
The fourth child was not feeling so brave. Kitty was cold, frightened, and worst of all, ignored.

She didn't want cake and her bladder was bursting. Jigging from one foot to the other she tried to get Hannah to notice. It was too dark and windy outside to go to the privy on her own, she wanted to squat by the back door, but she knew that wasn't allowed.

'Hannah, come with me to do a wee, the hens are outside, and they frighten me an' it's so dark. Hannah, please? Where's Mam, Hannah? Where is my Mammy? I want my Mammy....'

'Ah come on, Hannah, take the child outside before she pees the floor.'

'Will now, just a minute, I'm doin' the kettle first so I am.'

Moments after the girls left the room, their father walked in the door.

'Dada!', the boys cried out, delighted in his arrival home. It no longer felt like an empty house.

Looking around at the scattered food and untended mutton stew, Michael reckoned he had arrived just as they were getting bored with looking after themselves and once fed, they might begin to feel resentful, now their initial hunger had been met. He thought to take some tea with them before telling them about the afternoon's events.

A straight-talking man, Michael sometimes wondered where the past fifteen years had gone. He had moved from his easy bachelor lifestyle to this all-consuming responsibility of family man.

His mother, he reflected, had not been keen on Deirdre, but resigned herself, reminding her neighbours of an old Gaelic adage, 'The only cure for love is marriage.' She had died shortly after their first son was born, but Hannah bore her name.

He loved Deirdre and the children were welcome when they arrived, but sometimes he wished they had had more time to establish themselves before heading straight into family life.

There was no doubt in Michael's mind that Deirdre was the force behind the family, and his whole life, and her opinions were unquestioned. He wouldn't have it any other way, but he didn't want that to show and sometimes he made a point of refusing requests from the children or asserting his authority in small ways.

When Hannah arrived in from the yard, her first thought was to bring her father a hot cup of tea, letting him help himself to a roughly cut piece of cake.

Michael's thoughts were confused. He needed to share the news with his family, but he wasn't sure how to do that. He hadn't carried out Deirdre's request from that morning but had worked on through the day, not going to his brother's house at dinnertime but calling at Derryduff when he'd finished his day's work. Once he had seen Maud's pony and cart tethered by the doorpost and the scuffling taking place under the window outside the house, he'd known that Fiona's time had come.

Fiona and Joe's children and the young Hegartys had been climbing on one another's shoulders to see into the room where the birthing was taking place, and a running commentary on progress was being passed from one to another.
    'A second babby has come out.'
    'Get away!'
    'Let me see.'
    'Is Mam still crying?'
    'Did you see it come out?'
    'Was it her bellybutton?'
    'Never seen a cow calve or twin lambs born? You eejit!'

Michael had wondered, catching this last, how children brought up in the city would ever understand birth and death. He'd brought the youngsters inside where there had been no sign of Joe, but he expected he was with his wife and newborn.

With Caitlin's help he had found the meal which the women had prepared for the children and the men. Potatoes boiled in their skins, cabbage, butter, and a mutton stew. Identical fare to that prepared in most homes in the area, most evenings. The children had just been set down to eat, when Deirdre came through the door, carrying a bundle in her arms.

She'd taken him aside, not wanting the conversation overheard by the children or by Caitlin. He had been shocked when she told him, 'Mickey, Fiona has twins. It's one more than she can feed, so I'm taking this babby home with us.'

'For now?'

'Maybe, or maybe just not. I don't want ye asking questions now Mike. Just go home to the children and tell them, so.'

He'd wondered, only for a moment, whether he also had one more than he could feed, but as he gently lifted the bundle from Deirdre, folded back the blanket and looked into the baby's bewildered eyes he knew he couldn't refuse.

Turning down an offer of food from Caitlin, Michael had taken his leave, cycling home alone, letting Deirdre stay a while longer; she'd told him she'd travel home in the pony cart with Maud within an hour or so. So now he had to break the news. Never one for small talk, he took a gulp of tea then announced, 'Mam is bringing a new baby over to the house.'

'You said we weren't getting another baby now.'

'This is a different baby. It's Joe's and Aunty Fiona's. The baby will be your cousin, like a little sister.'

Kitty caught this last explanation. She was just in from the yard and hit by an unfamiliar emotion. Not frightened, but a sinking in her stomach. She felt a dread of what she was hearing, a creeping unease settling in. It made her feel lonely and sad.

'Dada, will I not be the baby anymore?'

What she really meant was 'will Mammy love a new baby more than she loves me?' but she couldn't put that into words. Instead she asked hopefully 'Will Hannah look after the baby?' and finally, 'Where's Mammy?'

But her father ignored Kitty's pinched, sad face and so did Hannah. He told them they would have to be big girls now to help with the baby and help their Mam. He told them to get the new baby clothes, which Deirdre had been sorting out earlier in the day and warm them by the fire.

'And lads, go out to the barn and bring in the cradle, then fetch in some fresh water from the pump for your Mam's tea.' Then, seemingly exhausted by all the arrangements, he lit his pipe and settled himself by the fire to wait for Deirdre to tell him what would happen next.

They named the baby Agnes and, years later, when Kitty was a young woman living in London, she would look back on those early years with fonder memories than she could ever have imagined at the time.

Kitty left home when she was seventeen, with a head full of memories of childhood. Her mother, Deirdre, continued to insist that her girls shouldn't be expected to have the same education as their brothers, but by some way of compensation she made sure they appreciated the city ways which she knew so well, taking them to Cork every year. They always travelled by train, whose arrival was an event not to be missed. It puffed and steamed into Drimoleague from Bantry, before being uncoupled to enable the wagons to be reassembled for the next destination. All the children had loved the bustle of the railway, with the coal being loaded and the fireman and drivers shouting their orders.

They viewed these men as almost another species; definitely superior beings. Fascinated by the uniforms and the names – Stationmaster Collins (no relation, they were told), and Mick the Coal, they would stare admiringly at them. There were three platforms - known as The Down, The Up, and The Back. This was a bit confusing for the girls but for their brothers it provided an opportunity to demonstrate their much superior knowledge in all mechanical matters.

'What train did ye go on for Cork then Kitty - was it the Skibreen train changed through The Back or was it the Bantry train which came in on The Up?' they'd query, confident in the belief that the answers would be wrong. Michael and the boys explained the logistics of the train lines to the girls on a regular basis. The lines merged and then separated again, running in all directions, on their way to and from those towns further west.

'Now girls', their father had explained, trying but failing to sound patient. 'The Back is the name of the platform where the trains come in from Bantry. Try again. If the Skibbereen train always comes in on the platform called The Up, then the engine detaches itself and the Bantry train goes under the bridge and back down to connect with the what, Hannah?'

'Sure, I couldn't care at all,' said Hannah, far more interested in what her mother was going to buy her when she got to Cork.

'I know, Dada, it's the Skibbereen train, an' that's the one we get for Cork,' Kitty was always pleased to be getting ahead of Hannah. 'An' I do always know it, Hannah, you should too. It's The Up we take for Cork and when we come home we arrive in on The Back, because that's us, all back!'

She'd loved the smell and noises of the steam engines, the whistling and the clanging of the buffers as the wagons coupled. Then when the engines charged up it made the station seem like a world apart from their regular routine and on the outbound journey, it felt like a great adventure.

She remembered how, when Deirdre and the girls arrived in Cork, onto Albert Quay, the first leg of their expedition was a riverside walk into town. They'd loved the anonymity of the city; enjoying the freedom of not having to stop and greet everyone and be politely attentive. When they were allowed to run ahead of Mam, they felt more carefree than they had ever done in Drimoleague.

Cork, built alongside the river Lee, had seemed an exotic destination then but now she thought its splendour diminished compared to the majesty of London. She recalled how they had all enjoyed following Mam's confident directions in her hometown as they were introduced to the market area. She knew the shops which sold the highest quality fabrics, shoes, wools, and embroidery threads. Their mother only ever looked at goods which could not be obtained locally, and she'd always tried to buy the best.

Kitty, Agnes, and Hannah had never left the city without their own parcels; material for a new coat maybe, or wool for a hat and gloves, and always a ribbon each. Then there had been the First Communion shopping. This was a very big event for the girls.

The boys only needed white woollen jumpers and were none too concerned with their appearance, wanting to get out of their impractical white clothes as soon as possible. The girls, however had to have new white dresses, with a head covering, usually a veil.

She was sure that her mother found it a challenge to dress such young girls in elaborate outfits without making them look like miniature brides. She had watched her mother pick out fine trimmings, turning Hannah's otherwise ordinary and plain Communion dress into something much prettier.

Kitty had known that everyone wore their elder sister's First Communion dress so when her own turn came, she had Hannah's and then of course Agnes had worn hers. It had been thanks to Deirdre that each girl had her own special trim or piece of lace, making the garment individual.

This had been a good arrangement for Hannah and Kitty, but when Agnes's turn came, she was much too small. Poor Agnes, the knee length dress had reached the middle of her calf. Undaunted, Deirdre lengthened the garment with a fine layer of organza and made a short dress into a long one.

'We are ahead of all the others,' Deirdre had declared. 'Long Communion dresses are just coming into fashion in Cork and Dublin.' No-one ever questioned where her mother obtained this information, or whether it was indeed a fact. And Agnes looked beautiful. In fact, Agnes had always looked beautiful, and regularly on their Cork outings well-meaning shopkeepers, singled her out for attention.

Thinking of Agnes, with her kind disposition and great love of life brought a lump to Kitty's throat. Although she had only been a child herself when the baby had been brought home, she felt guilty about the time when she had only tolerated the little newcomer. It had taken a couple of years for her to get over the jealousy which came from having her mother's attention diverted to a new baby. Eventually Agnes's unwavering loyalty to her as older sister won. Almost without noticing, she had come to love her very much and now missed her more than she missed any of the others, except Roisin, of course.

Roisin was her godmother. And now she had a letter from her, in her pocket, just waiting to be read.

Chapter 3

Kitty and Will. London, England
1921

'...Ooh, mind the Nanny, sorry Nanny, naughty, naughty us.'

Kitty, making her way through the crowds at the top of Oxford Street, shook her head clear of the reminiscing as she was jostled by a pair of brightly dressed young women, laughing and hanging onto the arm of a not a particularly good-looking man, but the white silk scarf and fine worsted wool coat caught Kitty's eye.

She felt a tinge of envy when she recognised the quality. She had been aware of the bright colours and flowing scarves which the Londoners were wearing since the day she arrived, and she often felt drab by comparison. She wondered, not for the first time, what it must be like to live surrounded by fun, sociable friends whose main aim in life was to enjoy themselves.

All three looked as though they had been to a party, a faint whiff of alcohol catching Kitty's attention, before they spun off down Oxford Street, lost in the crowds. She didn't much mind being referred to as nanny and it wasn't an uncommon assumption. She was pushing a perambulator, she had two small children on board, and she was a young woman who looked sensible and responsible in her dark grey coat.

But she was so enjoying her freedom. It was well beyond anything she had known in Cork. People here would be even less likely to be recognised than they would in the Irish city.

'How lovely to do what you want without anyone telling all the neighbours.' Kitty murmured to her four-year-old nephew, Finbarr, not expecting a response. She stopped for a minute, letting Finbarr down so he could look in the window of the elegant coffee shop, situated on the corner near Marble Arch.

'And now this is the place I will bring your Grandma and your Auntie Agnes for afternoon tea when they come over to visit next year. They promised they would. Finbarr, do you think so? Shall you come too? What cake would you like?'

This was a fine place, reckoned Kitty. Mam would approve and maybe find some cakes she had never come across before. Kitty, aware that rationing was still in place across England, was surprised by the impressive selection.

'Pardon Ma'am, didn't see you there'. A tall man, dressed in brown gabardine, and with a trilby hat lifted to acknowledge her as a lady, skirted around Kitty, pram, and nephews, before rapidly continuing down Oxford Street. This was another wonder for Kitty.

'Back home, Finbarr, people you knew stopped for a chat, people you didn't know were introduced to you by friends or they would put themselves forward. Strangers would, maybe, ask you to get to know them, but here in London it is so different. You know the lady next door invited me to call in anytime, but when I did call, she said she was busy.'

Other neighbours had occasionally invited Kitty in, maybe she'd get invited in for a cup of tea or maybe not. Kitty was more used to the formality of tea being served at a table with some sweet treats, scones, soda bread, jam or cheese.

She was learning that in London a cup of tea was just a cup of tea and sometimes the invitation to come in was only meant to be polite or the opportunity to start a conversation and find out more about the Irish girl; although she found that at other times it really did lead to friendship.

She noticed hardship too, and the elaborate steps people took to keep their poverty concealed. She had come to realise that the streets of London, contrary to the words of the song, were not paved with anything remotely like gold, and that people in her own home town, although it was not a prosperous place, had a better supply of food than had most of the people she came into contact with in London. She knew that the war, which had only ended a few years earlier had caused rationing but didn't know why, although basics were plentiful, there was still a scarcity of jam, sugar, and good cuts of meat.

She was still disorientated by her move from home, but she always made an effort not to let the feeling of being an outsider show. Six months ago, she had been learning to make the best of her skills as a seamstress in the girls' sewing and knitting school back home, loving it and believing that she was showing great promise.

Remembering the pleasure she took in mastering the structure and order of the craft; sorting colours, standardising sizes, shape, and style and learning the "measure twice and cut once", approach to dressmaking.

Certainly, it was a philosophy which suited her own approach, but mostly she had enjoyed the opportunity to inhabit another life where fine fabrics and colourful designs enriched her days and lifted her thoughts away from the drab and the ordinary.

There had been friends, a few admirers, and generally Kitty was happy with her life.

That was until the message came from her brother, Michael Og and she was whisked away; her own wishes not really being taken into account.

Her brother had moved to Chelsea in London, along with Gina, his new wife, five years earlier, having an offer of work near Battersea. Now he had two young children, and apparently

Gina was making a slow recovery from a recent bout of pneumonia. Help was needed and it was only natural that they would look to family. Hannah was already married and Agnes was too young.

Kitty recalled Agnes's tears when she had left for London, on the mail boat from Queenstown Harbour, just outside Cork. The pretty dainty child, with a full head of strawberry blond curls and with finer features than the bold strong frames of Deirdre and Michael's children, had caused other people, intent on their own distressed farewells, to look across with sympathy for the little girl. Agnes was stretching on tiptoes to see - she was too old for anyone's shoulders – and calling a heartbroken goodbye.

Tired of looking in the coffee house window, Kitty hoisted young Finbarr back onto the end of the pram and skilfully dodged a horse and cart, several bicycles, and a motor car. Having safely crossed the busy intersection, she wheeled the children through the imposing entrance of Hyde Park.

She thought that autumn in London was not too bad. Recalling how an Irish autumn could be wet with bushes stripped bare of colour, in London autumn gave the trees and parklands a great vibrancy - all red, yellow, and gold. She loved the creaking and swaying of the branches on the majestic old trees.

It was really very different from West Cork, although of course that had its own special beauty. Here she found a more predictable form of nature in the parks and enjoyed pointing out the squirrels and ducks to the children. In the wild fields around her home at that time of year she remembered how as a child, she'd just run and explore, no squirrels or ducks as far as she could remember, but it was a great freedom and no trolley bus either to take her back into the warmth of home.

Autumn nights in London also brought Kitty some excitement. There was an abundance of lights and illuminations in the city which amazed and pleased her. An additional advantage was that most of Kitty's clothes fitted better with the winter months than with the summer days, being heavy and dark coloured. She knew she would find it difficult to buy more when the season changed.

And she loved the London transport. She could travel easily from Chelsea to the centre of London on a trolley bus or tram, or walk along the streets if necessary, as she had to do with the pram. She planned to go with one of the girls who worked in the house next door to try out the new underground soon. She wrote regularly to her godmother Roisin, able to more honestly express her liking for the city than she could to Mam, who assumed London to be inferior to Cork. And now this unexpected, out of sequence, letter had arrived. Kitty felt in her coat pocket for the sharp cornered envelope and quivered with anticipation.

It was Roisin's handwriting, and Kitty suspected there would be important news, which was why she was saving it to read in the park. She could never find any privacy in her brother's house. It wasn't the lack of space, more an expectation that she wasn't entitled to a life of her own. That's what made her careful to select just the right place to read her letter, undisturbed and quiet. She did so treasure these contacts with Drimoleague.

Kitty recalled how, after Christmas the year Agnes was born, there had been no more talk about Roisin leaving the school; in fact she had been given an assistant teacher to help her. She'd told them all the exact conversation and Kitty remembered it as though it was yesterday.
'I've had the full backing of Father Daley in getting approval for further education for the local girls. He's right behind me these days, an' a powerful man he is too in these parts.

Sure, I've told him he can bring that man in from Skibbereen, or wherever he wants, to the school now, but as an assistant. I have the final say in what gets taught and who comes over to my school. Imagine, I'm a headmistress now. Oh, an' I also told him we would be staying in the schoolhouse, Mam and me. His new teacher will have to be found another house.'

Looking back on it now, Kitty wondered how she had ever managed that, but her mother seemed to find it quite natural for the priest to have changed his mind and attitude so quickly.

Walking swiftly through the park, with Finbarr impatiently kicking his heels against the pram seat, Kitty soon found a bench near a sheltered corner, close enough to the trees to protect her from an unexpected squall of rain. From there she let her gaze drift over to the pond, the surface corrugated by the breeze. Lifting Finbarr down from the pram seat and spreading a blanket for little brother Eamon, she settled herself on the bench and pulled the letter out of her pocket.

'Roisin is so great, she will tell me all the news which I don't get from Mam, and more gossip.' Slitting the envelope with the pretty letter opener which Roisin had given her as a leaving gift, 'So's you think of us every time you get a letter, wherever it is from.' It had an enamelled handle, engraved with a Celtic symbol of a horse, and Kitty always kept it in her pocketbook.

Roisin regularly brought news of developing national politics. Ireland had sought home rule for some years, which meant, as far as Roisin and Kitty were concerned, that the British might no longer rule their part of Ireland.

What happened in the north of Ireland was of little interest to them, but the fact that Ireland might one day be called a 'Free State' sounded exciting and liberating.

Neither Kitty nor her family had experienced any particular disadvantage from British rule, or disruption from the rebels either, but Kitty knew that they would all be relieved to see the end of the civil unrest.

'Dearest Kitty,

Some lovely news for you today, my darling girl. You will never guess it, and I want to tell you before your Mam does.

I have found a great love - imagine, me, at the age of 39!

I'm courted by Michael O'Brian, he's a widower who himself has no family. Although Mam has been dead these three years past I know I'd have her blessing. It's what she always wanted for me and the boys will come home for the wedding.

But it will be a quiet one Kitty, in the spring next year. I want no fuss and bother so don't be thinking about coming over. I'll certainly see you anyway, as Michael has promised we will have a honeymoon in England next year.'

Surprised and pleased for her friend, Kitty absorbed the news whilst watching some boys chasing the ducks too near the water to be safe.

'Yes, I am very happy for your news Roisin. I think I might know Michael O'Brian, he runs the Post Office in Drimoleague. Although I can't see his face now, I remember he was thought of as a kind man. He will look after you.'

'Some young men from the West Cork area have been caught up in suspicious activities around the troubles with the Black and Tans.

I don't believe they knew exactly what they were fighting for, they meant well. Anyway girl, fair play to them, they were enthusiastic, energetic, and fearless.

Of course, they were also easily led and even more easily found out.

Some are now in hiding, two are in prison. You know this is never going to change the face of Ireland, but it breaks families up, divides opinions, and I'm sorry to say there seems to be resentment against all types of authority now.'

Kitty folded the letter into her pocket planning to re-read the interesting bits at home later.

The letter made her feel unsettled again and brought back memories of the years before she left. Coupled with these thoughts was a conflict, a longing to be part of it, with her own home and family.

Kitty remembered how she had felt in turns insulted by her mother's insistence that she leave to look after Michael Og's family and relieved that she didn't have to make a decision about her future. She settled on insulted, for now.

Maybe she would turn her dressmaking skills to good use for Roisin's wedding. She was developing a bit of a name for herself and had recently started getting some orders from Michael's friends. She wondered whether she could obtain sufficient material to make Roisin a petticoat to wear on her wedding day.

With her thoughts on Roisin and a possible design for the embroidery on the wedding gift, she did not notice a man propped against a tree reading The London Post. He was tall and slim with a strong boned face and looked somewhat undernourished. His pale, carefully trimmed moustache was matched by a head of wispy blond hair and altogether he seemed grave and serious.

William West, recently returned from the war where he had served as a sergeant, was living with his family in the East End of London. He was exhausted, disillusioned, and usually a little short-tempered. He believed he had seen enough wartime battles to last him forever, and he wasn't keen to engage in any more confrontation, at home or abroad.

Glancing up from his paper, he surprised himself by liking the look of the neat young woman sitting under the tree, dressed in sombre winter clothes. And he didn't often like the look of much these days. He thought she was probably a nanny. At that moment, young Finbarr, always wanting to know what was round the next corner, ran off towards the pond, chasing a drake. Kitty leapt up from the bench, calling after him.

She was slowed down by needing to gather up Eamon first and then handbrake the pram. The squawking of the ducks and the cries from Kitty drew attention from other park-goers. William's irritation with the domestic scene before him tempted him to move to a quieter area of the park to continue reading, but seeing a child running towards the pond soon changed his mind. Soldier training had taught him to act fast and act decisively, so he did.

Two quick strides towards the child churning up the flock of frightened ducks in his high buttoned boots enabled William to catch young Finbarr by the collar, trapping a handful of woollen coat under his fist. Tucking his newspaper in his pocket, he used his free arm to lift the boy up away from the water's edge. Finbarr yelled as William looked around for the young woman, although he knew exactly where she was, he could hear her shouting. Passing the wriggling child across to Kitty he instinctively lifted his hat by way of silent introduction. She wondered, not for the first time, what Englishmen had done when faced with a woman before the introduction of headwear. In Ireland a person would be greeted by the obvious, a 'Hello, Missus' would have been sufficient.

She subconsciously assessed his clothing as she stood in front of him, noting the good quality woollen weave in his suit and the gloss on his brown leather shoes but neither had what she would consider style. Looking up she was pleasantly surprised to meet his sparkling blue eyes and, she decided, his moustache was attractive too.

Feeling grateful to the English stranger who had put himself out to save Finbarr from, at the very least, an impact with a muddy puddle, Kitty smiled. Not having to explain, apologise, and take responsibility for cleaning and repairing any damage was going to be a huge benefit when she returned the children to Gina. Anyway, that was her reasoning for responding more kindly to the man with the lifted hat than she would normally have done.

'Thank you so much, sir, we can manage now. It's time they were getting home anyway.'

Her soft Cork accent was one he couldn't initially place, but an opening gambit of, 'Are you Irish?' seemed a little forward even in his tetchy frame of mind.

'My pleasure and privilege to be of service, Ma'am, it doesn't happen to me every day now.'

Kitty sensed the bitterness in his voice and hesitated – should she gather the children up and head off, or encourage him?

Definitely not encourage him she thought, whoever is he anyway? She gave him another smile, the one she had recently learned. It suggested friendliness but not overt encouragement. She had seen it used in shops when unrequested conversations were attempted. The English Smile, she called it.

'Pardon me for asking Ma'am, but are these your own children? They are very handsome lads.'

'Ah no, I'm not married, these are my brother's boys. I came over from Ireland earlier in the year to help look after them, but I also work, I am a seamstress, fully trained and intending to be my own boss.'

William's heart sank, not another independent woman, London seemed full of them just now. It had been so different before he went away.

Returning from the war he had expected his own prospects to be brighter. But here he was, supplementing his war pension with an office job, which bored him, and a salary that was never going to afford a Morris Cowley motor car, never mind a wife and family. Now he thought he might take the initiative, just in case his prospects improved.

'Mind if I walk you to the park gates? The lad might decide to run again?'

'Thank you that is very kind, as long as you are sure it's not out of your way. Say thank you to the gentleman, Finbarr.'

'What is his name then?'asked Finbarr, looking up curiously at the stranger

Kitty flushed, but William stepped forward pleasing Kitty by giving the trilby a rest.

'William West, please call me Will.'

'Thank you, Mr West',

'And I'm Kitty Collins.'

Neither Kitty nor William mentioned the park gate again, and William enjoyed the sensation of walking down Oxford Street with a pretty girl and a couple of little boys.

He wondered whether passers-by would mistake them for a family and that did not make him feel uncomfortable.

Could he find a decent future here in London, he wondered? There was so much pessimism in the newspapers, the mood and expectation in Britain seemed to be declining, and he really did not know where his future might lie.

His experience in the army had opened his eyes to different lifestyle options and now he took a keen interest in national affairs. Attempting to engage Kitty in what he hoped was an interesting topic of conversation he asked,

'What impact do you think the coal strike had, Kitty? Is it much talked about in your house?'

Kitty looked up at him, quite bewildered. She couldn't think of a single response; the question was so unexpected and without context.

'Maybe you can tell me how your family feels about the increased IRA activity in Ireland then, Kitty. Do you know anyone involved?'

'Indeed, no William, you wouldn't know anything about it where I come from, a lovely quiet part of the country. I never heard tell of a thing.'

Kitty was irked by his questioning, and she certainly wasn't going to share any information with this awkward Englishman.

By the time they had walked down Oxford Street they were both wondering whether either of them had any common ground but when William bravely suggested a walk in the park on Saturday afternoon, Kitty surprised herself by readily agreeing, making a mental note not to bring the boys.

As for Will, he went home to East London feeling lightness in his step and a renewed kindness to the women in his life. Maybe underneath all this gaiety and independence they were really the same as ever - needing his gallantry to save them; from what he was unsure. He pondered his prospects again, he just couldn't get away from thinking about his expectations for the future, and maybe, he thought, this girl will be part of that future now.

'I really do want a motor car to impress this lovely girl, but it will set me back more than I earn in a year. Well maybe a cheap, well-used one could be found. Would she like that do you think?'

Walking into his home his good mood evaporated on hearing his sisters talking about the nightclubs and jazz clubs, which were opening in London.

'Do you not think there is more to life than having fun, Elana?' his brow furrowed grumpily. 'If you had been a soldier you wouldn't be carrying on like this every night. People lost lives for you. Is that what it was all about? Just so you and your friends can keep enjoying yourselves?'

'Give over, Will, you're not the only one who was affected, get out and have a bit of fun. Get yourself a woman. Learn the Charleston.' Elana, a solidly built twenty-two-year-old, snapped. Then, in an attempt to lighten the mood, she began to dance to a tune only she could hear, shaking her hands by her sides and making the soles of her shoes tap, rather heavily, on the yellow and black chequered linoleum.

Will, aware that he wouldn't glean any sense from his sisters, stomped upstairs with his newspaper.

The following Saturday Kitty was up early helping Gina with the boys, making sure there wasn't any doubt about her afternoon in the park.

'All right now Gina, I'll be back before dark and I'll help with the boys' teas. Just let me borrow your blue hat and scarf for today will you now, there's a bit of a wind out.'

Gina watched Kitty fixing her hair in the hall mirror, noticing with a touch of envy how the blue scarf knotted at her throat and the hat firmly pinned to her head looked so much better on the dark curly hair and creamy skin of Kitty than they did when she wore them.

Gina did not seem to share Kitty's interest in fashion or colour, her style was more about comfort. Kitty thought her rather frumpy as well as appearing to be exhausted by the whole business of family life. The two women had little in common.

Kitty set out early, glad to be away from the claustrophobic atmosphere within the house. She'd always loved being outdoors, enjoying the wind whipping up leaves and now she was tingling not only with the fresh air but also excited about the meeting ahead.

She hopped onto the trolleybus at the end of the Brompton Road, squeezing her slight frame into the half space of a spare seat, the other half taken over by an overweight woman dressed as though she was going house-cleaning.

The woman wore a faded floral overall, crossed in the front with grimy laces straining at the seams and her head swathed in a knotted scarf, giving the impression of an Indian turban but without any exotic appeal.

The bus was filled with people of all ages and styles, which always amazed and delighted Kitty. The equality and ease of movement, the ability to be anonymous, not needing to know who else was on the bus, or care.

A dark-skinned bus conductor asked for her fare and she silently scolded herself for being surprised by how clean he was compared to her seating companion, who smelled of freshly boiled cabbage and stale clothes.

Never having encountered a person of colour before arriving in England, Kitty had felt embarrassed in the presence of other races, not sure what to say or do, but soon discovered that she had more in common with them than she would have expected.

The signs on many of the lodging houses, 'No Dogs, no Irish, no Blacks', gave Kitty a sense of solidarity with those 'Blacks', which she did not feel towards the Chinese, Poles or other nationalities she was meeting for the first time. She heard rumours of drug trafficking and that Chinatown was becoming a hotbed for vice. None of her friends would want to venture too far into Soho. The tantalising thought of a night out in such a heady cosmopolitan area occasionally crossed Kitty's mind though, until she was told of the unbelievably high prices.

She was enjoying thinking about the range and variety of lifestyles she had met since arriving in London and, not paying attention to the journey, nearly missed her stop.

Jumping off and pushing through the waiting crowd at the tram stop, Kitty tried to quell the fluttering in her belly. She was nervous now, rather than excited and hoped Will would be there on time. Still early, she walked the long way through the park approaching their agreed spot, the pergola, from across the pond. It was worth Kitty having dressed carefully; she looked as elegant as was possible given the limits of her wardrobe.

William was watching as she approached. Leaning against the wrought iron frame, he eyed her tall but slim figure and healthy complexion appreciatively. He liked the soft blue hat and scarf, no cloche pulled down to cover her face or rouged cheeks, he noticed. He thought she was unlike any other young woman he had met recently and hoped to know her better.

'Oh, hello, Kitty - didn't see you comin'. Good to see you again.' This was as much of a greeting as William could manage. Kitty just smiled an acknowledgement. Silent walking took place for some time, although the usual cacophony of children, bicycles, and nannies filled the gap and made the silence less awkward.

'Shall we have some tea, Kitty?' The tentative invitation from Will broke through the cheerful boisterous background noises.

Kitty was glad to accept this diversion and, much to her surprise, she learned, over a pot of tea and Victoria sponge, that his experiences overseas made him rather more interesting than she had at first assumed.

She began to relax and listened carefully when he told her tales of France and Belgium; then gasped in horror when he told her, calmly and after a well-chewed mouthful of cake, how he had watched a fellow soldier choke on a piece of meat he had stolen from his comrade's plate.

'Was he alright, so?' she asked in alarm.

'Sorry to say not, Kitty, he died. That taught him a lesson and a few others around him also.'

Kitty sniffed disapprovingly and it was all she could do to stop herself asking whether, if a man choked to death would he benefit from that or any other lesson?

Will recovered himself by changing the subject and telling her about his plans for the future, including the bull nosed Morris, which he made out was a near future acquisition. The rest of the afternoon passed quickly and after having been "safely escorted", in Will's words, to the tramline, she agreed to meet him again.

During that autumn they met regularly, and in the weeks leading up to Christmas they began to explore more of London. Oxford Street, with its lights and shoppers, came alive and sparkling in December.

Kitty preferred Regent Street. And considered it to be a smarter shopping area, although it was adjacent to the bustling Oxford Circus it had a wider range of elegant shops, whose windows displayed the wealth and marvellous variety of goods.
She tried to remember the details for letters back home to her mother.

Her favourite store was Liberty's and exploring the magnificent interior became a regular pastime. Luxurious fabrics, elegant surroundings, and a quirky approach to presentation all suited her taste for colour and style. Will surprised them both with his willingness to accompany her. This was a state he found himself in more often than he would have expected. But it was mainly his interest in the construction of the Tudor extension, built so that trading would continue whilst renovations were being completed on the other premises, that particularly interested him.

'Did you know,' he told Kitty one afternoon, 'that the company wanted the front of the store to resemble the bow of a Tudor ship, and to achieve this effect they used the timbers of two ships: HMS Impregnable and HMS Hindustan.'

'Well, that's very interesting Will, but I prefer the inside, if you don't mind.'

Will, knowing that both had been naval training ships wasn't interested in their history but it was the construction and original approach to surplus maritime materials which drew his attention.

'Surplus material, you see Kitty, what do you think Britain could use me for then?'

Kitty really had no idea what he was talking about and climbed effortlessly up Liberty's oak staircase to the heavily accessorised upper rooms. She liked to immerse herself in the vibrant colours of the velvets, brocades, and silks, which were the store's trademark, it lifted her spirits and allowed her to dream.

Catching sight of her across one of the halls which created a central area within the bustling store, William smiled at the realisation that this quiet, reserved Irish girl had come to mean so much to him. Her naivety and wonder at the abundance of London was always offset by her practical down to earth approach.

'Will, I do like the way London people style themselves wearing nothing but the best, just as though it was Sunday every day, but I don't think they have anything put away in case their luck changes. I don't even think they consider what would happen if the landlord wanted them out or they had another baby, or there was no work. I think they just expect this to be a good time for ever.'

Kitty couldn't know how these words warmed William's heart. Ever cautious and prepared for the worst, he was growing increasingly distanced from his sisters and their friends, as well as from the other men in the office. In fact, he felt he had little in common with any of them in terms of a future lifestyle.

Now, as Kitty's dark head bent over a turquoise scarf, he moved through the room to get to her side. 'Oh look, I just have to buy this for Mam, for Christmas. Roisin's wedding is coming up and she would look so fine wearing this against her dark coat. I know it's expensive, but she will really love it and we never see anything like it at home.'

Kitty's flushed cheeks gave her sallow skin an attractive lift and Will thought he might lean across and kiss her in front of all the customers, then he remembered how she would hate such an act. "An exhibition" she would call it. In order to avoid her gaze he turned his concentration on the scarf.

'Do you have sufficient to buy it, Kitty? I can help if you would let me.'

'No, Will, I've been saving up for Christmas and everyone is getting something nice from me.'

Did that include him? Will wondered but did not say anything whilst Kitty made her purchase; he counted more than one package though.

As the weather was expected to be very mild over Christmas, William told Kitty that he would be able to meet her over the holiday period without too much difficulty, even though public transport would be reduced. He planned to walk if necessary. Kitty was expected to spend Christmas Day with brother Michael and the family, and William would be with his own people, but Boxing Day, she agreed, would be an opportunity for them to have some time together.

She was busy indoors now, finalising Roisin's wedding gift. A cream silk petticoat had been created from an offcut found in a bargain barrel in Selfridges and Kitty was spending all her spare time embroidering delicate trails of flowers across the bodice.

Her friend Eileen had provided the transfers and Gina found several skeins of embroidery thread, which she had purchased with good intention, but never used, before the children were born.

She had also been busy making paper-chains out of coloured magazine cuttings with Finbarr between embroidery sessions and she was pleased with the result as there was nothing else festive about the living room in Michael's house, save one small dry looking tree, purchased reluctantly from the grocer's cart and meagrely draped with thinning tinsel.

Kitty was not surprised when Christmas Day at Michael's house turned out to be a dreary affair. Up early morning for Mass at the nearby church then back through the unseasonably mild and foggy streets to the house she could never begin to call home. The boys, Finbarr and Eamon, were excited and wanting to open their Christmas presents, but Gina, pregnant again, was tired and irritable. Michael took, as ever, the stoical approach. Never one for a drama, Kitty was reminded of the time long ago when he and her other brother Dan had rifled Mam's cupboards for fruitcake, that day when they were all alone, the day Agnes was born. She and Michael had always had a good relationship, and he still made sure she was treated fairly in his house.

The house in Chelsea, with its brown paintwork and gloomy pictures, looked and felt a bit bereft of cheer all year round, and as it was Christmas the dour atmosphere was even more striking. What a contrast to Carrigmor, she thought. Mam would always make the house feel like home, there were little treats and delicacies and a good fire to make you feel comfortable and secure.

Kitty watched Michael light a fire in the grate when they came back indoors, accepting that it would be too late in the day to heat the room comfortably and missing, once again the presence of the peat fire which Deirdre had always kept banked and ready to offer instant warmth. She and Michael had worked together that morning preparing the vegetables and now they checked that the Christmas bird, a chicken, was browning before settling down with the children and Gina to open the gifts.

Kitty had bought everyone a present: a set of painted blocks for Eamon, a wooden train for Finbarr, a soft scarf for Gina - not from Liberty's this one, Mam's gift was to be special - and some tobacco for Michael. She was planning on getting Roisin's silk petticoat in the post very soon. It would still be in good time for the wedding and then it could double up as her Christmas gift. A parcel had arrived for Kitty from home. It was still wrapped in its brown paper and sat under the tree in the corner of the room.

'Go on, open it Kitty.' begged Finbarr, 'What are you waiting for?' Kitty looked at Finbarr and then around the room, as though seeing them all for the first time.

'What am I waiting for?' she murmured. 'What am I waiting for?'

'I'm waiting for better than this,' she inwardly answered herself. 'My brother's family - and I will always care about them - but they are not enough for me. This is not how I will be spending my life.'

She shook her head to clear her thoughts, putting on the ghost of a smile and reached for the brown parcel under the tree. There were three gifts wrapped together, with a letter from Mam. Kitty wondered briefly whether Michael and his family felt embarrassed by her receiving a parcel from home whilst they had not thought to buy her anything. She swallowed hard and reminded herself of the promise she had made earlier, not to make this her life.

First unwrapped was a gift from Agnes, an embroidered picture, 'Well, counted cross stitch actually,' Kitty noted with a smile, embroidery was never going to be Agnes's strength, but she assumed someone had suggested it as a gift. On the back Agnes had written. 'Dear Kitty. Happy Christmas. I miss you. Agnes.'

'Let me see, let me see.' Finbarr tried to grab the gift from Kitty.

'I'll hang this in my room, Finbarr, then you can look but don't touch, it's not made for little boys.'

'Now, Kitty, he only wants a look,' interrupted Gina, unaware of the significance that these gifts from home had for Kitty.

'You just don't understand do you, Gina?' Kitty snapped, 'Sure, you have your family and it's all about your family. I'm here, miles away from home. Lovely to be with you all, of course it is, but I miss my own and I'll always come second here, so I will.'

An uncomfortable atmosphere clouded the remainder of the day and the meal was less than festive. Kitty, pleading a headache, went up to her room after tea for an early night.

Over in East London, William was missing Kitty. Not an impetuous man, he had thought seriously about whether to continue seeing her or not. He really found her presence enchanting and over the weeks had come to view her as a woman who would make someone a fine wife and mother. On the other hand, he was reluctant to move into an area of conflict and he reckoned his family wouldn't be happy about him marrying a Catholic.

Religion was rarely discussed at home, but he remembered as a small boy his parents telling him and his sisters not to play with the Irish or the Jewish children in the area. He sensed it was a fear of losing their own identity and his Dad had told him often enough that it was his duty to marry respectably and continue the family line and name, with children who would represent his own London East End background.

'Sometimes,' he thought, 'I feel like an outsider in my own family. I'm really not keen to spend too much time in the pub with Dad; not interested at all in Eve and Elana's personal lives, frivolous and irresponsible as they are; and, Mum, well she's lovely, of course, but she never seems to know about anything outside our house. So, I can't really talk to anyone about what I want.'

Arthur, his father, had taken him to the pub on Christmas morning and over their pints of bitter asked him whether he was serious about the girl he had been seeing.

'No, Dad, she's just a friend,' Will replied anxiously, feeling an unexpected guilt towards Kitty as he lied. 'I have no money and it doesn't look like I'm ever going to get my Bull Nosed Morris, so a wife is really not on the cards.'

'Well son, you're back two years now, demobbed as I think they say, and there never is a right time; so maybe if you like her, think about it.'

'Drink up now, Dad', Will encouraged, 'You know Mum will have the Christmas dinner on the table sharp at one o'clock, we can't keep her waiting.' He didn't want to further discuss the possibility of his future with his father, time enough to let him know when it had all been agreed and decided.

He was looking forward to his date with Kitty on Boxing Day and to giving her the gift he had bought for her. He hoped she was missing him today. His sisters were chattering non-stop throughout the meal, shrieking with laughter as they recalled their friend's latest escapades.

'Funny how it's always your friends we hear about, never a tale about your own misadventures,' Arthur interrupted, 'Heaven preserve the country when you two get the vote.'

William thought his father had the right attitude. He considered it worrying that in another six and seven years both women would have turned thirty, eligible to vote if married and he wondered what sort of wives and mothers they would make. And if they never married then what on earth could their future hold?

After the meal there was the customary exchange of gifts. Will had made a real effort this year; taking Kitty's example of generosity towards family he bought both Eve and Elana silk stockings and his mother a faux fur collar for her winter coat.

Arthur was more of a challenge, so he had settled for pipe tobacco. In return he had a pair of gloves, a new pipe, and a wooden fretwork pipe-holder, carved by his father.

By the early evening he felt the need for quiet and his own company. Excusing himself, he left the house and lit his pipe as he walked cautiously through the East End streets, knowing they were dangerous once they began to narrow away from the main routes.

The electric lighting was poor and unreliable and numerous alleyways and side entrances held potential danger in every shadow. He had heard talk in the office about protection rackets, rival gangs, prostitutes, and illegal drug-running which made him determined to leave the area.

'I reckon,' he had told Arthur the previous November, who accompanied him to lay a wreath at the Cenotaph, 'I feel more in tune with these crowds outside Whitehall who have come to say goodbye to the unknown soldier from France, than I do with my pals here in London.'

'I know that, son,' his father had replied patiently, 'but sometimes you should be a bit kinder to your sisters and a bit less critical of the young ones. I know you don't like the way they dress, and you don't approve of them having fun. It's because you saw such terrible things. But they aren't doing any harm and you could have a bit of fun yourself now.'

Stepping into the middle of the road, avoiding the darker corners of the ill-lit street, he gave himself a stern talking to. 'Well, it's a new world now; no-one bothers any more whether you are the chief yourself or just one of the indians.

Indeed, being a black musician seems to be the very thing these days.' He even admitted to having been just a little bit amused the day before when he had watched Elana and Eve clumsily dance the 'Black Bottom' after dinner.

Recalling how they had described, with ever increasing excitement, the arrival of black jazz musicians from Harlem, he had really tried to share their enthusiasm but failed. 'If you keep that pitch up', he had cried in desperation, as their chatter reached glass-shattering levels, covering his ears with his hands, 'You will alert every dog in the neighbourhood.'

Dragging deeply on his pipe and skirting the puddles, he allowed his thoughts to return to his favourite subject. 'Kitty wouldn't be interested in that sort of thing,' he decided. 'She is like a beacon of light shining out across this murky city, a place which has gone completely mad.'

It was this enticing combination of factors, both real and imagined, that helped him make up his mind. The next day a sluggish mixture of smoke and fog filled the streets, shrouding the buildings in a threatening opacity. The atmosphere seemed also to shroud Kitty and William as they made their separate ways towards the meeting place in Hyde Park, dissatisfaction with their current lifestyle looming heavily over them.

'Kitty, Happy Christmas!' called William as soon as her dark coat became visible. Although it was much less smoky in the park, the foggy mist still reduced visibility down to fifty yards. She was early, but that didn't surprise William, he was beginning to get used to her ways and she was never late. He took his pipe out of his mouth and moved quickly towards Kitty, taking his hat off ready to offer her a kiss on the cheek.

Kitty, looking up, saw the young man who might change her future. Nicely spoken, considerate and kind and she felt she could rely on his interest in her. She had even begun to think about how life might be with him. But her thoughts had only taken the first tentative steps along that road and Kitty never did anything in a hurry.

Offering her cheek, she twitched her nose slightly at the damp musky smell of tobacco and responded shyly to his Christmas greeting.

They walked for a while, without speaking, through the busy park.

Today it was filled with the irritable squawking of the ducks, disturbed by excited small children trying out their new Christmas toys. Undeterred by the pea-souper outside the park some had brought their spinning tops, the chrome brightly painted, a few had tricycles, and barely-skilled fathers were demonstrating the complex art of kite flying.

The few who wanted to sail their new model boats further into the pond than was wise were continually being called to order by their nervous parents, most of whom were unfamiliar with the responsibility of handling their children, as Boxing Day was a holiday for the nannies.

Today it was the mothers who were pushing the prams and the fathers who were keeping an eye on over-excited young charges, making sure they didn't exceed their fun quota and return home overtired or, worse still, dirty.

With this informal family filled background, William was a little disappointed that when he reached for her hand, she moved it into her coat pocket. Eventually, damp and chilly, they arrived at the cafe and, once settled, both placed packages on the table. William's heart leapt as he realised Kitty had bought him a gift. He thought that offered a glimmer of hope and decided to state his intentions before he lost his nerve.

But what he actually said was 'Afternoon tea for two, please,' when he managed to address a white-faced waitress who looked reluctant to be working on Boxing Day, or possibly any day.

'Open your present then,' Kitty urged him, as she pushed the small parcel wrapped in red shiny paper towards him and fixed her clear brown eyes on his. A strand of dark curly hair escaped from under her hat, tumbling onto her flushed cheeks and he thought she had never looked prettier. William opened his gift, and a soft amber and cream scarf drifted onto the café table.

'It's lovely Kitty, thank you very much.' Feeling unaccountably disappointed, he realised that he had hoped for a more sentimental gift, something which might indicate Kitty's feelings and wondered in turn whether his gift to her would be well received.

Interrupted by the waitress slapping down the tray with the tea, then coming back with the cake stand containing a selection of dainty small cakes and sandwiches, William looked at Kitty without speaking, wondering how he could make her see what he saw. How his vision of a life together could be described in such a way as to make it irresistible.

Leaning across the table he passed Kitty his teacup and as she poured for them both he remembered his officer's advice and decided to take the bold approach. Meanwhile Kitty was enjoying the sandwiches and cakes, unaware of William's mood. He was often quiet and reticent.

'Mam bought me a leather notebook. She said I could use it to remind myself of all the tales of London I will tell her when she and Agnes come to see me next year. Hannah sent a writing pad and envelopes, with a pretty border, so she would always know my letters. Silly really, when no one else ever writes to her but it was a lovely thought, and then, from Agnes ... '
'Kitty, here is a little gift from me, I hope you like it.' William interrupted; he couldn't wait any longer.
The small silver-wrapped package had been lying on the table between them, and Kitty had pretended not to notice. Slightly shocked at William's interruption, she looked up sharply, her mouth filled with the sweet sugary confection of a lemon slice. Feigning surprise, she reached across and took the gift.
As she carefully removed the paper, thinking it might be used next Christmas, revealing an expensive looking jeweller's box from Bond Street she began to feel that events might be moving too quickly.

Her instincts were confirmed when she opened the padded navy leather lid and saw, lying on a tiny black silk cushion, a gold necklet - a small gold heart-shaped locket on a fine gold chain. Taken aback, she looked up, 'Thank you, it's lovely, but...'

'Will you marry me, Kitty?' William blurted before he could stop himself.

Kitty was completely dumbstruck. She realised that she did like him, quite a lot actually, but was several steps away from making a decision of that magnitude. However, she did not want to hurt his feelings and although this was what she might have been hoping for, she needed more time. Without giving herself time to think about a response, her words seemed to spring out, ill-considered.

'I could never marry a non-Catholic, so unless you agree to convert then no.'

William gasped; he had known there might be hesitation but hadn't expected such a clear rebuff.

'Indeed, that is an unusual request. Does that mean if I convert the answer is yes?'

'I wouldn't like to say. I don't like to be rushed into decisions and I need time to think. Will, I really do like the locket and I'm not saying no, I'm just not saying yes either.'

Kitty looked directly at him as she spoke, willing him to understand. Her deep brown eyes looked worried and pleading.

'Well now Kitty, I've never encountered such a reaction. Is it a no or a yes? When I was in the army men would have lost their lives over such a decision, I can't tolerate that sort of thing. As far as I'm concerned, I think it deserves an answer now.'

William, as Kitty had a few moments earlier, was shocked to hear himself speak so harshly. He wondered where these words were coming from and his anger grew as he reflected on his own situation. 'War over, my turn done,' he thought, 'no-one listens to me anymore. Well I'm not going to beg; she can make up her own mind now.'

Will's shock was similarly matched by Kitty's. She had not expected to be spoken to so harshly and this, coming on the heels of her feeling like an outsider in Michael's family over Christmas, felt unbearable. Fighting back tears, unsure whether they were generated by the insult or disappointment, she swallowed a hard lump in her throat before standing up from the table, gripping the edge with both hands.

She looked down at his pale bewildered face and heard herself say, more gently than she really felt he deserved, 'Sorry William, I really don't want this conversation to last any longer. I've given you my answer. It's obviously not good enough for you, so now I really think I'd like to go. And don't see me out Will, please,' she added, in response to his rising quickly to his feet.

Squeezing past a round table where the occupants were obviously enjoying the small drama before them, she left William sitting alone, in front of the debris of half-eaten cakes, sandwiches, and a small jewellery box. Feeling mistaken and misunderstood, he waited for the bill.

Heading for home, conscious of the rejected gift weighing heavily in his pocket, his anger grew. He felt she had never given him a chance. 'I guess she decided I wouldn't be good enough for her. Well she doesn't know what she's missed then,' he muttered, as he entered his house. A sharp slam of the door, caught by the wind, caused three heads to jerk up as he walked in.

'Easy William, no need to take your bad mood out on the furniture,' cried Eve. 'It's Christmas in this house, we're all having a lovely time getting ready to go to the Blue Jazz Club downtown. Oh, by the way, this is Missy, she's coming with us tonight.'

A small girl with smooth bobbed hair looked up from filing her nails as she heard her name mentioned.

'Say hello to Missy, William,' urged Elana. 'He's a dreadfully bad-tempered boy, Missy, nothing has pleased him since he came back from the war. Sometimes I think he wishes there would be another one.'

'Shut up Elana, just shut up, will you? You know nothing about my views and even less about war. I'm in no mood to listen to your chatter tonight'.

Feeling slightly ashamed of his outburst, he conceded, 'Hello, Missy', giving a slight nod in her direction. Missy nodded back, holding his gaze, unable to interrupt the two conversation streams running from Elana and Eve to their brother.
'Ooh, sorry I spoke I'm sure. And is that a new scarf you're wearing? Did you get it from that girl you are seeing? Very nice, very nice indeed.'
'So, what's she done to upset you then? Turned you down has she? Wise woman I'd say.'
William felt he had had enough for one day and turning around walked back out the door, straight to The Red Lion, where, after drinking several solitary pints he found no consolation whatsoever.

Much later, returning to the house, the girls were gone. His mother, stretched out on the new sofa in front of a dampened fire, stocking feet propped on a cushion seemed to be enjoying the solitude. Hiding her anxiety at his flushed complexion and slightly erratic gait she made an attempt to get up, greeting her son with, 'You're late home, son. It's cold leftovers tonight, Boxing Night, so help yourself.'

William waved her offer away impatiently and asked, 'Mum, Dad's advice - need some man's talk - where is he?'
'He's gone to bed, Will, it's nearly midnight. He's going to be digging the allotment over tomorrow. That's the end of his Christmas holiday, but I'm taking a bit of rest myself, if I can get it that is.
'Now, get yourself something to eat.

You can't go to bed staggering drunk, I won't have it. The talk can wait until tomorrow.'

William slept late the next morning and, with a slightly sore head, took his breakfast tea and bread carefully. Wanting to leave the house before his sisters were up, he left as soon as he was finished eating, gingerly walking the two streets between home and the allotment which constituted his father's daily commute.

Reaching the plot which the family shared with most of the neighbourhood he looked across and began to feel more relaxed. Pale blue wisps of pipe smoke rose up across the informally fenced sections, identifying several men who were already there, stringing fresh rope along and between their plots, or just sorting out their sheds. Something about it reminded William of the war and he wondered, not for the first time, whether the real attraction of the allotments was not the growing of vegetables but the camaraderie of men having a common interest. He had no desire to grow vegetables, but he did miss the company.

He thought back to his time in the army and a flood of loneliness washed over him. He was growing used to feeling like a misfit and he had hoped that feeling would lessen once his future had been, if not secured, then at least begun.

Finding his father didn't take long. The neat, fragile shed meticulously preserved with a glossy brown creosote coating stood out from its lesser preserved neighbours like a cockerel in the farmyard. His father was tidying apparently, although William couldn't see a misplaced flowerpot or uncoiled ball of twine on the shelves. Although he was usually comfortable around his father, he found this conversation difficult to start. After a bit of grumbling about the state of Britain, and London in particular since his return from the war, his father rubbed his hands along the legs of his gardening overalls and interrupted. 'OK son, I've a lot to do today. Do you want something in particular because if not I'd like to get on, unless you're coming to help, of course.'

'Well, actually, I did want something in particular. I've met a girl, a lovely girl and I want to marry her, and soon.'

'Didn't you speak to me about this on Christmas Day, Will? What's happened all of a sudden? Have you got a girl in trouble? This is a bit of a change of tune. I hope you're not going to disgrace the family?'

'No Dad, I told you, she's a lovely girl and she wouldn't allow anything like that, neither would I, she's a real lady.'

'And what has she said to you then, this fine lady? You with an office job and no savings?'

'She says she's a Catholic and she might marry me if I convert.'

'Yes, and I might throw my son out on his ear ... what has got into you lately? See no more of her lad, and don't mention it to me again.'

Walking away, he felt lonelier and more confused than ever. He had decided, before she turned him down, that he could marry a Catholic if he wanted to and his family could say whatever they liked. He knew his family were not concerned with any particular church, but it was a dilemma and William did not like dilemmas. He knew that if pressed his family would describe themselves as Church of England. However, Kitty's religion was not something to which he had really given much thought, although he had been curious to learn a bit more about Ireland.

He was still wrestling with these thoughts as he pushed against the unlocked door of his house. His senses were unexpectedly overwhelmed by a pungent haze which seemed to fill every corner of the room. The origin of such a rich sweet variety of scents and powders was soon revealed; his sisters were getting ready for a night out. His sad face and downcast appearance triggered an affectionate response from Elana, who leapt up from her place at the kitchen table and, putting her arm around his shoulders, urged him to go out with them that night.

'Please, please, darling, it will be such fun. We will be with friends. Missy is coming, you already met her, Will, so no need to feel out of place, just give it a try, you might enjoy it.'

It was with serious misgivings and some reluctance that William agreed. That evening, wearing his best suit, he entered the door of the club with his sisters. He felt disadvantaged and out of place surrounded by exuberant noisy young people.

'I don't know anything about these people,' he said to Eve, who was shrugging off her coat and indicating for him to do the same.

'Come on Will, a night out, people your own age, have some fun for a change, please ... Look, here's Missy. Give her a dance Will, go on.'

Fashionably slim with a head of glossy blond hair shimmering under the bright lights, Missy, in her sparkling red dress just covering her knees and her dainty silver shoes was looking hopefully up at him.

'Of course, if you don't want to...' Missy began, before William's sense of chivalry took over and he held out his hand to lead her onto the crowded dance floor.

'I think this one's a foxtrot.' Missy looked around at the other dancers as she placed her hand on his shoulder and moved closer. 'Not the best choice, but as it's crowded we can't move much anyway.'

Taken aback to find himself pressing so close to a woman he hardly knew, William began to relax and concentrated on his moves. 'Feet one, two,' Missy whispered. 'Slow, slow, quick, quick slow. Got it?'

William enjoyed the tempo of the music, finding it helped him to take his thoughts away from his conflicted emotions and he began to melt into the atmosphere of the evening. Missy seemed in no hurry to leave his side and so they danced on. Foxtrot followed by the Black Bottom. William surprised himself.

He couldn't believe it. He really was acting like a different person. Enjoying the ragtime beat of the Black Bottom, he caught sight of himself in the great arched mirrors which span the length of the ballroom.

Sweat had made his wispy fair hair cling to his head, his moustache looked sweaty and his pale features were pink and shining, although he thought his blue eyes did reflect the sparkle and energy of the evening.

'I'm such an unattractive cad, only my eyes pass muster,' he murmured, as his image bobbed up and down and was then reflected a dozen times off the walls, 'Why would anyone have me at all?' Determined to improve his chances he paid more attention to Missy than he had originally intended and before the end of the evening they had agreed to meet again.

Waiting for her at the South Bank exit of Victoria Station the following Friday evening, William was feeling apprehensive but hopeful. The evening was cold. A biting wind blowing over the Thames made him shiver and he was grateful for Kitty's soft warm scarf.

He had carefully checked his reflection before leaving the house and decided that he looked more the city gent now than he had when jigging and twirling gracelessly sweating at the nightclub the previous week.

He was early, of course, and he thought that leaning against the tobacconist wall just outside the station would give him shelter. It was cramped, squeezed into the corner between the exit and the embankment, but he had plenty of time to peer at himself in the mirror advertising Woodbine cigarettes, which was hanging inside.

'Nice scarf and this colour really does suit me,' he told himself ruefully. 'She knows a bit about style that girl; a chap could never have picked that out for himself. Anyway, no more Kitty, I need to think about Missy tonight.'

Hoping not to have much longer to wait at the draughty corner, he kicked sullenly at the loose sheets of newspaper fluttering over his feet and noted how everyone around him seemed to have somewhere important to go.

Half an hour later he was ready to go home himself when he felt a light prod to his back and turning around found himself face to face with Missy, who was arm in arm with another young woman.

'Hey, Will, sorry we're late, we got held up see ...'
'Hello, I'm Jean, call me Jeanie, I work with Missy and we just had to stop off ...'

William lifted his hat to Missy and Jean, hiding his surprise and mild displeasure at there being an extra in the party. 'Lovely to see you ladies, shall we get indoors out of this cold?'

'Good idea, Will. Actually we have already made some arrangements. There's a new place just opened round the corner. You have to know someone to get in, but it's such fun.
They have the most marvellous cocktails and we know quite a few of the people who are going to be there tonight so it will be wonderful. Do let's hurry.'

Not wanting to argue and feeling completely out of his depth, William walked in the direction Missy indicated, with one pretty girl on each arm.

Contrary to how it might appear to a passer-by, he was not enjoying himself at all. Arriving at an entrance, discreetly wedged between a dress shop and a pawn shop, Jeanie knocked and called through the crack between the door and door frame, 'Friends of Dickie and Bertie here. We were here earlier, and we're back now with another friend.'

The door was opened immediately, and a tall man dressed in shiny black trousers, bow tie and waistcoat ushered them in. Handing over their coats to a young female attendant in a spangled dress and bossily ordering Will to do the same they pushed their way through the smoke-filled room towards a brightly lit bar.

It was more glamorous than anything Will had ever imagined. There was glass and mirrors from bar counter to ceiling, topped with embossed brass decorations that under the lights and reflections from the mirrors resembled gold. The room was filled with small tables and more gilt chairs than he estimated would be needed to fill an opera house, their plush velvet seats giving the room an air of grandeur.

'Shall we have cocktails, Will?' asked Missy smiling up at him, one elbow on the bar the other arm stretched out to stroke his arm.

'Yes, of course, Missy, what would you like?'

'And Jeanie too, Will, you can't leave her out.'

'No, of course not' he stuttered; flustered and unsure of the etiquette required when a date with one girl suddenly expanded.

'I'll have a Bees Knees, please and Jeanie, your usual?'

'Just a Dubonnet cocktail for me please, Will, don't want to rob you blind!'

Will looked across at the barman who appeared to be busy with a metal canister into which he was pouring crushed ice and several measures from a range of coloured bottles in front of the counter.

'Do you have any beer?' he asked wistfully.

'I'll mix you a Highball sir, you'll enjoy that. Bourbon whiskey and ginger. Looks like you're going to need some fortification to get through the evening with two lovely ladies to look after. I'll just get your order next.'

'No hurry,' murmured Will, thinking the longer the barman took to get the drinks the better; he was hoping he had enough money to last the evening.

There was a jazz band playing and the girls had settled at a table just below the stage. Waving across, they indicated that he should bring the drinks over as soon as they were ready.

'OK, sir. One Bee's Knees, one Dubonnet Cocktail, and a Highball.' Handing William a tray with the drinks, replete with straws and glacé cherries he murmured, 'that will be one pound exactly, please.'

William was horrified. It was bad enough to pay six pence a pint when it had been three pence when he left for war, but he had never spent a pound on alcoholic drinks before. He wondered, not for the first time that evening, what Kitty would say if she knew.

Handing over his pound note he made his way carefully to the table where the girls were already engaged in conversation with a couple of young men in bow ties. He thought they were just the type he tried to avoid, assuming that they had never seen wartime action. He reckoned they probably claimed some kind of exemption through family influence.

'Here, Will, meet Dickie and Bertie, we were just telling them what a fine chap you are, and such a great dancer too.'

Will put the tray down very carefully before looking up just in time to catch the smirk on Missy's face as she finished the remark with a knowing glance towards one of the young men. Will didn't care whether it was Dickie or Bertie. He really wouldn't mind, he told himself, if he never set eyes on any of them again. Settling back in the empty chair he sipped his Highball and looked around, quite detached from the company at the table.

'Cigarette, Will?' offered Missy. Maybe it was an attempt to re-engage him, but he neither knew nor cared.

'No thanks, Missy, I prefer my pipe.'

'Darling, no one smokes a pipe in here', she cried wrinkling her nose as though horrified. 'Do they, chaps? You can have snuff if you want it or, I do believe, there is something a bit harder on offer if you are feeling brave enough.'

'Steady on there, Missy,' interrupted one of the men, possibly Dickie, he seemed to have more of an influence with the girls.

In fact, Bertie had a glazed look in his eyes as though he had already been a bit brave. 'Take no notice Will, this place isn't exactly illegal, but we don't want the coppers crawling all over us, now do we? Not when we are having such fun.'

'Dance, Jeanie?'

Alone at the table with Missy, William was stuck for conversation. Away from the glittering bar area, the soft lighting and the wafting smoke gave the room a dreamlike quality. Looking over at her, he hoped to see the fun, friendly girl he had met at Christmas, getting ready to go out with his sisters.

'Do you often come to this sort of place, Missy? Have you ever been here with Eve and Elana?'

'Well us girls've got to have a bit of fun, Will. We work all day and can't be expected to hold back when a chap is taking us out in town now can we?'

'But my sisters?'

'No, Will, your sisters don't come here. To tell you the truth I'm a bit bored with your sisters. They go dancing and have an occasional drink, but they really don't know how to let their hair down. Now you and I, we're different, aren't we? We can have a good time and no regrets?'

As she put her hand on Will's knee, he looked down at the brightly polished nails as though her hand were a foreign insect about to bite. Moving his leg away he blushed, thinking perhaps he had misunderstood.

'Look Will, it's like this. You're a nice guy and all that but unless you loosen up a bit no girl is going to want you, well not any girl I know anyway. Maybe some old frump would...'

Will's temper had been simmering, but now it boiled. He swallowed his Highball and rose from the table abruptly, knocking his gilt chair to the floor.

'I've a lot to do tomorrow, Missy, so I need to be getting home. Shall I walk you to the station or would you prefer to stay here with your friends?'

'I'll stay here, thank you very much for asking. And no need to get me another drink although I've finished this one, it was tiny! But anyway, I can look after myself, which is just as well. Some gent you are, Will, really.'

Feeling humbled and apologetic, but unsure why that should be, he left Missy sitting at the table and made for the door. Looking back, he saw Bertie leaning over her, swaying somewhat and offering her his handkerchief.

Interrupting the glittering young cloakroom attendant who seemed to be enjoying the doorman's company more than the girls had enjoyed his, he finally retrieved his coat.

Grateful for the blast of cool air, which hit him in the face as he left through a side door, he pulled out his pipe. Cupping his hands over the match to light it, he noticed them shaking while protecting the flame from the gusty night air. As he sucked gratefully on the smooth horn stem, he told himself that he had had a lucky escape.

'What a fool I was to think a girl like that would suit me, and what a fool she was not to see how she is wasting her time with those idiots. Well anyway, it's a long walk home for me tonight, not spending any more money. Do me good.'

The next few weeks passed slowly for William. He was taking his time, cautiously weighing up the odds before making a plan.

Once the decision had been made and the plan finalised, he wasted no more time. On the first Saturday morning of February he dressed carefully in a fine brown pinstripe serge suit, topped by a winter coat and he gave his shoes an extra polish. He was setting off to find Kitty and knew she would notice these small details.

The morning was bright and clear, and he felt optimistic as he checked his reflection in the mirror hanging at the back of the door. The same thin pale face smiled back at him as before, but unlike the night of his fateful date with Missy, he thought he looked more confident, more like himself now rather than the gadabout he had tried to be. He brushed his hair back, parting it once he had applied an extra slick of Brilliantine, combed his freshly clipped moustache, and pulled his shoulders back, battle ready. He shuddered remembering some of his battles, sensing a quiver of fear in his guts.

As he walked to the tram, which would take him to Chelsea, he ran through his intentions, and what he considered the objective of his mission. 'Time for me to go and get her. First order, she has to be found.'

All day he traversed the streets, past the new mansions along Cheyne Walk Row, past the Victoria Hospital for Children and then along Tite Street, up to the majestic facade of the Infirmary of the Royal Hospital. He had no idea where he should look and had just about decided to return to his tram when rising before him, he saw a fine red brick building with white portico pillars flanking the door. The Church of Our Most Holy Redeemer proclaimed the notice outside, advertising times of services.
'Of course, what a fool I've been, Chelsea, Catholic Church, must be a connection.'

Stepping inside the open door he felt the temperature change from cool February evening to a still chilly but less biting atmosphere. His shoes moved quietly across the soft wooden floor as his eyes tried to adjust to the dim light. He was barely able to make out the pews and aisles by a bank of flickering candles on his left and a small red light up ahead on the altar.

And he breathed deeply, aware of a strange smell, heavy and sweet, much heavier than his sisters' preparatory toilettes, more like some French perfume he recalled having experienced once or twice during the war.

'Well, this is my first step and I might as well see what it's all about.' Noticing a bustling movement at the side of the main altar, William saw a priest changing wooden numbers on a board near the pulpit.

'Excuse me, Reverend, I'm thinking about becoming a Catholic. Do you have a form I could fill in or something?'

'Father Murphy, Parish Priest, God bless you, my son. And you are?'

'William West, it's just an enquiry.'

'Ah, William, well now, son, I am delighted to hear you are wanting to join us, but we need to have a bit of a discussion first.'

William felt he was getting more than he had bargained for but he needn't have worried, it seemed the priest was not planning a lengthy prayer session.

'I can't stay long now, as the Catholic Women's Guild is coming in to Benediction at six, and I have to be ready, you know you can't keep the ladies waiting.'

Suddenly his heart beat wildly. His legs felt weak and he leaned against a highly polished wooden pew. Hoping his voice wasn't trembling, he asked,

'Sorry Reverend, I mean Father, did you say the Catholic Women's Guild? Is that the one Kitty Collins attends? Is she coming tonight?'

The words were still echoing across the cavernous nave when the door opened, and, arm-in-arm with another young woman, Kitty walked in. Taken aback, she looked enquiringly from priest to William and back again.

'I think we will make ourselves scarce, ladies,' said Father Murphy. 'Kitty and Mr West here have some talking to do. Kitty, I think we might not see you for the meeting tonight. Take your time and I'm here for you both when you need me.'

As Kitty and William walked out of the church into the dusky evening shadows, they moved together and this time, when he reached for her hand she did not pull away.

Three months later, they were married.

Chapter 4.

Ellen. London, England & Llandeileo, Wales.1939

'War, war, the talk of war goes on and on, nothing but yak, yak, yak, so bored of it all.' Twelve-year-old Ellen West felt overwhelmed by the constant discussions. Her father William tuned in to the radio every evening and they all had to be quiet in case he missed anything. He had even taken her to listen to Neville Chamberlain the year before - some treat that was - standing in the crowd at Heston Airport, everyone cheering and shouting.

She was told that there wouldn't be a war now; it was all going to be fine. a year later, everything seemed to have turned around and when her father said it was likely that there would be a war,

Ellen wasn't worried, if anything she felt pleased with the idea of a change. Her life, she believed, was pretty monotonous now and a war might bring some excitement. She sensed that her quiet, confident father was sick with anxiety, so she didn't declare her enthusiasm.

She had seen a photograph of him in uniform during the last war and he had told her that this time it was not going to be easy, but it would be quick. At first, she had been amused by the gas masks. A baby down the street had been taken to have one fitted, and it looked as though he was inside a leather container with a porthole to show his face.

She and Daisy, her younger sister, had small versions of adult gas masks, which they kept in small cardboard boxes slung over their shoulders with string and they were supposed to wear them, both indoors and out. Disgusted, they had kicked them under their bed once they came in from school and left them there as long as they could.

'Well, there is no war yet,' argued Ellen, on one of her frequent disagreements with her parents. 'So why would I go out looking silly with a box on my side?' Her little brother Billy however, had a Mickey Mouse mask. His was red, with a gentler face, two eyes instead of one porthole and a leather flap to imitate a nose. 'Yours looks just like Mickey Mouse,' exclaimed Daisy. 'I wish I could have one too.' This removed any doubt from Billy's mind. If Daisy liked it, then Billy was keen to wear it.

The following week the ID cards arrived in the post and there was much talk of ration books. On the 3rd of September, war was declared but most of the publicity related to food. 'Well, really,' said Kitty, 'it's food information we are bombarded with now, eat this, grow that. I'm sure I know all about good food, coming from our lovely farm in Ireland, I don't need all this advice from the authorities, but I would really like to know what's happening to us in London.'

William's father still kept the allotment and for years now her father had returned from his weekly visits with an armful of whatever vegetables were in season. Usually carrots, beans, and rhubarb wrapped in newspaper. Sometimes, memorably, there were strawberries and blackcurrants.

Ellen knew her mother never liked to speak about her husband's family, although his sisters visited occasionally. Ellen knew her grandmother had also visited when each of them was born. She had often met her grandfather in the pub, but he had never come to the house. So, when her father arrived home with the vegetables, there was never any mention of where they had been grown, although Ellen and Daisy knew.

The three youngsters soon got used to being at war. It was like a game and Billy started collecting posters called Spot Sight charts, showing enemy uniforms. 'As if a German soldier would come walking down Kilburn High Road! Billy, you are so stupid', said Ellen in exasperation.

'Well, if he did, Billy would know him right off,' responded Daisy, always ready to protect her little brother.

Billy was excited by the war, looking forward to seeing German planes and going into an air raid shelter. Then, it was decided.

They would all be leaving London and going to Wales. Well, their father wouldn't be leaving, having recently opened his own small shop. It would be just Ellen with Daisy, Billy, and their mother.

Ellen had known that her school was evacuating. She didn't really mind going as most of her friends were leaving London. There weren't so many teachers staying either and with never having enough butter or sugar and having been constantly told to make do, she thought Wales sounded just fine.

'We will be going to a place called Llandeilo, a village in Wales. Sounds very foreign doesn't it?' Her mother announced, not waiting for, or expecting, a response.

'We get the train from Paddington on Monday. We plan to stay there for a while and miss the war. So, make sure all your good clothes are ready, washed, and packed. You can wear your old things until Sunday, then straight after Mass we go and say goodbye to Uncle Michael, Auntie Gina, and your cousins in Chelsea.'

Now Ellen, help me get Daisy and Billy's rig-outs packed. We will be washing down in the basement, so you can show Daisy how to use the mangle, and Billy you come down as well, so we can watch you.'

Ellen's mother never seemed to expect a response, she was more a giver of information than a conversationalist.

Packing up the clothes into a metal bucket and with Kitty lugging the empty tin bath down the stairs, Ellen thought they were a funny looking group.

Little Billy, his straight wiry hair cropped short by William, somehow always managed to look untidy. Stubby legs with short trousers and boots with thick socks inside were making the gap between ankle and knee barely worth talking about.

He was carefully carrying the soap bar and the Blue, for cleaning the whites, wrapped in a cloth. Following him was Daisy with the washboard.

Her wispy fair hair was losing its baby curls and darkening to a mousy brown. She was the prettiest of the three, having her father's fair colouring and, like Ellen, she had inherited her mother's brown eyes.

She was also the most timid and Ellen knew she was happy to take a back seat, expecting her big sister to lead and preferring to play with Billy whenever there was a choice.

Ellen loved the basement. It was a shared area amongst the three flats, and they all used it as a laundry. There was more space here than in any room in the flat and she never knew who she might meet there. Her favourites were George and Stephen, the men who lived downstairs. They were always nice to her and Daisy when they met on the stairs, admiring their Sunday dresses and bonnets. They also spoke more softly and politely than most of the men she came across, either in church or at school. Her mother liked them too, she noticed, although her father always held back. But then she knew Dad usually held back. He wasn't much of a one for making friends.

'How long will we be away, Mum? I will really miss Dad.' Ellen, halfway through scrubbing the socks and pants on the washboard, looked up at her mother who was busy turning the mangle. Billy and Daisy were holding a nightdress coming out the other side.

'The war won't last long Ellen, girl; we'll be home by Christmas and you can get on with your schooling.'

'And then what will we do for friends between now and Christmas? Not stuck with you all day Mum, surely? That would not be much fun.' Ellen mumbled the last bit under her breath.

A few days later, still worrying about lack of friends or any young company during the evacuation, Ellen arrived with her family onto the main concourse at Paddington station. They were hours early, of course, but that was normal for her family.

Carelessly swinging her new cardboard suitcase back and forth she looked around at the crowded, smoky scene. 'Not so bored with talk of war now, are you, girl?' she asked herself as the noise from the trains was drowned by the excited shrieks from the clusters of children who were gathered in front of the departure boards. 'Lovely to see you all dressed in every winter garment you own, great labels too. Is that in case you forget who you are?'

'What was that, Ellen?' Her father bent down to hear her remarks.

'Nothing, Dad, just thought how lovely everyone looks with their labels and gas masks, don't you agree?' Her father, as ever unsure of his daughter's remarks, nodded without comment and turned to his wife for a last check of papers and details.

'Ooh look, Daisy, everyone your age seems to be hanging on to their sister's hands, not like you. Tho' obviously most do have the necessary teddy bears and dolls, they always help in times of war I hear.' Looking down she saw her sister's eyes fill with tears.

Ellen knew she understood her mocking tone and would be upset by the implied criticism. Clutching her favourite doll even tighter she looked at Billy, with his bear. Daisy and Billy were not clear about what was happening, but they could feel the anxiety of the parents and teachers around them, even though they were standing apart from the main groups of children.

'Oh, here we go,' said Ellen, 'turning on the old tear tap.' She watched as a group of mothers were openly crying and waving towards a line of little bodies moving down the platform to board the impatient, belching, Great Western steam train.

'You've no idea how I hate all this,' she heard her mother tell her father. 'It brings back memories of when we used to take the train to Cork City with my mother and sisters. Anything to remind me of Ireland makes me feel sad now.'

Ellen wondered why her mother always sounded sad when she referred to Ireland, perhaps she missed her family, certainly there weren't Sunday visits from grandparents like her friends enjoyed. She liked the sound of Ireland though and thought she'd like to go there herself one day.

Their small group was suddenly interrupted. 'OK, let's go now, West family join this queue please.' An official woman dressed in grey serge and using a clipboard as a shield marched through the clusters of families and luggage filling the platform. She stopped right in front of them. Ordered to kiss their father, the children then obediently followed the woman onto the platform where, once their mother arrived, they boarded the train. Ellen settled herself in the corner, leaning back gratefully into the padded seat. She remembered that one time she had been on a train before, the trip to the seaside. It had good memories for her, and she looked forward to a change of scenery. Maybe she would find animals and countryside, normally only seen through coach windows or read about in her favourite books.

The train pulled out of Paddington Station slowly and looking across to the seat opposite she saw Daisy squashing her nose against the carriage window, trying to hide her tears. William, waving from the platform, was soon out of sight. Now Ellen felt she could look around the crowded carriage without being accused of not waving goodbye for long enough. She smiled, recalling how her mother had insisted they sit in a ladies' carriage, but she needn't have worried, there were no men. The very few adults in the carriage were women teachers, their assistants, and then some mothers.

The train was tightly packed with pale-faced, tired-looking children, some already dishevelled. They were surrounded by anxious teachers who were constantly marshalling their small charges from lavatory to seat. Ellen hated it all and put her book over her face in an attempt to block out the noise and the smell of sweaty woollen socks and stale clothing.

'Don't speak to any of the children,' their mother had instructed. 'You don't know where they come from, they could have fleas.'
Ellen and Daisy concentrated on their books, but Billy was a different matter.

'Are you going to Wales?' he asked everyone who paused outside their carriage. 'We're going for the whole of the war. Are you coming with us?'

There were some young teachers standing in the corridor between the carriages smoking and exchanging anecdotes.

'Do you know, of my whole class only one child has enough to fill a small case, most have a paper bag with only one change of clothes.'

'I took Peter Brown to the lav' jus' now, an' 'e 'as brown paper sewn under his vest. 'E says it's not to come off 'til Easter.'

'They were supposed to have a packed lunch, most of 'em have nothing at all. Lucky for them they got pocket money from the school, but unless we can get something in Reading, we're stumped.'

'What address did you give your man? I was told we was goin' to Haye-on-Wye, sounds lovely, dunnit?'

'Mine has been called up already and is standing by for orders. I was quite glad really when they declared war. Get it over and done with I say, we are planning to marry next year.'

Two middle aged women, experienced teachers and assuming control, were trying to hide their impatience at the younger women's lack of engagement. They began to organise songs. Soon Billy and Daisy were singing along to
'Run rabbit, run rabbit, Run! Run! Run!
Bang! Bang! Bang! Bang! Goes the Farmer's gun....'

Ellen, embarrassed by all the jollity and high spirits, snuggled down into the corner of her seat and opened her book as high as possible to prevent having to make eye contact with anyone who might ask her to join in.

Once the journey was well under way, tears dried up and spirits were raised. In some cases, raised to bursting point. Boys were climbing over seats, girls squealing at every jolt and turn of the carriage, shoelaces coming undone, shoes being used as weapons to beat back an intruder and throughout all there were excited references to war and Hitler and soldiers.

More songs, some were 'rolling out the barrel' and they really did seem to be having a barrel of fun. This war was becoming a great adventure for the children.

'I remember how it was in '15,' one teacher sighed. 'No evacuation then, it was all happening in France, but they still dropped bombs from them Zeppelins over London. My man never came back. Neither did my father, and he was only a driver.'

The voice belonged to the stouter of the two senior teachers and as she was conveniently seated close by, Ellen was able to listen to every word. Miss Murphy, the label on her coat announced, and she looked very impressive. She was wearing a felt hat secured by an enamelled pin shaped like a bunch of cherries, held firmly above a tight bun.

Her companion, labelled Miss Roberts, was a thin woman with no hat and wispy hair, much of which had escaped from being tied back. Her strong cockney accent made Kitty check the label again, to satisfy herself that she was not a teacher but an assistant. Miss Roberts entertained the carriage with details of her family,

'Lucky for my brother, 'e 'ad a weak 'eart, 'e was never called up, but 'e broke a few once 'e was left behind.

''Ad the pick o' the bunch, 'e did, then got trapped by Florence Minns - a right Flossie she was an all, up the duff soon as 'e looked at 'er. Got two kids more now, he 'as, an' 'as taken up wiv a shop girl. His 'eart's still bearin' up just like 'is John Thomas!'

Ellen heard Kitty tutting at this last remark and realised that her mother underestimated how much herself and possibly even Daisy, could understand. Once the singing was over it was the 'Are we nearly there's', which could be relied upon to drown any conversation. It was a refrain repeated so frequently across the carriage that soon Daisy and Billy had made a game out of guessing where the next one would come from.

As the day drew to a close and the carriage darkened the children settled down and most were dozing, when Ellen was jolted awake by the train's abrupt halt. The noise from the train's engine, the orders shouted from the station staff, and the general confusion within the carriage made it difficult to know what was happening but Ellen could just make out the name 'Llandeilo Station' by the dim lights on the platform.

Stiff and tired they gathered up their suitcases and satchels and stepped from the recent familiarity of the passenger carriage onto a station platform in chaos.

'Families for Llandeilo, this way. We are going to the Methodist Chapel Hall for allocation.' They heard voices call through the semi-darkness.

'This way, Ma'am,' Ellen heard a male voice addressing her mother. His accent was different, she didn't know where he came from, but it wasn't England or Ireland. The only other exposure she had had was to an Italian family who lived next door and, remembering that Wales was another country, she asked, 'Are you Italian?'

'I'm from the valleys, born and bred,' came the response, not a reply – strangely emphasising the first part of the words. Bemused, Ellen followed her mother, who followed the man with the voice, until she saw the outline of the chapel hall ahead.

Squeezing past the cluster of smokers standing outside the door of the hall they found seats on a bench near the back. 'We'll be inside our digs soon, and get ourselves settled in,' Kitty reassured the children.

'I thought the Welsh would speak English, but if there are lots of Italians, how will we understand them?' asked Ellen, quite bewildered.

'Well anyway, the Italians are Catholics,' her mother murmured, not wanting to be overheard, 'So we will already have something in common with them.'

With surprising speed, names were checked off and pairings made, and they found themselves in the care of a red-faced woman with a pleasant expression, who introduced herself as Ness.

'I'm Mrs West, although please call me Kitty,' her mother replied standing up to shake the woman's hand' and you are Mrs..?'

'Mrs Jones, I am, but so's half the village. We're known as 'Jones-the-Shop', but there isn't much buying and selling going on. They told us yesterday to expect two boys, so I only have two beds, but you look right tidy. I'm sure we'll manage.'

They trudged along the main street, following many of their fellow travellers. Ellen repeatedly heard the strange accent she had mistaken for Italian. So tired now, all she could make out through the darkness was Ness's bright yellow check woollen scarf and black wellington boots, leading them up to a neat terraced house with a blue door. All she could hear was Billy; he was very tired and had kept up a low moaning grizzle all the way.

Not knowing, or caring, what was being said to her, she silently swallowed the bowl of soup Ness put before her and crawled quietly into bed, head-to-toe with Daisy. She was aware from murmurings and scoldings that her mother and Billy were settling down to sleep on the other side of the room.

Next morning the sound of a loud crowing cockerel woke Ellen. 'Listen to this, Daisy!' She shook her sister's shoulder. 'Do wake up. We must be in the country, come and see.'

Putting their school coats over their nightdresses, the girls knelt on the beds and looked out at the early morning scene. A pale sun was just visible over the terraced row of rooftops opposite with pale ribbons trying to reach across the street and breaking against the brick walls of the houses on their side. There were green hills on the higher land beyond and Ellen could just make out fields and sheep.

'Oh, Daisy, it's so wonderful, look at all those animals! Maybe they even have horses. We are going to have such a good time here.'

'What are you girls doing?' Ellen started as she heard her mother's tired voice across the room 'It's only six o'clock, you've woken us up and we don't want to be a nuisance in this stranger's house now do we, not on our first day. Go back to bed and rest your body if you can't sleep.'

Ellen lay down impatiently, irritably fidgeting to annoy Daisy who was trying to settle at the other end of the bed. It was another hour before her mother, hearing noises coming from the room downstairs, said they could get up and dress.

Downstairs the domestic scene was simple. One room, clean but sparse, washing-up in a bowl at the table, and a bucket by the door. There was a modern addition; a range cooker was built into one wall, efficiently sending heat into the room.

Ellen, looking more closely at Ness than at the room, saw a friendly looking woman, about the same age as her mother, she guessed. She noticed that this woman was quite a bit stouter and more plainly dressed, even without the wellingtons, which had been replaced by short leather boots. Ellen thought it was not a very fashionable look.

'I've porridge here for all now, if you want it. We are not short of milk in this place either so help yourselves.' Delighted, Ellen headed for the table, closely followed by Daisy and Billy.

'Thanks, Mrs Jones … Ness,' she heard her mother say wearily. 'The children will be glad to take some breakfast now and then get up to the school to see what's happening with the classes. Can I just trouble you for a cup of tea, please?'

'Now, Mrs West,' said Ness, pouring Kitty a cup of tea and taking one for herself, ' I was expecting two boys as you know, so I think they will only have places for two, but go you up and see from the schoolmistress yourself now.'

'Right, Ellen and Daisy, look after Billy between you. Once you have finished go and wash your faces and clean your teeth. Where should we do that, Mrs Jones?'

'The scullery out back here has a space for washing, use the bowl then empty it outside, not too near the back door, over by the vegetables is best.'

Ellen was embarrassed when she saw her mother purse her lips and raised her eyebrows, she knew her mother was not too pleased with what the scullery had to offer. She hoped Ness wouldn't notice.

Kitty fetched the washbag and towel from her suitcase, which they had been too tired to use last evening, and they didn't spend much time on the chilly wash. A metal bowl, fed from a single tap above a stone sink in the tiny back scullery, they considered an adequate ablution. Then there was another surprise.

'Wow, chickens!' cried Ellen, as she took the bowl of used water out the back door and with a squeal of delight threw the water as hard as she could amongst the flock of half a dozen hens, scattering them on impact. 'At least I can get near these without asking Mum,' she thought. 'Maybe I can even help feed them if I ask Mrs Jones later.'

At last, washed, fed, and muffled in coats and scarves they walked up the hill through the village and along Carmarthen Street, where the buildings petered out onto open land. On their right was a provisions market. There were high granite walls surrounding the building and noises from inside which sounded as though the market contained animals as well as people.

'There's not many about at this time of the morning,' her mother remarked. 'It's very different from London, so nice and quiet.' Ellen noticed the schoolhouse before the others and was surprised to see that the playground was twice the size of the ones in London and backed onto open fields.

'I would enjoy that,' she thought 'but I think Mum has other ideas, she always expects me to learn housework, and I know Billy will be sent to school.'

'It does look much nicer than St Joseph's,' said Mum to Daisy and Billy, as if on cue.

'You'll both be making friends and away playing in those fields before the week is out.'

'We don't know anyone here', grumbled Daisy, 'an' even if we did, they don't talk like us.'

'Looks lovely dunnit, missus?' A voice directed at Kitty caused them all to turn and meet the gaze of a tired looking young woman whom she vaguely recognised from the train. 'I'm Susan. Hello.' She held out her hand. 'My girl is starting today an' all, so I wonder if I can come in with yours, I'm not sure what to do.'

'Come on together with us then,' smiled Kitty, pleased to be taking the lead. 'We'll go in the entrance here.'

Over the doorway was a stone lintel, engraved with the words Merched. 'That's the girls' entrance, our landlady, Mrs Jones, told us to use that one.'

'Bechgyn is for boys, Billy, so when you come in and out from playtime make sure you use the right door.' Without waiting for him to reply, they all walked through the girls' door. Ellen was momentarily stunned by the darker interior. She was just able to make out a high-sided oak desk and a stern looking woman behind. 'Queue please, there are more of you than we were expecting.'

Looking around Ellen was surprised, and disappointed, to see women and children lined up along the wall, waiting to have their details added to the school register. Billy clung anxiously to Kitty, while Daisy and Susan's daughter - a skinny, pale child called Rose, had begun a stilted, shy conversation.

Ellen, left alone, began to lose hope of being part of this new school and wandered round the edge of the room, looking at the pictures on the wall, particularly those illustrating farming activities. Eventually she noticed her family had reached the front of the queue, so she reluctantly moved across the room to join them. She didn't want to appear disinterested and was still hoping she might be given a place.

'Two boys from Jones-the-Shop's house?' asked the woman at the desk.

'No,' she heard her mother reply. 'We're the West family, with three children. If you can only take two, here's Daisy and Billy.'

'I'll make the decisions around here, thank you, Mrs West.'

Ellen's heart sank as she saw her mother's face flush with embarrassment at being undermined. She knew anger when she saw it; a raised head, a stiffened body and no response. She stood very quietly, shifting her weight from one foot to another on the hard tiled floor. 'Please God, please let me have a place, please,' she prayed inwardly. 'I'll be very good I promise.'

'Right, Mrs West, we have too many children here for our school so, as I said, it's two places and those will be for half a day. The evacuees take the mornings and our own children take the afternoon. You can teach them at home in the afternoon and we will set you homework, so they don't fall behind.'

'My children will not fall behind I can assure you.'

'We speak English and Welsh here, but all our signs are in Welsh so they will just have to get used to it. You can bring them their dinner at midday, and they can play in the schoolyard after the break before they walk home or you can fetch them, but we don't wait to see who's collected, not like your London schools.'

'They can't walk home alone; they've only just arrived. They might get lost.'

'Mrs West, we know our children are safe in the village, so you can take your choice.'

Ellen looked away, feigning disinterest, when she heard her mother bend down to Daisy and Billy, 'I will be here at dinnertime with your dinner and I'll stay around in the park over there until school finishes to walk you back to the Jones's. Don't leave the school gate without me now, do you hear? I don't care what the others do.'

Turning to Ellen she murmured, 'You know, girl, this town is very like where I came from when I was about your age but Roisin writes to say it's changed a lot. So, there can be good changes and bad changes.'

'What's a good change Mum?'

'Well, I was only Billy's age, but I was able to run home from school with the bigger ones over the gorse, it would scratch your legs, but the thought of Mum's tea and the warmth of the home kept me running on.

D'ye think the children here can run freely home? I'd never say it could be done in London but maybe it's a bit safer here. That would be a good change.'

'It's a bad change for me not going to school.'

'What did you say, Ellen girl?'

Without waiting for a reply, and still ignoring her daughter's downcast appearance, Kitty turned away from the schoolhouse and, grabbing hold of Ellen by her hand, left the schoolhouse and the children behind.

Although determined to maintain an aggrieved and dejected attitude, Ellen found it impossible not to be distracted once they approached the market. Sheep were bleating their confused conversations and men in flat caps with long sticks and poles were attempting to herd them across the road into the pens.

Her mother held back whilst the sheep and men overflowed their route, leaving behind fresh sheep droppings and snags of wool on the wooden railings alongside. Ellen, anxious to see more, pulled her hand away from her mother's tight grasp. At the entrance she was hit by the smell of warm manure mingling with the smoke from the men's pipes. The novelty and mix of animals and unusual activity was thrilling.

'Please, Mum, can I stay and watch?' she pleaded. 'You said it was to be a holiday and we haven't seen anything yet, I was hoping for horses, but sheep would be nice.'

Ellen could hear the cries of owners and auctioneers. She so wanted to be in there getting close to the animals and the bustle of activity, but she reckoned that her mother was in no mood for lingering today.

Above the noise she heard her mother call, 'Come on now girl, we'll go down into town and ask where the Catholic church is, then we will know where to go and make new friends; not much hope of getting any help from them here.'

Unsure why it had been decided that there was no help to be had, but expecting it had something to do with the scullery and the schoolmistress combined, she reluctantly gave a last look at the sheep market, before joining her mother.

On the corner of Carmarthen Street they stopped at an imposing stone building, with a swinging Bear Inn sign set high on the wall. Ellen thought there was no way her mother would go in. She knew she had never set foot inside the Red Lion when her father went in for a pint. She hated the thought of the money wasted.

'I'm just going in for a minute to ask about the church, you stay right here outside and don't speak to anyone, you hear me?'

Ellen was shocked. Her mother rarely surprised her family by a change in habit. She sat on the bench outside to wait. She didn't have to wait long. A minute later, flushed and reminding Ellen of one of Ness's affronted chickens, her mother swung out through the door of the bar.

'This is a dreadful place, girl, we won't be staying here. I went in and there were two men standing up at the bar drinking, and they stared at me. Then when I asked where the Catholic church was, they started speaking in Welsh. They knew I didn't understand. They turned back to the bar, which was none too clean I can tell you, and they left me standing. And drinking stout at this hour of the day, no wonder they haven't any money.'

'Have they no money, Mum? Is that why they are selling the sheep?'

'Well does this look like a town with money, girl? Where are the coffee shops or the beautiful stores like we have in London? Where are the buses taking people to work, if there is any work at all, at all? Did you see a picture house or a dance hall yet? No, ah no, they have no money here and, safe though it is, we won't be stopping long.'

Disappointed, Ellen walked alongside her mother, digging both hands into the pockets of her best woollen coat, not really needed on this mild autumn day but which Mum had insisted she put on this morning "to make sure people knew they were dealing with respectable Londoners."

She thought she might quite like it here, the wide-open streets with few cars and no buses. She hoped there might even be a bike she could borrow. She was wondering whether she dared ask, when the grim set of her mother's face made her decide to postpone that one for now.

'Just when I hoped there might be a bit more interest in my life, she's turning against it,' she muttered, lagging behind, 'And once turned she's very difficult to unturn.'

'We're calling in here now.' Her mother's voice broke Ellen's train of thought, and she looked up to see an all grey building, with the name carved on a lintel above the door Horeb Wesleyan Methodist Chapel. 'You come in too, girl.'

Stepping through the arched doorway, Ellen blinked as her eyes refocused in the gloomy interior. No lights, candles, statues, smell of incense here. There was just a bare room and benches. No flowers or coloured glass windows either, she noticed. 'I think you're right, Mum, the people here really are very poor, not even flowers on the altar.' She heard a man's voice asking what help he could give. She heard relief in her mother's voice as she asked him for the Catholic church.

'Not around here, Ma'am.' The reply was clear and quick, leaving no room for doubt. She heard her try again.

'We've just arrived, evacuated from London you know, my three children all brought up Catholics and we will need to go to Mass on Sunday.'

'There's no Catholic church here, over at Ammanford there is one hall where they have a Mass on Sunday and confession once a month, but not here.'

'And how would we get there on Sunday, is there a bus?'

'No bus, you would need a bicycle or a horse and cart, or a car. But there's very few of us runs cars here and I don't know any Catholics who would be going over.'

Ellen saw her mother bend her head and as she noticed the silent tears roll down her cheeks, felt suddenly afraid. Hardly ever seen to cry, Mum was the strong one. What were they going to do here in this strange town far away from Dad with Mum crying?

'Let's go back now, Ma,' she pleaded, her voice as quiet as she could make it, hoping to restore some calm. 'Let's go back to the house and ask Mrs Jones, she will know what to do.' Ellen had sensed reliability in Mrs Jones, and she felt sure they had the local woman's support. Reluctantly, Kitty agreed and followed her daughter's lead out the chapel door and down the street to the home of Jones-the-Shop.

Entering through the side gate, as Ness had shown them that morning, they found her at the back door, sleeves rolled up and plucking at the body of a scrawny looking chicken. She greeted them with a curt nod of her head and when they didn't move, not being sure where they should move to, she said, 'Take yourselves indoors now, it's getting cold out here today, and stoke up the range for me.'

'Anything else I can help with Mrs Jones?'

'We'll be organising some dinner for the men in a bit and I dare say you've some unpacking and sorting out to do. I can't be chattin' an' carryin' on as though there was all the time in the world. I've work to do, and I don't see that stopping just because there's a war on.'

A while later, Ellen and her mother heard the sounds of pans being clanged onto the range top and chopping noises coming from the kitchen below.

They hoped this meant they could venture downstairs without being in Ness's way.

Entering the small steamy room Ellen saw Ness kneading dough in a bowl at the table who, without looking up, addressed her mother.

'You'll be wanting to make the babies some dinner to take to the school, use these vegetables and the chicken carcass here for soup and I've a can you can borrow. Maybe young Miss here will help me, all right, cariad?' Ellen did not know that 'cariad' was a term of endearment, but she guessed it was a kind word and so, looking first to her mother for approval, she took the apron Ness handed her. She was soon busy trying to keep up with the instructions.

'Fill the bowl from the pump, it's out the back, clean the *tatws* now, give them a good scrub with this cloth and put them on the range here to boil while I do the *bresych* and *winwns*. Soon realising that the *tatws* were her job, she set about scrubbing the small welsh potatoes with a damp cloth and wondered what dish Ness would be making with the cabbage and onions.

Not being too keen on cabbage and onions she hoped the dough would lead to something sweet. Watching her mother out of the corner of her eye, she saw her angrily pulling apart the chicken carcass.

'Now put any peelings into the bucket by the door,' Ness told Ellen quietly. 'We keep all the leftover food scraps for the pigs. Mind you remember that but ask me first as there's some you can't put in, eggshells for example, they're no good at all. Now I need to talk to your Mam a bit.'

Realising that this meant she was to keep out of the way, Ellen made very quiet, scraping movements over the bucket, reckoning that unless she drew attention to herself, they would keep talking and not notice her.

'Now Mrs West, I know you are not happy with what we can offer you, but it's as good as we have and we won't let your young ones do without, but it won't be grand. At school here we all learned about how Welsh people had to give up the coal mines to the English, we've seen our countryside destroyed and we don't like it. So, you won't find many friends here.'

'I'm used to that. I came from a farm myself and I know people don't like strangers.'

'The sheep farmers had it a bit easier but many of them were rehoused into the mining villages and set to working for the English.

'Are you a mining family then, or a farming family would you say?'

'Well, our own family had once belonged to the farms, but Geraint, my man, worked in coal mines up in the valleys. Not any more though, we're much more comfortable in the town.'

'Both really then?'

'That's right, missus. I won't be unkind to you now, but we had it tough to get here and I can't be givin' away to strangers. My boys work for farmers now, they are registered as agricultural students, keeps them from conscription. I couldn't do without them see, as my poor Geraint, he's not well.'

'We haven't met your husband yet, have we? Is he here now?'

'Yes. His chest is bad after a lifetime of coal dust, so he only does the shop when he feels well enough. But you can see for yourself it's only the front of a house and I think most times 'tis more of a meeting place for the men than a business.'

Ness stopped to draw her breath and looked up at Kitty as though expecting more questions.

'I don't care about the school not giving Ellen a place, or sharing a bed with Billy, but I really don't know what we are going to do about Mass.' Kitty's voice sounded near to breaking again and Ellen, head down, hated to hear the pain.

'It's no trouble to me doing these chores, Ness, and the pump by the door are just like I was used to as a girl, but that was a long time ago and I left Ireland for a different life. But I don't mind any of that, being here keeps the children safe, and I am grateful to you, really I am.'

'We will manage to help you find a Mass, Kitty.'

'And now I'm here I can get used to it. I can stand at a sink all day and I can wash in a bucket; this really is what we women do – England, Wales or Ireland. Maybe there will be more for me in years to come, but for now I'd just like to know we could still go to Mass on Sunday.'

'Well now, I know that's what's troublin' you and I have good news. You struck it lucky when you came to Llandeilo, more ways than one. I've heard that there's evacuees coming, a lot more, and you'll be wantin' to know them I reckon.'

Ellen moved over to where Ness and her mother were standing and, leaning her elbows on the corner of the table, she saw Mum's expression soften and lighten. Ness explained that a convent school from London, which had been evacuated to Eastbourne, had to be moved again for safety and were being billeted in Llandeilo, along with their teachers, the nuns. They were expected by the end of the month.

'Now I don't know what arrangements are being made for them, but I do know that the Kings Head are going to give a room over on a Sunday morning, and you might like to know the girls are all being taken into the County School.
So, if I was you, I would see if they can't get young cariad here a place in with the convent girls. Now shall we get on with the dinners?'

Indicating to Ellen, Ness pulled three bowls across the table 'You can help me with the men's dinner while your Mam takes the can up to the school. We will eat after they have finished, if there is any left.'

Later, with the cooking completed, a huge bowl of potatoes, large pat of butter, dish of chicken broth, and a pot containing the cabbage and onions was placed on the small wooden table in front of the range. Ellen eyed the butter in wonder and hoped the men wouldn't eat it all.

She watched her mother anxiously. Her shoulders weren't so tightly hunched under her neck now, her colour had returned to its normal faint blush and Ellen thought she seemed pleased by Ness's news.
She peeled off her apron, folding it carefully before returning it to the rack above the range from where Ness had reached for it earlier.
Having wrapped a scarf inside her winter coat she took the dinner can and, with a brief 'goodbye now' to Ness and Ellen, went out to climb the steep street to the school, with her head turned to face the grim drizzly afternoon.

Moments later, two young men, caked in mud and rain-soaked, arrived in through the back door. Introduced by Ness, Ellen learned that they were her sons, Walter and Fred. They nodded a greeting. Then, to her surprise, they stripped to the waist, washing themselves in the bowl on a chair in front of the range.

'It is as well Mum has gone out,' she thought, as Ness's sons dried themselves unselfconsciously before replacing their shirts and, once Ness had taken away the bowl with their dirty water, moved to the table and set about heaping their plates with food.

'Will we tell Mam about Sammy Davies?'

'Aye, when Dada's here.'

'Wait your dinner, boys, wait for your father,' implored Ness, although she looked as though she expected to be ignored. They had taken several mouthfuls before a stooped elderly man, fussily closing the door behind him and carefully replacing the mat which served as a draft excluder back into its exact position, arrived in through the shop door. Ellen guessed this must be Ness's husband, Geraint, and wondered whether he would be stern or soft, whether she should be wary of him or whether he would be easily persuadable, like her father.

'Hello young miss, what's your name then?' Geraint asked.

'Ellen West, sir.'

'No need to 'sir' me, girl. No English ways here. Geraint Jones they call me, Geraint is fine. And did you enjoy your morning in Llandeilo? Isn't it a grand town?'

'She's not got a place in the school, Dada, so I told her Mam what we heard of the convent girls and maybe she can go with them.'

'Maybe, girl, maybe. We can help with the reading here if you want it. Good to have a tidy miss about the place. Will she help you with the chores, Mam?'

Reaching for the bowl of potatoes he settled into his dinner and no more was said to Ellen.

'Sammy Davies, Da.'

'Gone missing he has, they saw him off last week, but he never turned up at the camp. Police been to the house an' all, big trouble there I'd say.'

'Who telled you, Walter? Don't be listening to any gossip now. 'Specially war gossip.'

'It's all over town, Da. After his leave was up, they took him to the station and waved him off.'

'An' he was talking about getting hitched next time he was home. He's been going with Betty Allen a while now and she don't like him being away, thinks he might meet another girl.'

'He's mad, so he is, I heard there ain't no girls on the front line, well, there are girls but not those available for marryin' I'm supposing.'

'No more now, not in front of ...' Ellen saw Ness widening her eyes, indicating in her direction.

She was listening carefully, of course, not wanting to draw attention to herself but mostly hoping for her turn to eat. As soon their plates were cleared, the boys pushed their chairs back, going upstairs without a word.

'They need a sleep after their dinner, as has been up since four-thirty, milking starts at five.' Ness explained whilst clearing away the men's dishes, filling the swill bucket with the scraps and, to Ellen's relief, putting three plates on the table.

'We have some fresh dumplings and tatws for us dinner now along with the remains, come on girl, get started. It's cold enough already.'

'Where's Mum? I don't think she will want me to start without her.'

'We'll go ahead now, cariad, and I'll keep some back.'

Sensing the wisdom of doing, in Ness's house, as Ness suggested, Ellen began to eat.

Obeying the mother was the same in her own home after all, and she was very hungry.

After dinner, Kitty still wasn't home. When Ness asked Ellen to walk up to the school, just to make sure, as her brother and sister would be due out soon, she reluctantly dressed in her gabardine and boots and headed out into the blustery wet weather. She was not used to walking through unfamiliar streets alone, but once she started, she found she was not unhappy at the chance to explore her surroundings. Meeting her mother on the way, she asked her where she had been.

'Trying to find out more about this Catholic school and to see whether we can get another billet with an extra bed. But it seems with this big number of evacuees due we can't move, girl. People here have their own troubles, or so they say, and we have to put up with it or go back. I'm sure she means well but how does she know you will get schooling when the nuns get here?'

Ellen, ignoring Kitty's outburst, began to plead. 'Mum, can we walk after we've collected Daisy and Billy? Can we look at the sheep and cows and pigs and chickens? I'd love to do that before we go back, please Mum!'

So began the slow assimilation. Ellen, Daisy, and Billy enjoying the novelty of countryside and animals, Ellen wasn't too sure that her mother felt the same way.

One afternoon, when they had been living with the Jones' family for several weeks, and there was still no sign of the convent girls, Ness asked Ellen whether she would like to do some reading, to keep her schooling up. 'I've read all the books in the bedroom, and I read to Daisy at night too. Have you any others?' she asked hopefully.

Geraint, not well enough for the shop that day and quietly resting in the corner, offered a suggestion. 'We have a fine bible here. Read it before all else. If ye read all that's in the Good Book you'll never tire of it, not in a hundred years. I go back to it again and again, and always it gives me guidance and peace from the Good Lord.'

'No, I never read a book like that,' said Ellen. 'We have books of the saints at home and of course the missal for Mass but I never read a bible.'

'Now don't start preaching, Geraint,' interrupted Ness, looking up from the mixing bowl at the other end of the kitchen table. 'You know they are Catholics. I don't know what they believe or don't believe but I know you can't preach to them, and her mother is a fierce worshipper, breaking her heart as she can't get to Mass on a Sunday, and them prayers upstairs every night, I hear them tho' they thinks I don't.'

'Well, child, we are Methodists, Christians like yourselves; but I say you can take the book, mind you keep it clean and put it back when you are done.'

Reaching to a barely visible shelf high above Ellen's head, Geraint grunted as he heaved down a square brick-thick object. It was a leather-bound book bigger than anything she had ever seen before. She knew she would never read it all, even if there were lots of pictures and puzzles and she wondered how she would ever be able to put it back. On the front it read 'Glorious Gospel of the Blessed God.'

Ellen rested the book on the table, and carefully opened the gilt clasps holding it shut. To her delight, the first page was a full colour print of two barely clothed men on what looked like a Welsh hilltop. The title was Abraham offering up Isaac.

'Who are these men; do they still live around here?' Ellen asked, interested to know who would walk around the hillside without a hat and coat. Horrified at her lack of biblical knowledge,

Geraint attempted to tell her the story of how Abraham, a wise man, agreed to God's request to kill his son to prove his great faith.

'Is that Methodist? Do you have to kill your sons? Did you have to kill any of yours?' and, not waiting for an answer from the red-faced Geraint, not even noticing his annoyance, she grinned 'Well I'm glad I'm a Catholic then, we believe in the one true God, and we never have to kill anyone.

We don't know of anyone who did either - well except for the Jews who killed Jesus, but they will never get into heaven now.'

'OK, that's enough, *twp* you are. Holy Bible goes back on the shelf until you have more respect.'

'Oh please, I really, really do want to read it. I will have respect.'

'Geraint, tell you what, I'll go through it with her and see to it she doesn't make light of it, nor get nightmares neither,' interrupted Ness. 'Last thing we want is the missus getting in a tymer.'

Ness reopened the book and Ellen sat alongside her at the table in front of the range. Before the light had faded, they had looked it through, deciding to only concentrate on the illustrations.

That became the pattern of their lives for the next few weeks.

Her mother would go to collect Billy and Daisy from school whilst she and Ness enjoyed a quiet hour of education.

They read the Bible, although somehow it was never mentioned.

The one hour stretched to a further hour as Kitty became more familiar with the village. Knowing her mother would leave early each afternoon, arriving in good time at the school and then taking the children the long way round the village gave plenty of time for reading.

On their return from school, Daisy and Billy would tell Ellen how they had leaned on barnyard gates to admire the pigs, mucky and snuffling, pink, grey or spotted.

Sometimes they had looked out onto fields of sheep, or over the coops alongside the lanes which were filled with fat, fidgety hens.

No one wondered why Ellen always refused to join them, and although she was curious to see the animals, she also treasured the hours with Ness and the bible stories.

The afternoons were short enough with the light fading quickly outside - and often the days were overcast and grey. She was happy working through the enormous book, choosing the illustrations and letting Ness explain the text. Although Ellen was a competent reader, most of the reading was done by Ness, who could then put her own interpretation on the parable wherever possible.

Once Ellen was allowed to choose another title and so she found a colourful illustration which read So Abraham Departed and Lot went with him.

Ness explained 'There was a wicked city called Sodom which God was planning to destroy, but he let Lot leave before the destroying began and allowed him to take his wife and daughters, on the understanding that they did not look back to see what was happening to the city. Lot's wife had friends there and she couldn't help but look back. That was when God turned her into a pillar of salt as a punishment.'

'What about the others then?' Ellen asked, unfazed by Lot's wife's fate and not really convinced. She turned the heavy page and was not surprised by the scene with Lot and his daughters.

Ness was growing uncomfortable at this stage, also mindful of Kitty's imminent return. However, she saw no option but to take a short cut.

'They needed to have babies so they made their father drunk with wine, which was very bad of them indeed, then each took a turn and visited the father, so they could have a child. They had two sons and Lot didn't know he was the father of the babies. He thought he was their grandfather, so everyone was happy.'

'Why did they tell it in the bible then?'

'Oh Ellen, maybe it is not a story we should talk about, let's find a better one tomorrow.'

The next day, once her mother had left the house after dinner, the big leather book was again brought down from the high shelf.

Ellen quickly turned the thick pages until she came to one she liked - Joseph sold by his brothers.

'Good choice', exclaimed Ness, so pleased to have moved away from Abraham and Lot. 'Here we have him then, a young lad, a seventeen-year-old, old enough for the army now, see, and his father's favourite. His father made him a wonderful many-coloured coat as a gift.

One night he dreamed he would rule over his brothers. He was foolish enough to tell his brothers about the dream. They kidnapped him, tore off his coat and dipped it in goat's blood, to make his father think he was dead. Then they sold him into slavery.'

Ellen slid down from the table, put her hands over her ears and declared she couldn't stand any more illustrated tragedies.

'God still punishes those who do wrong, Ellen; it's just not seen by an unbeliever.'

'Am I an unbeliever, Ness? What do I have to do to be a believer?' Ellen was now so enthralled by the possible tragedies that lay ahead for her if she made God angry that she needed to know more.

'Repent of your sins, girl, stop the idolatry and come to chapel with Geraint and me. There is a great preacher coming next week, listen to him speak and you will want to wash away your sins in the blood of the lamb.'

'I don't think Mum will let me, but thank you very much, Ness, anyway,' Ellen thought it might be fun to go to the chapel but knew the visit would never be agreed.

Every afternoon, when the book was returned to the high shelf, Ellen thought about her status as an unbeliever.

She did not think she would ever be converted to the strange religion and God of the Jones's, but she was wholly converted to the heady mix of suspense, terror, and wickedness which she had found in the bible.

One day, hoping to cheer her mother up, she began telling her about the bible stories and Geraint's kind offer of helping her to become a believer.

'They're great, Mum, really exciting, and the book is so old, older than English Granddad or even his Dad I should think. Once I go to school with the convent girls, I won't have time to read them, but I'm sure Ness would let you have a look.' She didn't add that she had already told Daisy, and Billy had overheard a watered down version of the stories. She kept them for bedtime and every night dealt out a little more detail, with her sister begging for more.

She watched anxiously as her mother turned to Ness, her cheeks flushed, and her shoulders raised in the stance that was usually, in Ellen's experience, a sign of an impending angry outburst.

'I'll thank you to keep your Methodist beliefs to yourself. I don't know what you've told her but she's talking about needing to get her sins washed away at your chapel. It's bad enough for us to be beggaring ourselves and sharing beds where we are not wanted, but to bring such confusion into their lives. That's a sin, so it is, and I don't like it.'

'Now Mrs West, we only meant to give the girl something to read; see, here's the Good Book, look for yourself, she needs an education. She didn't know any of it. Even our youngest ones know the Bible.'

'No, Mrs Jones, of course I know the Bible, but we don't use it much ourselves. We think more on the saints and prayers. It's difficult enough for us to be here. You don't have any idea, do you?'

'I know you're upset Mrs West, but we thought we were helping the girl, see?'

'But your children are not evacuated, you don't have to leave your comfortable homes and live amongst strangers. And your strange Welsh words, when you all speak English anyway.'

'Now Mum, it's not their fault, I just wanted something to read,' Ellen interjected, trying to smooth things over.

'Anyway, Mrs Jones, I've just had a letter from my husband. He says that since war has been declared the fighting's all in France, so I think we will just go back.'

Ellen watched her mother sweep angrily from the room clutching her glossy black leather handbag, which Ellen assumed contained the letter, leaving Ness wordless and red in the face.

She waited a few moments before following her mother, feeling the need to be peacemaker between the two women.

'Mrs Jones - Ness, I'm really sorry. I did like your Good Book and I would like to read other stories. Have you anything I could share with Mum without upsetting her?'

'Your mam is angry so let's leave it for now, girl.'

'She doesn't mean to be angry; she's just worried that's all. Mum came from Ireland you know; there was a famine there and everything. Lots of people died, but she calls it a land of saints and scholars. They have stories going back hundreds of years. I think Mum would like to think she was living with people who also had long stories, and I know you have lots in your bible.'

'Tomorrow, Ellen, not now', replied Ness curtly, still smarting from Kitty's outburst. 'Leave it girl. I will find you something later.'

The next day, breakfast was taken in an awkward silence, Kitty didn't eat at all, concentrating on preparing the soup for the school dinner before urging Daisy and Billy to be ready for school.

'And you'll come with me too, Ellen, you're not staying here on your own.'

Glancing an apology to Ness, Ellen pulled on her coat and scarf. Tucking her hand into Billy's, they left the house together, an unhappy little group.

Kitty was striding ahead, still fuming over what she thought of as the Jones's attempts to corrupt Ellen. Daisy was trotting beside her mother, a bit bemused by the dejected attitude but looking forward to hearing more about the trouble brought on by her sister.

Ellen looked down at her little brother, they weren't able to keep up with the others and she could sense he was miserable.

There were red marks where his shorts chafed the backs of his knees raw, his balaclava was pulled down over his face to keep out the wind, and she knew he was missing his friends and the promised wartime drama of aeroplanes.

'We are all unhappy,' she told him, 'but most of the unhappiness is felt by me. I've done nothing wrong, but I feel a whole heap of misery has been brought on the Jones's too. They really are very kind and I love those afternoons and the stories. It's such a pity Mum takes these things so badly.' Billy just looked up at her not understanding why she was making such a fuss when he was the one who was lonely and miserable.

They walked along the now familiar quiet roads of the village. They had several times been allowed to explore after school, or at weekends, and to run in the fields outside the town. Ellen would join them on Saturdays, always looking for animals and scaring the younger ones with stories of beasts and demons.

They usually passed a field in which a shepherd's hut stood. It seemed a mysterious home. Dark green paint flaking off the sides, and wheels beneath to allow it to be moved. Ellen thought it was halfway between the gypsy caravans she'd occasionally seen horse-drawn through the lanes nearby and the garden sheds on the London allotments.

One day, shortly after the incident with the Bible, the three children decided to explore the shepherd's hut, quickly crossing the field and clambering inside. It smelled of musty, damp bedding and old wood-smoke, making it seem exciting and mysterious. There was very little inside except a rough platform for a bed and a wood burning stove with a kettle. They thought it had a sense of fairy-tale.

'Maybe Hansel and Gretel had a home like this in the woods?' suggested Daisy, wide-eyed, half-scared, half-amazed.

'Ah no Dais', it's like Little Red Riding Hood's grandmother's cottage. See here, I'll gobble you up.'

Billy wailed, Daisy screamed and all three ran out of the hut. They jumped down the steep ladder-like steps, and across the field, not stopping until they were over the gap in the hedge and onto the road again.

The following day, as Ellen and her mother were beginning their chores and before the men came in at midday, Ness handed Kitty a scrapbook of newspaper cuttings.

'I'd like you to read this, Mrs West,' she said quietly, 'before you make up your mind about the Irish and the Welsh. Maybe it's not as tragic as the history of the Irish, I don't know about them, but it is what my grandfather collected, and I think you will find we have a history together you maybe did not know about.'

'I will later, Mrs Jones, thank you,' Ellen heard her mother reply, her tone cool and abrupt. Ellen had to bite her lip to stop herself explaining that her mother was insecure and frightened and that she always needed to look like she was in charge. She reckoned that wouldn't really help.

Ellen leaned on the back of the chair so she could look over her mother's shoulder as they both read an extract from the Monmouthshire Merlin on 'The alarming and lamentable appearance of the streets of Newport, crowded with many hundreds of famishing Irish'.

Looking further, Kitty found another cutting: 'Those who are arriving in Wales are fleeing the Irish potato famine, and often arrive in a very desperate state. The Wanderer, which docked in Newport in 1847, deposited 113 destitute men, women, and children in the town, with 20 of them said to be close to death.'

Ellen pulled back quietly and watched as her mother looked up surprised and responded with a softened tone of voice, 'Mrs Jones, Ness, this is such a surprise to me. I never knew Wales and Ireland had any common experiences, especially not the famine.'

'We are closer than you think, Kitty.'

'The famine was always an important part of our history, although it was just about finished by the time my grandmother was born. Did you know about this connection before you offered to take us?'

'No, I never knew much about the Irish and I wasn't told your family were Irish either. And, of course, Newport is a long way from here; but anyway, I'm not sorry to have you and I think you should know that we never wished you harm, in fact many of us probably have Irish blood. Maybe I have too, Kitty.'

'I think you might have, Ness!'

'Now, shall I make us some tea before you go to the school for the babies?'

Ellen was delighted. This seemed to be the first, tentative start of a friendship between Kitty and Ness. She noticed how they were now considering themselves on first name terms and spending more time together since they'd shared a piece of history.

She could see similarities between them, as both were women who believed they were independent, and she knew neither of them would have admitted to seeking support from each other. They enjoyed the companionship that was developing, working together in the kitchen during the hours when the children were at school.

She hoped this would delay their return to London. Then her mother received a second letter and she read it upstairs when her mother was out of the room.

24th November 1939.
Dear Kitty,

Thank you for your letter. I look forward to the post every week, it is so lonely here without you and the children, but I'm sure it won't be long until you are back.

Mother has been looking after me, I go there for dinner every afternoon, and hear news of the war.

It still seems that all the fighting is in France, although there has been some bombing in Edinburgh, so maybe we were too hasty in sending you away from London.

Maybe you should come back before Christmas, we can see how it is going then.

I am so sick of war. The last war seems only months away to me now, I feel as though my whole life has been taken. First it took me from being a schoolboy to fighting as a soldier, now it has taken my family.

Sometimes I think I am all alone here and I feel very low.

Mother and Father say I can stay at the house while you are all away and I plan to move over from next week, although I will keep an eye on the flat. I don't want you to worry.

I'm glad you are enjoying the countryside. It sounds lovely. I've never been to Wales, maybe after the war we will take a holiday and you can show me where you stayed.

Please write soon and tell me of your plans.

Kiss the children for me, tell them to be good and help you through these difficult times.

Your loving husband, William.'

'Oh, Ness, what should I do?' she heard Kitty ask, although of course Ellen knew exactly what her mother was intending. 'My husband needs me back in London, his parents are not well, and we will have to return sooner than I thought.'

The letter was ill-timed, the long-awaited convent school evacuees had finally arrived, there was Mass once a week and Ellen was on a promise to join the classes.

They had all started to enjoy Wales, and Ness was taking Kitty round the shops on Saturday, to get a few items unobtainable in London, so the children would have some surprises on Christmas morning.

Sweets were more readily available, so was wool and coloured felts, and Kitty's skills at sewing turned these into small toys and novelties.

Now William's letter would have to put a stop to those outings and Kitty sounded reluctant to prepare for the journey in her usual single-minded way, asking Ness,
'Can you help me with transport arrangements? I can get us travel vouchers, but I need to know what the best trains are.'
'Well now, Kitty, tomorrow the council offices are open, we can go by and see what is available. Once you're back from the school we can sort it out then. I'll help you get the clothes washed and aired ready for packing again.'
Ness, in her chequered pinafore and solid footwear, an unlikely soulmate for the fashion-conscious Kitty, sounded sadder to hear of their departure than anyone had expected. Daisy and Billy considered it good news that they were to return to London soon, but Ellen was not so pleased.

'Oh Mum, can I not stay on here? I'm enjoying the time to read and now that the new evacuation party are here it will be good for my education,' Ellen knew that was a card which just might sway her mother's intentions. 'Ness's arranged it so's I am available to show the girls around and stop them from being homesick.'

'Sorry, Ellen', her mother replied with a stiffening of backbone which indicated there would be no more discussion, 'You will come with us, the family will stay together, you are not yet even thirteen and can't be left on your own.'
Ness, as usual, managed to reduce the tension between them. 'Let's all have some tea now. I've just put some dough onto the griddle, the cakes will be ready in a minute and they don't keep long.'

Grateful for the change of subject they gathered around Ness's scrubbed wooden table and shared the tea. No one noticed Ellen putting her share of cake into her apron pocket.

Bedtime was the usual round of washing in the cold back pantry, prayers on their knees beside the bed, and then Daisy and Ellen in one bed, Billy and Kitty in the other and no talking allowed.

Ellen lay on her side listening for the regular breathing which would indicate a room full of sleeping family, before quietly sliding out of her side of the bed.

She pulled her nightdress over her head, having kept her knickers and vest on underneath.

Then she tugged her jumper on, wriggled into her skirt, and with socks in hand began to tiptoe towards the door.

'What's going on, Ellen?' Daisy's little white face peered up at her from between the blanket and the overcoat they used as bedding. 'Where are you going?'

'Shush Dais', I'm going to be like the children in the books. I'm running away. If Mum asks you just tell her I've gone to join the fairies, she can go back to London if she wants to, but I'm staying here.'

Ellen slipped out the door and crept downstairs. She fumbled in the dark looking for her boots and coat in the kitchen before putting on her socks and, wrenching open the heavy front door, stepped out into the night. Her heart missed a beat as she heard the door close behind her, knowing there was no going back.

Hastily lacing up the boots and shrugging on her coat, she was suddenly encased in bitter frosty air and she shivered as she pulled her old red scarf from her pocket, carefully tying it over her head. She looked up gratefully at the moon, its faint light came and went as the clouds moved.

The blackout prevented any leaking of light from windows and she hadn't been prepared for the feeling of loneliness which washed over her.

Pressing her hand in her pocket she felt reassured by the two small crumbling cakes earlier smuggled from the tea table. Just knowing they were there gave her some confidence as she started walking up the hill.

She knew where to go but the lack of light made the journey feel longer and more difficult than she had expected. Tripping over a hole in the road, she grazed her knee and, struggling to her feet, felt blood trickle down her leg.

It wasn't really painful but anyway she decided to tie her headscarf around the wound as a makeshift bandage.

'Last thing I need to do is leave a trail of blood,' she muttered, 'wouldn't take long for the dogs to track me down would it? And then back to London in a shot.'

Limping stiffly, she walked until she came to the gap in the hedge, which she recognised as the one they had used before for their visits to the shepherd's hut.

Struggling through, she snagged the scarf covering her knee on a thorn in the bush but was able to rip it free. Underfoot the ground felt soft and spongy, soaked by the recent rain and she had to creep slowly over the field towards the outline of the hut, just discernible through the trees.

Ellen was glad to take a brief rest when she reached the wooden steps of the hut and sat down to examine her injured knee before going inside.

'This will need a wash before it becomes infected' she told herself, in a voice imitating her mother's. 'Well anyway, I'm here now, so let's get inside into the warm and have a bit of a rest.'

Opening the door of the hut she peered inside to make sure it was still unoccupied.

The bench and wood burner were exactly as they had been at the last visit, the kettle was missing but that wasn't any use to Ellen, and she breathed a sigh of relief.

In a loud voice, hoping it would make her feel more confident, she spoke to the empty room. 'I will stay here until they've gone back to London, then I'll go and see Ness. She'll keep me, I know she will.'

The hut was not quite as empty as Ellen had expected. A rustling underneath suggested field mice, or hedgehogs, or badgers. Each time she put a foot to the floor the boards creaked. Even a faint hooting owl seemed ominous to her, and she was becoming increasingly frightened.

Her knee hurt and her coat wasn't warm enough to keep out the damp of the hut.
She swung herself up onto the bench, which, she assumed, served as a bed and looked out the grimy window onto the faintly moonlit field.

Fishing a broken piece of griddlecake out of her pocket she nibbled on it, more for comfort than out of hunger and began to wish it were morning, hoping a search party would come and find her. Lying down she closed her eyes, unable to relax whilst her mind was buzzing with the adventure and, before drifting off into a light sleep, she began to wonder whether she could make her way back to the house unnoticed.

Ellen woke startled and disorientated. Cramped and cold, the brief sleep hadn't been enough to refresh her. The moon was gone, and the night sky turned to grey. Bladder niggling for release she carefully opened the door, made her way outside and squatted behind the hut before climbing back in to finish the second griddlecake. She began to feel braver and ready to face a day in hiding.

Dozing lightly again, with her head against the window and using her scarf as a pad against the grimy glass, she was jolted awake for a second time by a noise outside.

No longer grey, the sky had a hint of pink and the birds sounded busy and cheerful.

Through the small glass pane she was able to make out the figure of a man ducking through the same gap in the hedge, which she had used as an entry the night before. Moving her head cautiously down below the window she tried to remain calm, waiting quietly. The loudest sound she heard was her heart thumping loudly in her ears.

It might have been the sound of hooves on the road which had woken her this time, and now she listened carefully, bravely peering over the lower edge of the windowsill.

She could see a herd of cows emerging around the bend, lumbering and heavy with milk, followed by a dog and a youngish man, hardly more than a boy, walking nonchalantly behind the herd as though still half asleep.

The other man looked older and was definitely much taller. He was skirting the field staying close to the trees, attempting, it seemed, to keep out of sight.

As he moved closer Ellen could see he was probably about the same age as Walter and Fred. He looked dishevelled, his unshaven face giving him a scrawny beard and his clothes, even from a distance, looked dirty and torn.

'A tramp probably,' Ellen spoke aloud, thinking that the sound of her confident voice would bring her some reassurance 'I hope he doesn't come in here. If he does, I'll scream and run.'

She looked again towards the young herdsman following the cows and she thought he might be the saving of her. Should she run out and attract his attention? But then, how would she explain herself and anyway she didn't know him. And both Mum and Dad had always told her not to speak to strangers.

As the tramp figure moved cautiously towards the hut, she realised she really needed help. But the cows had receded round the next bend by the time Ellen knew there was no way out.

Terrified, she cowered on the bench-bed attempting to make herself shrink, pulling her knees up to her chin and wrapping her arms tightly around her body.

The door opened with a creak and Ellen found herself gazing into the wary and shocked eyes of the tramp.

'What are you doing here, girl?' the man's voice sounded anxious. 'Are you waiting for me? Did someone send you?'

'No, really I'm just going, I need to get back to the Jones's, my Mum and Ness will be looking for me.'

'Are you a spy then? And don't lie to me; I don't want any of that nonsense, I'd not put anything past the ones around here. It's just as their own men are gone away that they want to be sure I'm caught an' handed over. Now you come here out of nowhere, I don't know who you are, and you expect me to believe you when you say you're not a spy?'

'No sir, I'm not a spy. I'm just here for a bit.'

He pulled the flap of his coat back to reveal a gun tucked into his belt. He looked directly at her as his hand moved towards the gun handle.

Ellen felt so frightened she thought she would be sick. Still looking angrily and suspiciously at the girl, he reached under the end of the bench and to her surprise brought out the kettle and a small cake tin.

'I'm goin' to the stream to fill this and make some tea now, and you don't move from that bench or I'll shoot you. I'm a soldier, see, and I'm used to shooting people who don't obey orders.'

Ellen blinked hard and wordlessly agreed by nodding her head, terrified by his threat and wishing she had never left the comfort and security of Ness's house.

He was only gone a few minutes and when he returned, he didn't speak to her but muttered and swore at the wood burner until it reluctantly delivered a feeble flame which licked the base of the kettle. Ellen knowing it would take a while for the water to boil, felt trapped. Rocking back on his heels the man gave her a long, careful stare before asking,

'Let's have your name then, rank, and serial number, please. And tell me why you are here.'

'Ellen West, age twelve and a half, evacuee from London, staying with Jones-the-Shop in Llandeilo.'

'And why are you here, Ellen West? You say they didn't send you to find me?'

'No, they don't know where I am. I only ran away because I don't want to go back to London. But now I do, so I need to go home. Please let me move and please, please don't shoot me.'

As he looked up at her, she saw a flicker of sympathy cross his face.

His battered old hat, wet from dew or rain, was pushed back towards his ears. He wore a collarless grey shirt which may originally have been white and a heavy brown coat over baggy trousers secured by a cracked leather belt. Now she had time to observe him more closely she thought he looked more like a workman than a tramp.

She'd seen plenty of soldiers in London preparing for war, all smartly turned out in dark green, and of course she'd watched Billy with his uniform Spot Sight charts. Only having seen his gun made her believe he was a soldier.

Handing Ellen a mug of tea, 'Sorry, no milk or sugar,' he opened his tin and offered her a grimy looking biscuit.

'No thanks, just the tea is nice.' Ellen's hand shook as she reached for the hot tea.

'I won't shoot you girl, I just needed to know you weren't sent to find me.'

Ellen braved what she intended to be just one question, promising herself she wouldn't ask again. 'So, if you are a soldier why aren't you at the war? Why haven't you got soldier's clothes? And are you living here in this hut now?' The soldier seemed unperturbed by the barrage.

'My name's Sammy Davies. I've a sweetheart, name of Betty, lives over in Ffairfach and we want to marry. I'm just waiting now for the banns to be read. We'll marry next week and then I'll go back to my regiment. So, it's really important for us that no one knows I'm here just now. You can keep a secret can't you, girl? For the course of true love to run smooth?'

Ellen waited a moment before answering. She thought the name was familiar, and then recalled how Walter and Fred had told their father of the young man who had gone missing. It all made sense now and she began to feel sorry for him and a little less afraid.

'I can keep a secret, I'm very reliable, but I do want to go now.'

'Tell you what, girl. Stay here with me today, let's both get some sleep, then I am going to ask you to do me a favour.

If you do as I say you are free to go, no shootin' and no questions asked.'

Without giving Ellen time to respond he continued,

'Get over to Trapp tonight. It's a long walk, mind, but you won't be seen when it's dark. Get yourself to my parent's house and ask them to give you food and some clothes for me. Don't tell them where I am but say they're to come to the chapel in Ffairfach on Wednesday next week, see me and Betty married.

Well, then if they want to hand me over, an' if that's for the best, they can do. If I go myself I've no chance, but they don't know you and you won't tell them where I am. I know I can trust you.'

'But why must I do that, Sammy? I'm scared of the dark and I don't know the way and anyway why can't you get married next time you're home? You've really made this a big problem for us all.' Ellen remembered how her mother always won an argument with their father by reminding him of the problem his standpoint made for 'us all'.

'Well, girl, are you not aware of the facts of life? … Where babies come from?' he repeated his question, looking at her bemused and shocked face. 'There's a baby on the way girl, and babies don't wait, see.'

'Oh, right, of course,' replied Ellen, still unclear, but wanting the conversation to finish before it became even more uncomfortable.

And so the day passed. Ellen lay on the bench, listening to Sammy snoring. He was lying on a pile of clothes or blankets, she couldn't be sure which, that were now blocking the doorway on the other side of the hut. She did wonder whether she dare make her escape before he woke up. Then she remembered the threat, not only of shooting but also that he could find her wherever she went, and she dismissed that idea.

Thinking the walk to Trapp might not be too difficult, the combination of boredom and lack of sleep overcame her and it was dark outside when she was woken by the noise of the kettle boiling on the wood burner
. Sammy had made more tea.

'Here's a map,' he handed her a torn page upon which he had drawn a rough route from the road outside the field to his parent's house.

'It will take about four hours to walk there, young miss, so you need to leave soon. It's getting dark now and you should be there before they turn in for the night. Stay inside the fields, follow the hedges along, and don't walk on the road, you might be seen. Here's a stick for you and a letter to give them explaining.'

'Do I really have to do this Sammy? Or can you come too?'

'No, I can't. But I've told you what to say and once your mission is over you are free to go. You can come back here if no one is following you, or go back to the Jones's, whatever you want. Just don't tell them where I am, right? Always remember I have a gun and I am a soldier and I will come for you if you betray me.'

'Yes, of course.'

'Oh, and here's tea. Drink it now and take this piece of loaf with you. And remember my promise, I mean it, both ways.'

Having swallowed a mouthful of tea, which she didn't really want, Ellen wrapped her dirty scarf over her head, checked on her scabbed knee with its crusted blood and decided she needed a dry head more than she needed a bandage.

Putting the bread in her pocket and silently taking the letter and stick from Sammy, she left the hut and limped cautiously towards the road, skirting the trees as she had seen him do earlier. The light drizzle soon soaked through her clothes. She felt damp and miserable and her knee hurt. She followed the road towards Trapp, keeping into the hedgerow just as Sammy had told her to do.

She had no way of knowing how long she had been walking, only that the night grew darker, wrapping itself around her, heightening her sense of isolation.

She'd never liked the dark and the fear that someone might see her and ask questions added to her anxiety. She was convinced that if Sammy was discovered he would 'come for her' and her life really would be in danger.

Gritting her teeth, biting her lower lip to distract herself, she tried to recall the details of the Bible stories she had heard from Ness.

The sheep looked up at her in amazement as she passed them by, they seemed as anxious as she was and, although Walter had told her they nap at night they seemed alert and ready to scatter.

And of course, these twitchy creatures were an essential part of Abraham's story too. She'd been convinced that the Methodists believed in Abraham's sacrifice, and that slaughtering lambs and threatening to kill sons was part of the life in Wales. So of course, she reckoned, shooting her would not be too unusual.

Round the next bend she passed the small hamlet of Ffairfach. The Tabernacle chapel where Sammy and Betty were to marry loomed square and forbidding along the roadside and she increased her pace, although the boots were rubbing up blisters on her wet sore feet.

Her knee had begun to bleed a bit where the scabs broke. Walking on into the countryside without signposts or lighting she felt homesick for the London streets.

'Why, oh why, did I do this?' she asked herself, stifling a sob. 'Mum and Daisy and Billy will be so worried about me. Maybe Ness will know where to find me or the boys might come looking along the road and see me. But anyway, I mustn't tell, I'll never tell.'

The moon broke out from behind the clouds, the rain eased, and the fields became more visible. She could see mountains, hulking and unfamiliar on her right and ahead were the faint outlines of houses.

The improvement in the light gave her a chance to squint at the map again and leaning her stick against a hedge she decided to take the left turn leading to the Trapp chapel.
She could see some buildings ahead and felt a renewal of energy at the thought of reaching the soldier's parent's house and delivering the message.

She hoped they would be kind people and not be angry with her or with Sammy. They might even let her rest before she began the walk back.

Her head was aching now, and she felt her skin prickling as well as shivering. 'A hot mug of cocoa or Ovaltine would be lovely,' she murmured 'but no such luck for me, it's a crust of dry bread. I'm like Lot's wife, can't look back or I'll be turned into a pillar of salt.'

Her steps began to falter, she was so tired. Then she stumbled and fell on uneven stones as she took the left turn, hitting her head on the ground. She closed her eyes, exhausted and stunned, she collapsed in the ditch.

Back in Llandeilo, her mother discovered Ellen missing when she went to wake the girls for breakfast.
'Where is she, Daisy?'
'I don't know, Mum.'
'You must know, Daisy. Did she say anything at all?'
'No, Mum, just that she has gone away with the fairies and she wants to stay in Wales, not go back to London.'
Ness was quickly told of Ellen's disappearance and she decided to send Geraint to the Police Station, offering to mind the shop until he returned. Walter and Fred had already left but would be back at midday and Ness assured Kitty that once they had come home, she would tell them to go straight out to look for her.
'I've read about evacuee children running away, Kitty. They usually find them near a railway station…'
Kitty felt grateful for Ness's reassurance but not convinced. She knew Ellen didn't want to go back to where she came from, but she said nothing. She was feeling quite ashamed of her earlier dismissive feelings towards this kind family and grateful for their support now.

'Geraint is calling at the police station, then he's going down to the railway to see if she's there. So, we'll stay here for now. The police will come to question us first. Once they're done, we'll go out and search.'
'I need to send a telegram to Will. He has to know what's going on.'

141

'After the police have been, we'll do that at the Post Office. It might be all right again by then. As I said, I believe this does happen a lot with the evacuees.' She didn't want to say anymore, she could see Kitty was close to tears.

Not knowing what more she could do, Ness set the pot of porridge on the table, sliding three bowls across and avoiding catching Kitty's eye. Daisy and Billy were very excited. Police and a runaway sounded as though they were characters in a book and Daisy even ventured to say, 'Bowls of porridge, just like Mummy Bear, Daddy Bear, and little Baby Bear', before she was stopped by her mother delivering a sharp tap to the back of her head.

'How dare you make fun at a time like this, Daisy? Your sister could be anywhere, captured by the Germans, drowned, injured even, with no one to look after her. Oh, she is a naughty wicked girl. She's breaking all our hearts.'

Waiting for the police, watching by the window, Kitty felt frightened and alone. She needed William to be with her, he always knew what to do for the best, and she was sure Ellen was in danger.

Several hours passed before the policeman arrived, on his bicycle. Kitty had expected a car at least and more than one officer. This man looked too young; his fresh face unlined. Inappropriately the thought that he might not have started shaving briefly flashed across her mind.

'P.C. Williams, Ma'am. I've come to take a statement. I believe a young girl has run away. Any idea where she might be?'

Kitty, frustrated by his officious attitude, tried to impress on him the importance of setting up a search party immediately.

'We'll give it 'til nightfall, Ma'am, they usually come home by then. Short of manpower at the station, for obvious reasons, and a runaway evacuee is not uncommon. Not a priority here either. I'll file a report immediately I get back.'

'Can you get word to my husband in London? Tell him our girl is missing and ask him to come down?'

'As I said, if she's not back by nightfall, Mrs West, we'll set up the full search procedure. That's when we will let your husband know.'

Kitty immediately went out into the village after the policeman's visit, leaving Daisy and Billy behind with Ness. There was no question of their going to school. She headed straight for the Post Office and sent Will a telegram -

'Ellen missing. Please come at once. Kitty.'

Out in the street, her usual reserve gone, she asked everyone she met whether they had had any sight of Ellen. She walked the route to school and back but was anxious to return to Ness's house by midday, hoping the boys would help in the search.

When Walter and Fred arrived home at midday, they were given a hasty bowl of stew and their orders from Ness.
'Get straight out there now, boys, and find that girl. Don't come home until you've got her and treat her gently when you do find her. She'll be scared, all alone, and probably soaked through.'
'Right Ma, we'll get her back.'
'Remember Dada has already been to the train station, so go the other way. Start up by the school, go out of the village.'
As soon as they had finished eating, the two men pulled their coats from the peg at the back of the door, laced up their boots and, grabbing a walking stick each headed back out into the wet drizzly day confident that they would find the missing girl.

Once they had gone, the house seemed to be holding its breath. No one spoke much and all attention was on the sounds from outside. Daisy and Billy became bored and irritable so Kitty took them walking outside the village, partly to tire them out but also to help pass the time until the police set up what they had called their full search procedure.

Walking by the gap in the hedge where Ellen had snagged her scarf, Daisy's eye caught sight of a fragment of red cloth. She looked away quickly and distracted her mother by pretending to notice 'something moving' on the other side of the lane.

'It's only cows, Daisy; she won't go in a field with cows, she knows enough not to do that. Sheep maybe, we could look in fields with sheep.'

Daisy felt relieved, and proud of her ability to keep a secret. She knew Ellen would be pleased with her when she came back.

It was growing dark when they returned to the Jones's and as Kitty rounded the corner, she saw two policemen outside the house. Heart in mouth she ran to the open front door. 'Have you found her? My girl, have you got her?'

'No, Mrs West, but we are going to set up a search party now. Can you give us a piece of her clothes, something that hasn't just been washed, a nightdress maybe? It helps the dogs to have a scent to follow.'

'I'll get it now, straight away.'

'With your agreement Ma'am we will be asking for volunteers from all across the town. We expect to start a search just before midnight. You can trust us to be very thorough and ask you to stay here, so if she returns there'll be someone home. Don't be too worried, they nearly always do come home, Ma'am.'

Bringing Ellen's nightgown down from the bedroom, Kitty felt she was living a nightmare. She had a physical coldness in her stomach when she realised the implication of the 'nearly always', and she couldn't bring herself to wonder what happened to those who didn't come home.

Ness pulled the heavy blackout curtains closed, then lit all the lamps as well as leaving the electric bulb burning upstairs, giving the house an illusion of comfort.

Kitty wanted to be out, with a lamp, looking for Ellen but knew this was not going to be possible.

'I'm going to stand on the street so I can see and hear if there are any developments,' she told Ness. 'You've been so good to us Ness, God bless you. If there is ever anything we can do for you in return when all this is over...'

'Now, now, cariad, I'll give the babbies their tea and they can sit up with me a while, they won't sleep while we're waiting for news,' Ness replied gently, not arguing with Kitty and knowing how frightened she was feeling.

Kitty stayed on the doorstep in the dark, listening to the men calling Ellen's name around the village. Dogs were barking somewhere also, and she wondered whether they had picked up any scent from the nightdress or whether there had always been dogs barking without her noticing.

It was too cold to stand outside all night and she turned into the house after midnight and dozed in a chair. At dawn she was woken by the sound of a motor car and rising stiffly, opened the door. Her heart leapt when she saw William, his face pale and anxious, behind the steering wheel of the car, which had drawn up outside the house.
'I came as soon as I got your telegram, Kitty. Petrol on the black market. Never broken the law before but had to get here. Brought someone else to help too.'

Kitty was surprised to see Will's father clamber out of the passenger seat.
'I couldn't have got here without him, my love. He knows the right people and got us the fuel, as well as helping with the driving.'
'Well then I'm grateful to you, Arthur, thank you. Both had best come inside then and meet Ness and Geraint, it's their house. Their sons are out searching for her now, as is most of the village. D'you hear them? With the dogs?'

Will and his father cautiously approached the lamp-lit house, uncertain of their welcome. Daisy and Billy, who had been sleeping upstairs, were woken by the sound of the men's voices.

'Dad, Dad!' they ran towards their father, although Billy looked fearfully at the older man at his side.

'This is your Granddad', Will explained, focussing on Billy; Daisy had met him before. 'He's come to help us find Ellen.'

Gratefully accepting the hot sweet mug of tea, which Ness - arriving down to the kitchen shortly after the children - offered, they asked where they should look first. A knock on the door interrupted their discussion and as Kitty opened the door she saw two policemen, one of whom was the officious young P.C. Williams.

They had torn Ellen's nightdress in half and had something else in their hands. She forced herself to look at what was in their hands, and with a control she didn't know she had, managed to convince herself that this wasn't real. Creasing the corners of her mouth hard to prevent herself from crying out she thought that it shouldn't be happening. Not here, not to this family, to her daughter, to these lives. She knew it was happening to other families, other lives, but they had left the danger of London; she had not expected the war to reach its tentacles to here.

'Found a scrap of cloth, could be a scarf, Ma'am, do you recognise it?'

Kitty reached for the fragment of cloth and knew immediately that it was her daughter's scarf. Seeing the dark brown bloodstains crusted on the fabric she let out a wail, which seemed to echo across the valley.

'Where, where did you find it? I have to go there. Now.'

'Okay, Mrs West we'll take you, it's a gap in the hedge and there's a shepherd's hut, which the men are searching right now for any traces of her.'

Pulling her coat on roughly and wrapping her arms tightly around her thin body, Kitty turned to Will. 'It's hers. She's been hurt. We need to go.' Along with Arthur they ran between the two policemen, out of the village and up the hill to where the scarf fragment had been found. They saw someone being chased. A big man, taller than William or Geraint. Then they saw him stumble and fall.

William had been at her side as she ran, but now he hurtled past her to the man they had been chasing. Reaching him at the same time as the police, Will grabbed the man by the torn and dirty collar of his coat and brought his face down to within an inch of the man's own. They were both equally frightened and sweating.

'Where is she? If you value your life, you'll tell me where my child is. I don't care what the police do, I want my daughter. Tell me, tell me now.' To the shock of all the onlookers, police and dogs, William punched him hard in the face.
'Trapp, she's gone to Trapp. I'm sorry, I'm so sorry.'
Throwing the man to the ground Will ran down the hill towards his car, followed by his father.
'Trapp,' he shouted, 'Trapp. Anyone tell me how to get to Trapp.'
'I'll go with you,' offered a young man running alongside.
'I'm Walter Jones, one of Ness's sons.' He panted, as he kept pace with the older man. 'I know where to look. His parents live in Trapp, take me with you.'

All three men jumped into the car, which started at the first pull of the choke and sped down the hill away from the commotion of the village. Kitty walked slowly back to Ness's house feeling cold and frightened. It had all happened so quickly. One minute William arrived, the next he had gone again, and where on earth was Ellen?

Ellen opened her eyes. She hurt all over. She was shivering with the cold and one side of her face felt swollen and numb to touch. Looking around it took her a moment to remember where she was and what she had been doing. Pulling her torn scarf off she dropped it and shook her hair free.

'Need to get up, see Abraham, tell him where his son is,' she scolded, as she pulled herself out of the shallow ditch. Walking unsteadily up the road, pushing her hands into her coat pocket she felt the damp paper envelope in her coat pocket.

Her memory began to return as she fished out the letter. Although a bit wet, the envelope was still sealed and appeared undamaged by the journey. She moved it into her skirt pocket where she thought it would be safer and drier. 'First house I come to, that's the one', she muttered. 'And then he won't shoot me, he'll let me go.'

Passing the chapel, she knocked on the first house door in the row, set straight onto the front of the road. A middle-aged woman, wearing a coat over an ankle length nightgown opened the door a crack and looked suspiciously at her. Ellen couldn't have known how concerned this woman, who was Sammy's mother, became, with every late night visit.

They had had several recently, occasionally from the police but mostly young men in the village.

Home on leave, they would have a few drinks then, full of Dutch courage, they'd want to make sure his parents knew how shameful they considered Sammy's desertion.

Looking down at the girl on her doorstep, Vera Davies knew this was a very different kind of visitor. Soaking wet, with the side of her face swollen, the young girl had a brightness in her eyes which looked like fever and confusion.

Ellen was close to falling as Vera held out her arms to bring her inside.

Not asking any questions, she helped her into the kitchen, stoked up the range until she had a good fire burning, then removed her wet, cold coat. Giving Ellen a blanket to cover herself with Vera hastily filled a bowl with hot water which she set in front of the fire.

Ellen, watching the flames, was too tired to speak. Her confused thoughts jumping from the soldier to Abraham, then to her mother and Ness. She relaxed a little as Vera gently brushed the tangled hair away from her face before taking a warm flannel and lightly washing her forehead and nose. She winced as she felt the flannel cloth edge near the bruises which were beginning to form around her eyes. It was more a comforting caress than a cleansing, and the frightened young Ellen began to feel safer than she had done since she'd left the Jones's house.

'Sylvester, come down here right now, we've a problem, come and help me.' She called out whilst her eyes never left the girl's face, all the while wondering what could have possibly happened to her; closely followed by the suspicion that this might be linked in some way to Sammy. Ellen thought she was dreaming when Vera spooned a few mouthfuls of hot sweetened milk into her mouth.

The sensation was better than anything she had imagined. Better than the Ovaltine or the cocoa. The warmth and the hot drink made her feel drowsy again and she leaned back into the blankets before gradually drifting off to sleep.

Vera and Sylvester watched their unexpected visitor and, with an uneasy sense that this would very likely bring trouble, decided to let her sleep first before asking any questions.

Waking in the armchair some hours later, Ellen remembered why she had made the journey and pulled the letter out from her skirt pocket.

'I've to give you this, please, and you've to give me food and clothes for Sammy, then I won't get shot and then I can go home.'

149

Vera's face paled when she heard her son's name and called for Sylvester, who had gone to bed. Now he stood in front of Ellen, barefoot, hastily half-dressed, and looking shocked.

'What in heaven's name has he done now?' he asked, snatching the letter from Ellen's outstretched hand and ripping it open with his teeth.

'I'll swing for him, willingly. Has he touched you, girl? You can't be more than a child.'

'I'm twelve and a half, sir, nearly thirteen. Ellen West is my name. I'm an evacuee from London and I'm staying with the Jones's family in Llandeilo. That's all my rank and serial number. I'm not allowed to say where he is or he'll shoot me.'

'He'll not shoot you child, he's always full of big words, but he's in big trouble now. He'll have the law on him this time.'

'No, please don't, there's going to be a baby and it won't wait. He's marrying Betty next week.'

Vera crouched down in front of Ellen, gently stroking her arm.

'Listen to me child, you are safe now, no one is going to shoot you, but we have to take you home and we have to know where our Sammy is before this gets any worse.'

Turning to her husband she pleaded.

'If they find Sammy before we do, they'll maybe think he has hurt this child.

You've said it yourself; the men in the villages feel the need to take control now that there's so few police around.

Desertion is bad enough but kidnapping a child, now that's quite another, see.

Quickly, man, get the horse out, we'll need the cart to get her back to Llandeilo straight away and then she can tell us where Sammy's hiding.

Her mother will be beside herself and one thing I do know is how bad that feels.'

Before they could get any further with their plans there was a loud hammering at the door and the voices of two men could be heard shouting, 'Where is she, where is our Ellen?' Vera and Sylvester opened the door and staggered backwards as William and Arthur shoved their way into the house, followed more hesitantly by Walter.

It was daylight by the time they reached the outskirts of Llandeilo. Ellen was huddled in the back of the car and Walter gave directions to the Jones's house, although they couldn't have missed it, as there was a small crowd outside waiting by the doorstep when they pulled up.

Pushing past the watchers, Geraint was first out of the house. His usual feeble demeanour nowhere to be seen as he made his way straight to the car and with a shout of 'Lord, be praised,' lifted the blanket-wrapped Ellen out of the back seat and into the house where Kitty was waiting.

William later recounted how he had seen his daughter in front of the fire in the Davies' house looking up at him, her face bruised and swollen, bewildered by the noise.

Ellen would later report that her father had broken into the house and saved her life. Arthur would tell his wife how he felt when he saw their son rush towards the young girl, his granddaughter, whom he barely knew and fold her in his arms. Vera and Sylvester would insist that they were returning her to her family, but no one would believe them.

Walter, of course, would claim he had won the day.

The few days following Ellen's return were taken up with reassuring William that all was now well, and that he and Arthur could go back to London.

Sleeping space was very cramped at the Jones's, although the boys had given up their room to the two men and had decamped to a neighbour's house.

Ellen had to have several interviews reassuring the police that Sammy hadn't harmed her - and reassuring her mother that she would never, ever attempt to run away again. William was also interviewed. He had, after all, assaulted a member of the public and then taken the law into his own hands, bypassing the police.

He was reluctant to say too much and while he was planning his response Arthur stepped in, 'If we hadn't gone to Trapp and found her torn headscarf in the ditch and then made our way to the nearest house, you just never know what might have happened,' he explained to P.C. Williams, somewhat twisting the story.

'Now, young lad, I suggest you go about your business, get that defector sorted out and leave us alone. We saved your bacon, y'know. You might have had a murder on your hands or at least a kidnapping. We found your culprit and your victim for you, so I'd say no more about it.'

P.C. Williams looked, if it were possible, younger and less confident than ever, thought it best not to disagree.

Kitty was keen to get back to London now. The trauma of Ellen's disappearance had made her anxious to have the family together and away from what she described as 'the crime scene.'

A couple of days before they were due to leave, Ness brought the Bible down from the top shelf again.

Her plump face was flushed, not only from the exertion of reaching up whilst her tight pinafore strained over her substantial frame but flushed also from the emotional effort of offering her Irish-English lodger an insight into her life.

'Kitty,' she panted, slightly out of breath, 'I want you to see something, so's you'll understand better how things were with us in Wales, and you may be surprised, or maybe not. This Bible belongs rightly to the eldest son and is passed through the family. It is only a loan to me, because my father died last year, and his effects are still being settled.'

'I'd like that Ness, thank you.'

'I want to show you the names of my brothers and sisters and tell a bit about where we were brought up and how life was for us in those days. Have you time to listen while I tell you, Kitty? I feel you understand us better now and I want things to be clear between us before ye go.'

'I have time now, I think. Shall I mash the tea when we're ready?'

Ellen had always felt that the family Bible and Ness were her special territory and expected to be included.

'Me too, Mum, don't leave me out.'

'Ellen, this afternoon, you will go to the school to collect Daisy and Billy, take them for a walk to see the animals one last time and make sure to be back before dark. Don't speak to anyone, mind.'
'Mum, I will go, but don't you trust me now? I thought you said we put it all behind us?'

Kitty sighed. Her eldest daughter would never give an inch. A note of caution will turn into an implied criticism and before she would turn around it was all-out warfare again.
'No, I never thought that girl, on you go now and wrap up warm, it can turn wet and cold before you know it.'

Ellen grumbled whilst loading on her coat and boots. Slamming the door behind her, she was gone.
'Well, tea-time now, I think we have the kitchen to ourselves, Ness.'

Moving over to the range Kitty busied herself with the kettle and realised, with surprise, how very much at home she now made herself in the Jones's house.

'I never knew anything about England before I was sent there as a girl. Thought they were all high and mighty, but I found some were much poorer than we Irish were and many not as well educated. So now I'm to learn about the Welsh, Ness. Will you be more like us or more like the English, I wonder?'

Looking at the brown leather-bound Bible, with its ornate clasp, Kitty assumed that it was likely Ness's family came from a wealthy heritage, and maybe Ness had fallen on hard times. Married a poor man was more likely.

Opening the heavy book, Ness spoke sadly,

'It's our family tree I want to show you, Kitty. See here's my father, Charles. He was born in 1856, and here are the entries of all his children. You can judge he was around twenty-three when his son Walter was born. Walter is a grandfather himself by now of course and we think of him as the head of our family. He lives over in Llanduff, we don't see him much. Our Walter is called after him.

Kitty and Ness read in silence the list of children born to Charles and Megan between 1879 and 1895. There were nine in total, including twin boys, over a period of sixteen years. Kitty read the entry lines carefully.

She was used to seeing the names of recognised saints, often Gaelic names, although she had chosen not to follow that route for her own children. However, these names were less familiar to her and she marvelled how each child was given two names with rarely any duplicate.

'What a houseful,' exclaimed Kitty, 'Your poor mother, she must have never left the kitchen. And your father, all those mouths to feed. I never thought Protestants had more than a couple of babbies. Did ye have a grand house so?'

Ness did not reply, so Kitty continued 'Lovely names, though. I can just hear their mother calling - Walter, Leah, Vanessa - was that your full name, Ness? Elizabeth, come on in for your dinner. 'All three less than five years apart. Did she light a candle in the window to see you all in from school I wonder, like mine did? And did you look after the baby twins?'

Silently, with a shake of her head, Ness poured the tea. Then she turned the page.

The top of the page was embossed with gold and crimson illustrations, featuring angels bearing children up into clouds and the heading, above a list of names and dates which filled the page, was 'Deaths'.

'Indeed, Kitty, look at this now. It breaks my heart every time. William Thomas and Edward Percy, twins, died aged two days and three days. I never remember seeing them.

'Little William John was born two years later. Now I do remember him and see he died aged thirteen months, the same year that Betriss Lizzie was born. She's not on this page; thank the Good Lord, she lives over Amanford way with her family.

'After Betriss Lizzie came Frank, the last one and the only child without two names. He died the day he was born. My Mam never had another baby after him so Betriss was really our baby. So it's Walter, Leah, Betriss and me left.'

'Oh Ness,' Kitty was stunned by the tragedy of their lives. 'You know, I've really misunderstood all this time, I am so sorry. I thought the Irish had it bad enough, but this was happening during my mother's childhood, they could have been her cousins. I never heard of such tragedy outside of the famine.'

'Aye, well, enough for now Kitty, the four of us as survived have all lived long lives, and we trust in the Good Lord who giveth and taketh away'.

A blast of cold air hit the kitchen as three children stumbled in the front door, keen to escape the wind. 'It wasn't a day for wandering, Mum,' said Ellen, curiously eyeing the Bible and the two women sitting together at the table over a pot of tea long cooled. Even to her untutored eye, they had the comfortable air of two women who had been sharing some conversation over a book.

'Surely they haven't been reading those stories now, the ones there was all the fuss about?' grumbled Ellen to Daisy, making sure she was within earshot of her mother. Actually, she was rather pleased that the trauma over her running away had brought both families closer.

She hoped and expected that the new friendship between her mother and Ness would work in her favour.

Taking a deep breath and sensing the time was right for a softening of her mother's determination, she burst out

'Mum, the nuns from the convent are coming to the school tonight after teatime to take details of new pupils an' they said I can definitely have a place with them if I come back after Christmas.

'What do you say Mum? Please, Mum, please say yes. You did say I could help them settle in, didn't you, Ness, before.... Anyway, I can stay with you can't I, Ness? It would be so exciting and Mum, I'd be very good. No more running away, I've learned my lesson for sure this time.'

Kitty was unable to speak for a minute, looking from her impatient headstrong girl to Ness, both of them waiting for her response.

'I'll speak to your father when we get back to London and if he is happy about you returning then you can. Will that be alright, Ness?'

Ness, recognising they had all come a long way since the start of the billet, and, determined not to appear emotional, simply nodded to Kitty in agreement.

Ellen threw herself at her mother, knowing who made the decisions in their household and prematurely thanking her for agreeing.

Daisy and Billy looked on in amazement, not sure when or why the change had come about but realising that for Ellen at least, the billet with the Jones's had been much more than an evacuation holiday.

A few days later, surrounded by their suitcases and a bag of sandwiches for the journey they stood together in a little group with Ness and Geraint at Llandeilo Railway Station.

'I shall be glad to get home, Ness,' Kitty told her friend, 'but I'll always be grateful to you both. It's given my children a real sense of living in the countryside; they've done some of the things I did as a child and they have had freedom here. I would have liked them to be here in the spring. Maybe when the war is over...'

'Indeed, you'll always be welcome. And young Miss here will be back soon, she can write to her brother and sister and tell them all about the spring.'

The shriek and hiss of the approaching train made further conversation difficult and having said their goodbyes they climbed on board without noticing the police van parked at the end of the platform or the handcuffed young man being bundled into the guards' van at the rear.

Nor did they notice the girl standing dejected and apart from everyone, her eyes never leaving the prisoner's face. If they had, they would surely have known exactly who they were.

Chapter 5.

Eddie. Eglinton, Northern Ireland, 1942

The noise in Maloney's Bar on the evening of Market Day filled the air as completely as the men, dogs, and chicken crates filled the floor space. There was no room for an extra feather on the bar counter.

'Hey Ed, c'mon over here will ye, listen to this, your big chance, man.' A cheerful voice carried across the room.

Twenty-one-year old Ed, Eddie McCann, ready for a big chance wherever it came from crossed the room to hear more. Turning in the direction of the voice his heart sank as he saw it was Kieran, an over-confident fellow whom he knew slightly but avoided where possible, waving his pipe in the air to attract attention and beckoning him over.

He had no enthusiasm for spending time with the other man, but, pint of   Guinness in one hand and pipe in the other, he crossed the room to hear what it was that had got Kieran so excited.

'The old Maydown airfield has been taken over by the Americans and they're looking for drivers, so they are, signin' up's on Saturday.'

'Na, Kieran, I'm not going to Derry, no way. There's a barrage balloon above the city the size of a cathedral and I hear there are more sailors, soldiers, and war ships than has ever been heard of in the city before.'

'You're not wrong there, Eddie,' came a voice from behind; a small crowd gathered to hear the news.

'My sister lives in Derry so she does and she told me there was more army and so on than there were Derry men and women, swear to God.'

'Naw lads, we aren't talking of Derry. They're wanting drivers, so they are, an' Maydown camp in Eglinton is recruiting. All ye have to do is be able to drive and to hold yer nerve if there is a commotion going on.' It was his friend Michael, a generous hearted, popular man, one of those friends who was always first to the bar to buy a round, elbowing through the group to reach his side. Eddie looked up as his grinning, red haired friend, already a few pints down, pinched his shoulder, persuasively.

'C'mon Ed, we're all going down on Saturday, are ye up for it or no?'

It only took a moment to make up his mind. He had been driving farm vehicles and horses and carts since he was eight or nine-years-old and more recently his cousin Harry had loaned him his own car to take to the dances on a Saturday night.

'Aye, alright, I'll join yez on Saturday, but I'll want cash in hand like, and no involvement with any situations.' Being not quite sure what situations there might be, he felt the need to clarify his reluctance in case the others would think him too keen.

Eddie was a farmer's son. Living very contentedly where he was born, on a small Northern Ireland sheep farm, he felt he was part of the wild open spaces of the rough mountaintop land. He knew that his mother Margaret had been relieved when, aged fourteen he had started working for his cousin, hoping he would settle nearby. Ed hoped he might see a bit more of the world before settling down.

It was early morning when Eddie came back from the market, meeting his mother before she began her day's chores.

Explaining about the American offer with a 'I'll try my hand at it, see if I like it', it told her that he had made up his mind.

She was there when Saturday came, her kind round face flushed from the heat of the fire and the steam of the kettles as she poured him hot water. He had risen early, stripped to the waist and washed over the tin bath in front of the peat fire, wanting to be ready for the camp. She sounded anxious as she handed him the red, pungent slab of Lifebuoy soap.

'Sure, you'll be good and settled here before too long, Ed. I always hoped to see you stay close by, there's nothing for ye out there with the Americans, and once they get ye, you'll want to be emigrating just like all the others did, and never come home.'

She remembered sad farewells when her sisters had left the farm, unable to get employment around home. She had missed them, although she knew they were doing well in Philadelphia. Doing well or otherwise, they seemed like strangers to her.

'Eily and Mags went and never came back, son. Sure, they're very good sending letters at Christmas and the dollars are helpful but they are my sisters and I feel I don't know them anymore. I don't want that to happen to you Eddie, we already lost wee Annie, please don't go to America, son.' Not usually given to making requests, Margaret sighed.

'Easy on, Ma, I'm staying here. Sure, Maydown now, it's only a few miles down the road and driving lorries isn't emigratin'. Give over the towel now, I've soap in my eyes.'

Scrubbed clean, and wearing his Sunday suit, he waved out the car window, knowing his mother was watching as he drove along the winding mountaintop road towards the newly erected Maydown Camp on the horizon.

Slowing down before the approach he felt an unexpected sense of pride and belonging. Benevenagh, the mountain, loomed in the background and the ever-present lough on his right was as familiar to him as his own family homestead. Rounding the bend, the concrete runways and newly erected Nissen huts surprised him by their sense of permanence. As he drove closer and saw the rows of Spitfires lined up neatly against the edge of the runway, he realised that this war was real and close to home. Now his country, 'The North,' was joining something bigger, something he could never have experienced without leaving home.

Parking alongside several other non-military vehicles and a greater number of bicycles he walked quickly towards the larger of the huts where a queue was forming. It was dim inside, and narrow dusty beams of weak sunshine from the barred windows were struggling to light on the restless Irishmen, some of whom were wearing outgrown suits, others mismatched jackets and trousers; almost all the shirts were, like his own, collarless.

Hoping to see a familiar face his eyes searched the queue, a shuffling line of young men, waiting to give their details to the smartly uniformed Americans who were formally positioned behind three desks in the front of the hall.

Ignoring the protocol of queuing he stepped in behind a clean bareheaded Michael, his red untamed hair newly washed and catching the light. He was barely recognisable as the flat capped and muddy booted man from Maloney's with the sister in Derry.
'What's the craic, Michael, are they wanting many drivers or what?'
'They need men who can keep calm under pressure, Eddie, an' our Maureen says they give a test for yer nerves.'
'Well my nerves are good and so's my driving, I'm giving it a go and we'll see what happens; time to move on anyway, the family's getting a bit keen on me settling down and I've no notion for that yet.'
'Girl trouble is it then, Ed?'

'Aye, might be an all,' Eddie stopped the discussion, having no intention to engage in any woman-related conversation and anyway he was reaching the head of the queue.

'Next, please.' Even without the strange accent, the crewcut and a fading tan were enough to mark the American out from the Irishmen around him and Eddie felt a shiver of anticipation, hoping he would soon be moving into this unknown territory.

'Now, sir, we give you a test. Please take this pencil and paper and step into the next room.'

Eddie's heart sank. He had expected the test to be a physical demonstration of his fearlessness and his ability to remain calm under pressure, not a paper and pencil one.

In the next room the men were asked to line up on a platform whilst an American attendant placed a plate on each man's head. On top of the plate he balanced a pencil pointing upwards and secured it to the middle of the plate with a piece of chewing gum. The pencil tip then pressed hard against a small sheet of folded paper which was wedged tightly to the ceiling directly above.

Amazed, unsure whether this was some kind of joke or an American rite of passage, he stood absolutely still for half an hour whilst horns were blown, doors banged, and various orders were barked unexpectedly by the attendants.

Altogether it was a bizarre experience and Eddie was mesmerised, never taking his eyes off a crack in the plaster on the wall in front of him.

His back ached and his knees, unaccustomed to any form of immobility longed to flex. He remembered how he had maintained his balance by fixing on an object straight ahead when he had learned to ride his bike and he thought the same rule might also apply here.

The exercise seemed to last forever, but he soon heard the final order. Not barked, as he would have expected, but in a leisurely American drawl.

'All stand down now, you guys, be very careful with those plates. Then remove your sheet of paper, write your name on the paper with the pencils you have and hand them all over, please.'

'Did ye ever?' he asked in wonder, to whoever would hear him.

'How can they tell a good driver from that test?'

'Well that's the Yanks for ye' Eddie, we'll soon be saying 'Gee' and calling the girls dames if we get through this one!'

'Will the following men step into the briefing room – Michael Toomey, Gerard Kelly, Eddie McCann. You guys have kept still and calm throughout this exercise, now that's what we need in our drivers.' Hearing his name called he stepped into the briefing room, still unsure about the recruitment process but relieved to be called, as behind him he heard 'The rest of you can go now. Thanks for your time, guys.'

That afternoon, along with Michael and Gerard, he was fitted out with his driver's uniform and led out onto the forecourt, where the Spitfire fighter planes were banked in front of rows of lorries and small trucks, all in green camouflage.

'Now, men, here's the deal,' coming from an American in uniform, whom he later learned was the Commanding Officer, the casual drawl seemed to belie the importance of what he was about to say.

'You drive as fast as you can - we are under pressure here - transportation is one of our most essential resources and y'all stop for nothing on the way. That includes animals, vehicles or people. None, y'all hear me now? None. And no speed limit here, you're with the American Army now, so foot down and straight on, got that?'

'Yes, sir.'

'Any questions?'

'No, sir.'

'Horse and cart, sir, they don't move too fast. What happens, sir, if they don't get out of the way?'

'Then make sure they stay off our roads, lad, or there will be trouble.'

'Everyone clear? OK, come back first thing tomorrow and onto your stations. There'll be a list outside the Mess Tent.'

Eddie was unhappy about what he had just heard but excited by the opportunity to drive a Fast Willy's or Ford GP, or Jeep, as he would soon learn to call them.

The following morning, he was led over to a truck, not a Fast Willy's. He was a bit disappointed, thinking these trucks were more in keeping with the old farm vehicles he had occasionally used.

'Your first run, Driver, is to Nutt's Corner Camp, get your truck there before the blackout, unload, stop overnight in the camp, and be back here by midday tomorrow. Your AAF - that's American Air Force, boy - sergeant here is Bailey; He'll give you any more details you need.'

'OK, guys?'

Looking across at the sergeant waiting beside the truck he saw a clean-shaven, smartly dressed black soldier who was bigger and better groomed than his friends, but who looked about the same age.

'Hi Driver, I'm Herbert Bailey, always known as Bailey. Pleased to meet you. We won't need to rush this job, an overnighter. I was thinking to stopover in Ballymoney, it's not out of our way.'

'Aye, we'll have time for a party an' all, if he doesn't want us back before midday tomorrow. It's not much more than sixty miles and it's daylight here in this country until ten or eleven o'clock, And the name's Eddie.'

'Right, OK. Let's get going, Eddie, I'll tell you later'.

Climbing up into the driver's seat of the truck he looked longingly across the yard at where the Jeeps were parked.

'Head out fast, Driver, let them see you making good speed,' urged Bailey. The gravel flew behind them as they sped out of the camp but once around the corner, he suggested Eddie should slow down to a more moderate pace.

'We'll stop and have a cigarette and get to know each other a bit,' said Bailey unexpectedly, a gentle grin filling the lower part of his face. 'I've sure bin lookin' forward to meetin' you. We haven't worked with too many Irish guys up until now.'

Eddie slowed the truck to a stop beside the road, pulling as close into the ditch as he dared, remembering the earlier warnings of the Commanding Officer and not wanting to get involved in any accident on his first day. Eddie switched off the engine and Bailey pulled a packet of cigarettes out of his breast pocket, offering one to Eddie, who shook his head.

'Where're you from, Eddie? Do you have a girl back home?'

'I am back home, sir, and I have all the girls I want.'

Bailey tried again.

'The Northern Irish girls are real nice, I like them a lot.'

'Do ye now, and any one in particular?'

Eddie sensed his jibe had hit home, and there was a noticeable silence before Bailey filled it.

'Well, since you do ask, I've met a lovely girl, name of Iris. Lives in Ballymoney so I think you will meet her soon, but I'll expect you to say nothing about it in the camp.'

'Nobody's business but yours, Bailey.'

'Not as easy as you think, Ed. Mind if I call you that? They don't like us to mix with whites back home and they kinda want the same over here.'

'Well ye won't find any black girls here, Bailey, so it will be white girls or nothing at all. Your bosses better get used to it.'

He didn't add his immediate thought which was to wonder why a girl from the small market town of Ballymoney, would want to court a black soldier when there were plenty of good-looking men like himself around with no 'complications'. But he soon left that thought far behind whilst he listened to Bailey describe the discrimination he encountered in his homeland.

'I'm from Alabama, Ed. It's a fine state but due to its being part of what they call The South they have a bad view of black Americans.'

'Why's that now, sir? You been misbehaving?'

'Nah, comes from the slave days. They never look back to where all their money came from. Anyway, that's all history but what isn't history is that it's still illegal for a black - or coloured, as I like to say - and a white person to marry.'

Eddie knew of people who couldn't marry because they were different religions and even knew of a girl who was unmarriageable because she had had an illegitimate child, but he had never expected that a person's race might be just as big a problem.

Alabama did have a familiar ring to it though and he remembered the words of the song, giving an impression of waiting Susannas and soldiers with banjos on knees. Unconsciously, he began to whistle the tune softly as he turned the key in the ignition, aware that time was passing and needing to be sure he would get to Ballymoney and then on to the Belfast camp by nightfall.

'Hey, man, that's great, you sure can hold a tune, we could do with you at our Mess parties. You play the guitar?'

'Mouth organ, harmonica it's called, and you'd hear more fiddle than guitar where I come from.'

'I'm more of a jazz man myself.'

Looking in wonder at this friendly confident, dark man, of similar age to himself he thought they were a world apart.

'What do ye like about jazz? Sure, you can't dance to that music with a girl. I prefer a waltz or a quickstep at the dances, then you can talk to them and ask them how they are doin,' so ye know if there's a chance or not.'

'Ahh, man, we could really beat our gums over this one. The jive is the thing now in America, not the waltz, it's not up to the mark at all. You come to our Mess dances next week, and you are in for a real treat.

The dames are real nice, well you know that of course, and the bar has neat prices; just make sure you get to practice your steps real good.

An' we expect the best manners to the dames, no bad language and be sure to say something complimentary, whatever they're like.'

Eddie was somewhat taken aback by this advice; he was respectful to the girls he knew but small talk was never his strength. 'I'm only tellin' this because last week we had a bit of a problem with one of your sorts.'

Starting up the motor and driving more slowly now into Ballymoney, Eddie felt he had passed some kind of test of comradeship as Bailey talked more freely. He talked a lot, Eddie thought, amused by the unfamiliar drawl and the unexpected confidence, about how he had 'really fallen for her,' his girl, Iris.

'This is the real thing now, Ed, an' I'm planning on keeping her for life.'

Eddie didn't know how to respond. Talking freely about girls and emotions was not something he was accustomed to and most of his friends kept their feelings to themselves. When they stopped at the Diamond, in the middle of Ballymoney, Bailey climbed down.

'Meet me back here in a couple of hours, Ed and we'll head over to the Nutt's camp, wherever that is.'

With a wave and no backward glance, Bailey's distinctive uniformed figure strode confidently towards the tea shop where he had planned to meet his Iris.

'Does he not think the whole town sees him? I never saw anyone who looked more obvious, and more like an outsider,' muttered Eddie, slouching down into the driver's seat. 'Nice bloke but no idea what he's up against. He'll be the talk of the neighbours for sure. No laws here about not marrying other races, but I think her folks will think it a bit queer.

An' then where does he think she's goin' to live? Not Alabama it seems. Maybe they'll go to Belfast or somewhere else.' Pulling his new American cap down over his face he was soon dozing.

Woken by a tap on his head, he sat up smartly to find Bailey laughing at the side of the truck, his arm around a slim pretty girl in a light summer dress who looked no more than a teenager. Brushing back loose fair curls and securing them behind her ear, the young woman blushed as she was introduced as 'my beautiful gal, Iris.' As she held out her hand to Eddie, he found himself thinking that she was indeed a beautiful 'gal' but one who would need looking after if she was taken far from home.

'Iris knows I plan to marry her, don't you, Iris?' Bailey asked, bending forward either to catch Iris's attention or to ensure passers-by didn't hear.

'I know your family's seen us courtin', maybe they don't think it's serious? Well, you haven't told your family yet, Iris, but soon as you do I'll ask my Senior Officer to give my evidence so's the Registrar will be happy.'

'What's that all about then Bailey, is it still this illegal thing? Excuse me for asking him, Iris, it's just a whole new world to me.'

'Nah, Ed, it's just there's been a few marriages here recently which turned out not to be good, as the guy was already married back home. So, the Registrars won't wed us until they get confirmation now, fair enough really. An' as you know, it's even worse for me, man,' Bailey complained, 'I don't have to live in Alabama State when we go back, but if I have to spend some time there, say for a funeral or the like, then as I said marriage to a white girl is illegal, so I really need the army's support.'

Eddie was looking at Iris whilst Bailey was explaining his predicament. He was all too familiar with the difficulties between Catholics and Protestants when it came to what was called a 'mixed marriage', but he thought that this was surely more than the young girl before him could be expected to cope with

. Iris's expression had remained unchanged, calmly meeting his gaze, but the chewing of her lower lip betrayed her calm. He thought it was likely not new information.

'Well, you don't need to bother wi' the whole Catholic-Protestant thing now, marryin' an American will not be too bad at all, will it, Iris?'

'I don't want to tell Mammy yet, but soon as I do, she will tell me Da. We'll wait to see what they say,' replied Iris stoically. Eddie couldn't be sure whether she was hopeful, resigned or indifferent. Something about her attitude concerned him. Definitely stay out of this one, he thought, his foot already hovering over the accelerator, 'We need to head off now, sir. Good to meet you, Iris.'

Bailey gave Iris a kiss and jumped into the truck, whilst Iris, not waiting to wave them off, turned away and walked back towards the town. Eddie, hoping Bailey wouldn't notice the slight, whistled a tune. The day had been good. He liked the sound of having plenty of girls for the dances, cheap bar prices, and chewing gum. He was enjoying Bailey's company and he couldn't fault the wages. Maybe he'd even drive the Jeeps soon.

They arrived at Nutt's Corner well before dark and had ample time to admire a magnificent extended sunset. Bailey was particularly impressed, being more used to sudden nightfall than the long, cool evenings of a Northern Ireland summer. After supper, they took a couple of bottles of beer back to their Nissen hut,

'We call our huts after the big hotels, Ed, you'll see back in Maydown, on mine it's the Waldorf Astoria. It helps us when we feel brassed off and lonely.'

'I've heard ye don't be lonely for long, sir.'

'Ah, Eddie, Eddie, we are not all oversexed and over here, we don't all want to take advantage of the pretty dames or lie to wives back home.'

'Do some of the men do that Bailey? You said the Registrar was very careful now. Has there been much trouble?'

'There's one in particular I'll keep my Iris away from. Bud Willis, he's a charmer but married with a couple of kids back home.

Good looking fella' though, always at the dances and always leaves with a different girl.'

They slept well in the hut and Eddie was very impressed with a hot breakfast provided by the canteen. His usual fare was porridge or bread and tea so he happily took advantage of the bacon, eggs, and pancakes and, comfortably replete, he started up the truck, driving carefully and slowly, he was enjoying their conversations and keen to learn more.

'Bailey, what did you mean about the 'bit of a problem' they had had with a driver at one of the dances. Was it someone pushing their luck?'

'Man, this guy was so useless with the dames; he never knew what to say to be nice. He taxied up to dance with my Iris's friend. Now she is a well-built girl, I give you that, and not so well favoured in her looks, but there must be something better he could say to her.'

'What in the name of God did he say to her, Bailey?'

'He took her for a jive, not really the best choice for such a big dame, an' her hair was falling all over her face. Then he stopped, looked at her and said, 'You don't sweat much for a fat girl.' At that, Eddie, my man, she left the floor in tears.' Eddie swallowed hard, determined not to show he could see the funny side, but ever so slightly shocked by the poor behaviour of his fellow driver.

'I'll look forward to the dance on Saturday night, so I will,' he said, making a mental note to stay away from any of Iris's friends.

That Saturday evening as he cycled to the camp through the pass and with the lough on his right all the way, he watched as pools of sunlight showed up swarms of midges. He occasionally swerved to avoid the swallows swooping low in front of his bike.

'Man, this is great altogether,' he told no one in particular.

'I can enjoy a dance and a few beers; sure, I'll think I'm in America itself, then home tonight to my own bed.

Jazz, they tell me, I'll give it a try.'

Turning in to the barracks he heard music coming from the larger of the Nissen huts and Eddie parked up and sauntered casually towards the sound, not wanting to appear keen but eagerly anticipating the evening's fun.

Pushing his way towards the bar her ordered a beer, considering that to be a more likely drink in American company than his usual Guinness. Across the room he caught sight of the sergeant called Bud. True to his word, Bailey had pointed him out earlier and now he was difficult to miss.

A tall muscular man - his blond crewcut complemented by a golden tan - with eyes scanning the dance floor like a searchlight, it was little wonder, thought Eddie, as he's making such a big effort here, that he has his pick of the girls.

'Hello there, sure, it's my old pal, Eddie isn't it? Isn't this grand altogether?'

He looked up from his pint to see Michael Toomey, whiskey in one hand and arm slung around an attractive girl wearing a bright yellow full skirted dress and an enquiring look on her face.

'Can I get you one, Ed? Ah, go on, and how's it going with the driving? I'm getting experience with cards - poker and rummy; but mostly hanging around waiting to lift this, move that, not much driving really. And these guys, boy can they gamble, lose more money than I ever seen.'

'Hello Eddie, I'm Geraldine. Is this your first night at the dances here? You might be surprised to see how some of the girls carry on, a bit desperate some of them. I'm only stopping by because Michael wants me to, and he knows better than to try it on.'

Eddie was shocked by her outspoken approach, he thought that his generous straightforward friend deserved better and hoped she was not a permanent sweetheart. Before he could reply, he felt a heavy hand land on his shoulder, and he was relieved to hear the familiar voice of Bailey.

171

'What's your poison, man? Have one on me.' Out of the corner of his eye he saw Geraldine frown, wrinkle her nose, and indicate their departure to Michael. Bailey seemed oblivious to Michael and Geraldine and dragged Eddie willingly up to the crowded noisy bar.

After topping up both their drinks, he enthusiastically engaged Eddie in a discussion on which were the best dance numbers, which were most popular back home, and how the evening would be expected to unfold.

The band was playing Boogie Woogie Bugle Boy of Company B, and Eddie was wondering how he was going to dance to that, when he noticed Bud Willis approach Geraldine. He looked around for Michael. The hall was smoky as well as crowded so he felt he couldn't be sure, but it looked to him as though Geraldine was pleased to see Bud and before he could look again for Michael the pair had taken to the floor.

'That your friend with Bud?' asked Bailey. 'Hope she knows what she's doing, 'cos he sure does.'

'Nah, she's not my friend, she's my friend's girl but I never met her before. Bit stuck-up I think.'

'Is Iris here tonight, Bailey, or is she at home telling her folks about you?'

'I'm meeting her later. Her Daddy will drop her over and pick her up again. He has a motor and they sure like to keep a close eye on Iris.'

'How do they take to you, Bailey? Is it not a bit difficult with her family?'

'Her Pop was dead against her seeing me at first, probably still is. Her Mom soon came round when she realised I would take good care of Iris, but it might not be so easy once she tells them we're gettin' hitched.'

The music changed to an unseasonable I'll be Home for Christmas, but as it was a more familiar ballad, he left Bailey and bravely crossed the floor to where the girls were waiting to be asked for a dance.

'No thanks, I'm waiting for someone,' and again, 'Sorry, I'm sitting this one out,' until finally he spied Geraldine.

'Dance, Geraldine?'

'Don't mind if I do.'

'Are you having a good time? I can't see Michael anywhere.'

'Ah well, I've moved on from him now, that's my new boyfriend getting me a drink from the bar so I can't stay long.'

Looking up, concerned by the sudden change in his understanding of his friend's relationship, his gaze fell directly on Bud who was talking to Iris.

'Is that your new boyfriend talking to Iris there?' he asked, uneasily.

'Yeah, that's Bud; everyone is after him, even that little slut who goes with your friend the black man.'

Her voice changed pitch as she began to sing 'But he only has eyes for me...' Eddie was suddenly really angry. How dare she call Iris a slut?

'You need to watch what you're saying, she's a lovely girl so she is, and my friend has a name, he's called Bailey. You take that back now, Geraldine'.

His face reddened and his jaw set as signs of anger creased his brow. Geraldine looked up at him, widening her eyes and raising both hands as though to feign surrender.

'Well, she went with Bud happy enough a few weeks back and he certainly gave her a rake of drink, she was no' fit to go home. Lucky her Da didn't collect her that night, she slept in the back of the Mess kitchen an' I've no idea what she told them at home, but she's been gurning after Bud anytime she sees him.'

'Well she's not gurning after him now,' observed Eddie, seeing Iris shrug Bud's hand off her arm and make her way out of the hall. He left Geraldine where she was in the middle of the dance floor and went out to find Iris. Behind him he heard the music change tempo again. The strains of In The Mood leaked out from the hall door and he was caught against the general flow in a flurry of skirts, elegant heels, and a heady mixture of cigarette smoke and Yardley's Lavender talcum powder as the girls, accompanied by some of the men, moved excitedly in from the yard and towards the dance floor.

It was nearly midnight and the late summer light was fading. Looking around for Iris or Bailey, he could only see a few courting couples, their outlines accentuated by the glowing ends of their cigarettes. He took a stroll across the yard towards the nearest Nissen hut before deciding that the people he could hear giggling and murmuring inside would probably not want to see him. He felt like an intruder and moved away, retrieving his bicycle and making his way home.

For some weeks he continued working with Bailey and nothing seemed to have changed between him and Iris, and Eddie had no intention of interfering. He began to look forward to the trips to Nutt's Corner via Ballymoney.

One morning in September he was called aside by the senior officer in charge of transportation.

'Now, McCann, we are very happy with your progress and you're to be assigned to drive the GP vehicles from now on. Keep your foot down, make sure you don't let anyone get in your way and you can take Williams with you as your sergeant Bailey stays with the trucks and the lorries.'

Eddie was pleased to have his driving skills recognised and hoped it would mean more money, but he was sorry to lose Bailey's company. Going in search of his friend before reporting to Williams he saw him leaning against one of the trucks, cap pushed back on his dark curly head and smoking a cigarette before starting his day's work.

'Did you hear, Ed, about the accident?' asked Bailey, his usually cheerful face looking troubled. 'There was a guy driving a horse and cart, he didn't get out of the way when the Jeep approached. Whether he had heard the warning or not, we don't know, but the whole camp is buzzin' now, one of your locals with a gunshot wound.'

'Get away Bailey; sure, I never heard a word.'
'Reminds me of home, always the poor man who gets shot.'

'Bailey, enough man, enough. You're off to France soon, so you are. Now keep the head down. I've come to say g'bye, at least for a bit, I'm working to Williams now, driving a Jeep.'

'Well done, Eddie, you'll enjoy the Jeeps. Williams is a fine soldier, and a white man too, so maybe you'll feel more at home with him?'

'Bailey, you are the first black man I ever met, and I don't see any difference between us - all God's creatures. I'll miss seeing you and Iris.'

'Now my man, I had good news this morning. The Registrar approved our marriage, and she has persuaded her family to agree. I'm away the week after the wedding, two weeks next Saturday.' And unexpectedly, he then asked, 'Will you be our witness? Most of the others are not too happy about it. Well, you know why.'

Eddie was startled, shaking his head in disbelief. 'Sure, I never expected the men would react that way to you, Bailey. I've never met anyone except the Irish or English before now and for sure we say we hate the English but that's just talk.'

'What's that, Ed?'

'Well, sometimes the Prods now, I'm not too keen on their marches, but they leave us alone and we leave them alone.'

'I heard you all get brassed off with each other, that right?'

'Maybe, but even with all that going on, I still can't see marriage being criminal, but then what would I know? I'm just a boy from the mountains.'

'Well anyhow, Ed, Iris and I will marry, and her family are putting on a tea for us afterwards, back in their church hall. I get two days off, so we'll be doin' real good.'

Eddie was pleased at Bailey's obvious happiness and thought Iris a lucky girl. What would happen after the war he didn't know, but he thought they would work it out.

His mind still on Bailey's news, he walked across the camp to the building where he was to meet Williams.

Maydown camp was bustling; trucks, Jeeps and lorries constantly on the move between Nutt's Corner or Crumlin, near Belfast, and Eglinton in Derry. He had come to realise, with some surprise, that Maydown was a useful stop-off point on the way to most places.

'Williams over here. Are you Eddie McCann, my driver? Are we ready to go, man?'

Hearing his name being called he looked up to see a thin clean-shaven man in his mid-twenties, wearing his cap pulled low over the hairline, covering what Eddie knew had to be a crewcut, the same style they all wore. Running his hands through his own full head of gently waving hair, he thought it was untidy, probably unfashionable, but he also reckoned he wouldn't want to be taken for a US airman or serviceman of any calibre, especially now since the shooting.

'Aye, I'll be right with ye' now, sir,' and, jacket over shoulder and lunch-packet under arm, he strolled over, deliberately relaxed, to join his new boss.

'I'm sure you are mighty glad to drive a Jeep and no darkie to bother you today.'

'I'll drive a Jeep, but I don't want any remarks about 'darkies', if you mean Sergeant Bailey, he's one fine man. I've been asked to be his witness later this month, he's getting married.'

'Well, maybe he is and maybe he ain't. Now get in, Driver, and do what you are good at, we're heading for Crumlin.'

Bolstered up by Williams confidence in his driving he had little time to consider his remark about Bailey's wedding as he climbed up into the driver's seat.

Williams jumped in behind, armed with a machine-gun which he directed to the side of the vehicle. Raising a cloud of dust, they drove out of the camp and onto the road leading to Belfast.

Eddie was relieved to find that conversation was impossible over the noise and debris generated by the Jeep.

176

They were driving on rough roads and the vehicle bounced and jolted over the uneven surface more than the truck had done. After twenty minutes, Eddie felt a jab in his back.

'Pull over here, Driver, I need a smoke.' Parking on a grassy flat patch, which served as a lay-by, he wondered whether Williams would improve when he got to know him better.

'Got a light, bud?' asked Williams. Rifling in his trouser pocket, Eddie pulled out his pipe. Offering Williams a box of matches, he tamped the tobacco down into his pipe and leaned back against the Jeep waiting for the matches back.

'Do all you guys smoke those darned things? No one on the roll-ups over here? Jeez, it's like stepping back in time, no wonder you're matey with Bailey, 'cos his lot don't live like us none either.'

'Listen, Williams.'

'Sir, to you, buddy.'

'Well, anyway, sir, what's your problem, he's a good man, and he treated me well when I was his driver. He always has a lot of respect for the ladies too.'

'Oh, man, you don't know it. They'll shaft anything. Your women ain't safe with them around, they go mad for white flesh, can't help themselves, 'cos they're brought up wild most of 'em. Once your women've got a taste for 'em there's no going back, an' before ye know it there'll be half-caste kids runnin' all over the place, an' your own kids won't know what's hit 'em.'

'No kids I know would even notice.'

'Keep 'em down or they'll get above themselves, Driver. We got good reason for our laws; he'll have told you of the miscegenation law? It forbids negroes and whites from marrying. Leastways it forbids a black man marrying a white girl, an' back home he can be charged with rape or assault. Never heard of it the other way though - I guess if a white man wants it, well ...'

'Well far as I see it that's just a damned stupid law against good people. Is it really everywhere? I know Bailey comes from Alabama, and when he said he won't be able to go back with Iris, I thought he might be exaggerating.'

'Felonious adultery or felonious fornication, that's what he'll be tried for if he shows his face in Alabama, only place I reckon he can scuttle off to is Ohio, no penalty there. Course, you might have colour yourself and not know it, boy.'

'My family on both sides came from Northern Ireland as far as anyone can remember, so I would say divil a bit chance o' that, interesting though it would be.'

'Well you never know, Driver. Accordingly, a person with seven white great-grandparents would be defined as black as long as the eighth great-grandparent was black.'

'May as well say the same for yourself then, sir', concluded Eddie, mockingly deferential, tapping the side of his pipe against the door of the Jeep and preparing to climb back in.

'Gum?'

'No thanks, it's not to my liking,' Eddie turned the key and felt a subtle satisfaction at having been able to stand his ground. However, he was deeply uneasy at what he had just heard and began to wonder what other opinions lay hidden under the friendly faces of the US servicemen.

It was a long silent journey and Eddie was to leave Williams at the end of the day. Outside the base he waited at the roadside in the rain, bicycle propped against his leg, for his friend Gerard Kelly, who, although he had been hired at the same time as himself, seemed to be consigned to lorries en route to Derry. Reflecting on the racist remarks he had heard during the past couple of months he remembered that these opinions had not been confined only to the American soldiers, he had heard some of his driver colleagues joining in the discussions too.

'Hey Ed, here's yer lift.' A lorry stopped in front of him. Lifting his bicycle and heaving it onto the back before climbing in beside his friend, he was glad to get out of the rain. The warmth of the cab was already making him conscious of the creeping cold damp in his trousers. Eddie, knowing Gerry would give him an inside view of life in Derry, asked after his sister Assumpta, who lived in Derry with her grandmother during the week..

'Well, that big balloon is still over the city. The kids love it, girls love the soldiers, but the men aren't too happy.' Assumpta is going with an American soldier and won't come home after her working week, but stays in Derry, supposed to be with her grandma, all weekend. Da is furious, so he is, and me mother doesn't say much but I know she is worried about her. That's why I am calling to see her, got a wee consignment here might keep her safe. Don't let on but I'm filchin' the Yankees Frenchies.'

'Where did you get them from?'

'All part of the consignments we deliver, Ed, me boy, from Maydown to Derry and back. It's preventatives as well as preserves, maybe ye didn't know that, good Catholic as ye'are?'

'I had no idea,' replied Eddie, feeling ever more miserable. 'I would have a real problem delivering those things, it's against the faith, you know that Gerard.'

'Aw, get on man, get real. Anyway, we don't want little Yanks, or worse still you-know-whats playing in the streets of Derry after the war now, do we?' Eddie's silence was enough to stop the conversation and he jumped off the lorry after a few miles, glad to tramp the last distance alone.

The light rain had continued and, heaving his bike alongside, he took a short cut over the fields. The cold from the mud, caking his boots soon filtered through to his feet and, as he lifted his bicycle over the last ditch before home, he wondered how much, or how little, of his experiences he would share with his family.

This is like another world, he thought, and it would take more than the introduction of gum or barrage balloons to make it change. As he made his way across the yard to the back door of the farmhouse, he caught sight of his mother closing the hen house door, wet apron slapping against her legs, calling across the field to her horse with a bucket of meal.

Maybe nothing needed to change after all?

'Hey, Ma, I'm home. Any grub in the house?' his words were lost over a sudden gust of high wind tossing tree branches and farm implements alike across the yard, but she heard his voice and turned quickly in his direction.

'Eddie, son, come on out of this,' she cried, ignoring the weather herself but shielding her head with her hand as she sought his face. He moved towards her, this kind and reliable woman. He was sure she had never encountered either a black person or a condom. It was her love for her family and animals, particularly horses, which gave her a straightforward point of reference from which to view the rest of the world. He, so much the taller person, put his arm round her and hugged her.

Calling her 'wee woman,' he matched her pace as together they faced into the wind and walked to the farmhouse door.
'An' I'm to be witness at a wedding next week,' he told the family, later that evening.
'One of the soldiers is marrying a Ballymoney girl. I've got to know them, and we've had some great craic together, so we have.'

Across the table his mother caught his father's eye. Maisie and Maureen sensed some tension and were quick to make the most of it.
'Sounds great, Ed. Is he gorgeous? Will everyone be jealous?' asked Maisie.
'There's a bit more to it than that, Mai, she's white and he's black.'
'Oh, dear God!' his mother's hand flew to her mouth. 'Is she in the family way?'
'Not at all Mam, she just loves him, and he is a fine man to love too.'
'All well and good, Eddie,' said his father, speaking last, and expecting everyone to listen. 'But to bring up a family away from your own people is not easy, not for him or for her, so wish them well; but son, don't be getting any ideas yourself, will ye now?'

'Not easy at all, Da, you're right there. D'you know it's illegal in America, well some parts anyway, for a black and white person to marry? So, they might have to stay here when the war is over.'

'And what will a black American soldier do here in Northern Ireland, with a wife and family to support, do ye reckon? Eh?'

Eddie sighed, he had said more than he intended, he had hoped his family would give some hope to Bailey's marriage and he had no one else to tell. He was beginning to believe that the future for the young couple would be very bleak.

Eddie slept poorly that night, sharing the bed with his brother James was a noisy affair, and he rose when he heard his mother in the kitchen.

'We've eggs here, Ed. Would ye like some to take to the bride? Maybe her own Mam will be making a cake and provisions aren't too plentiful in the town I hear. We won't have ye go empty handed.' His mother hit the right note again, he thought, glad she hadn't asked more about his new friends, and the eggs showed she was offering them her support.

'Aye, I'll take some, sure enough, but I'll take a cup a tea here with ye before the others get up. I'm here now till tomorrow morning anyway. An' now tell me, how are the horses?'

His mother seemed pleased to have some quiet time with her son before the family rose, smiling and shaking her head as if in disbelief that her son really wanted to hear about horses.

He knew she could just about make her way around the kitchen, but was happiest outdoors, and discussing horses was her favourite topic.

Eddie left his home the following morning, with a dozen eggs, wrapped in straw and paper, in the saddlebag of his bike. He planned to call at Iris's house later that day to deliver them.

Eddie really liked Iris, he thought she was probably younger than him by a couple of years, but he reckoned she was more sophisticated than his older sisters. Most likely, he considered, living in a town gave youngsters more time for amusements and for the meeting of others.

He thought back on his own young life. Schooldays at the country school in Ballyrowan, which was just two rooms with one fire in the hearth in between.

The trudge across the fields, around a mile and a half from home, and then activities with his friend Connor.

Late afternoons lying on the damp grass leaning as far over the riverbank as they dared, using roughly crafted fishing rods - twigs, string, and pin or bent wire. Whatever they had for bait - a bit of bread or sometimes a worm. Staying in that position until the damp seeped through their pullovers to their shirts and the warmth of the day faded, they shared their great ambitions. And plans were tested out on each other whilst they waited for trout, or anything, to bite.

'Will we go an' see the world before we settle down?'

'Aye, we need to do that so. Long as we don't get caught by some woman, like Bernard did. He's not goin' anywhere now. Married at twenty and that's his lot.'

'Sure Connor, you're the adventurous one in your family. I'd say you'll make a great name for yourself. Just keep away from the women.'

Both boys had roared with laughter at the thought of themselves at nine years old being in any way attractive to the opposite sex.

Shaking his head to clear his thoughts he tramped over the top of Scout Hill, hoping to catch a lift back to camp, but ready to use his bike if needed.

Scanning the horizon, he wondered what it would have been like to stand and watch for the Redcoats coming to look for the people on the Mass Rock.

He had been shown what remained of the rock by his grandfather many years ago, told stories of the penal laws as though they had been in force only yesterday. They forbade the hearing of Mass and should have been a faded memory. Now, one hundred and fifty years later, the stories surrounding the events were recalled and cherished, becoming the legends of his childhood.

To others it might look like a flat granite outcrop, somewhere to sit and admire the view, or enjoy a smoke, but not to Eddie. It was where he went to in times of need, he reckoned the history inspired his thoughts.

The sound of a vehicle rumbling in the distance reminded Eddie of his inclination to get to Maydown the easiest way, and a cloudy haze appeared on the pass.

'Hop in there, Eddie, throw yer bike in the back.' Recognising Michael's voice, he gratefully clambered in, first carefully taking the parcel of eggs out of the saddlebag.

'Grand t'see ye, Michael, how's your sister in Derry? I was speaking to Gerry earlier; his sister is having a great time I believe.'

'Ah, our Maureen, she's home now, Ed. Me Da thought she'd be better here, what with all the carry-ons.'

'Maybe just as well. I'm heading back on shift now after a wee break there over at Dunbeg. Hoping to get to Ballymoney later today to give Iris some eggs from Mam for her wedding cake. Do you know if there is a run going that way I could ask for?'

'A word of advice, Eddie, jus' don't be always showing yersel' the friend of the coloured's, d'ye hear me? The Yanks don't like it, an' they think you're criticisin' them, and, well you don't really know do ye? We've never had them here, so we haven't.'

'I'll do what I want Michael, an' you can drop me off here, I'll cycle the rest.'

Eddie's surly response and an attempt to open the lorry door whilst they were still motoring caused Michael to steer aside to an abrupt halt.

Eddie had thought of Michael as one of his closest friends and felt disappointed. The two men parted silently, and it took an hour of uphill cycling to reach the camp. Almost late for his shift he missed the opportunity to catch Bailey before he had to report for duty.

'Hey, are you Eddie McCann? I heard you were with me today, we're heading east again, usual route. I'm George, Sergeant Antony Riley George, call me George.'

Eddie looked at the short red- faced officer, glad to be away from Williams, and thought he would be able to plan a detour to Ballymoney that afternoon. George, newly arrived at camp, looked kindly at the young Irishman before him. He didn't appear to be more than eighteen and he had a slightly naive way of looking the serviceman straight in the eye as though he didn't know how to defer to a superior.

The sergeant told Eddie that he came from Chicago, and whilst they were driving, bumping and jolting, choosing the mountain road from the camp, taking a route through Garvagh to get to Ballymoney, he began to ask Eddie about tracing his Irish ancestry, hoping to fill in some gaps in his family history.

'Daddy's family were Rileys, Mom's were Dwyers and they'd sure be happy if I could find some relatives still living back here. Don't know what part of Ireland exactly, but it's always worth a look.'
'I don't know any Rileys or Dwyers, sorry to say and the whole of Ireland is a big place, this is just the north.' Enthusiastically he suggested, 'Maybe you could start in the cemetery in Ballymoney? We've time, I'll drop you off. Great idea! Now what's Chicago like, tell me?'

'Chi Town, never heard of it, man? Heard of Al Capone, have you? Never met him myself, dead now of course but I guess you know that.
We're just setting up a new airport where they're building the Douglas C-54s for the war.

. Would have liked to get work there but anyway here I am, training in the rain.

Boy, is it wet here just now! Got three sisters at home, all married so we should be well supplied with parcels. Man, they are knitting like crazy!'

Eddie wasn't really listening, but he did respond to the one which he thought criticised his country.

'George, most of the time you're here you'll be training in this weather, so you better get used to it. I've watched them marching all day up and round the lanes, then they have to put their gas masks on inside six seconds. Doesn't seem much like war here, but I guess you'll soon be off to Europe for some real activity.'

Eddie had no response to give to George's questions about Chicago but was keen to keep the conversation going. 'Saw Major Hartley here the other day, I heard him called a Big Wheel. Think he might visit again?'

'Oh boy, Driver, do you ever get impressed? That's Major General Russell Hartley, he's Commander General of the American Forces over here in Northern Ireland, doesn't mean damn all to you, does it?' Ignoring the comment, which Eddie suspected again did not require an answer, he played his card, 'Mind if I call in with a friend of a friend in Ballymoney while we're going through, George? It's a really good place to stop if you want to do some lookin' around for ancestors and I won't be long?'

Motoring carefully into the town, wary of meeting any civilian traffic and dreading a repeat of the incident a few days earlier when a local farmer had been killed by an American jeep, he pointed out the cemetery to George, then left him at a curb side nearby without giving him any chance to object.

He headed round a couple of bends before arriving at the tidy narrow street where Iris lived. The terraced houses all looked the same with blackout tape across the windows, nets just visible behind the tape.

Bringing the Jeep to a halt, Eddie jumped down as a small-framed, neat woman, with an apologetic look to her face, opened the door before he had a chance to knock and, realising that she had probably heard the engine outside, he thought she'd want to keep the neighbours out of her affairs.

He knew there would be plenty of difficulties with this wedding and plenty of opinions also. She motioned him inside, nervously closing the door almost before he had time to squeeze through and led him down the narrow hallway into a small, well-ordered kitchen. Unnecessarily introducing herself as Janet Grey, Iris's mother, Eddie was struck by the difference in appearance between her and his own mother, Margaret whose stout figure and untidy hair gave her a relaxed and healthy appearance.

Janet's face was pale, and her hair was tightly drawn into a bun at the back of her head.

'I'm Eddie McCann, Bailey's friend. I'm to be witness at the wedding.' he introduced himself more confidently than he usually did, the driver's uniform helped. 'A dozen eggs from my mother to you, Mrs Grey. She thought they might be handy for the wedding cake.' The smile Janet gave him didn't reach her eyes and he sensed her unhappiness and decided to make his visit brief.

'So very kind, Eddie, do thank her for me. Iris is not feeling too well today, so she won't come down and thank you yourself but I'm sure you'll see her soon.'

As Janet reached her hand out for the eggs, the sleeve of her blouse inched back up her arm revealing a smattering of small bruises, in a range of hues from purple to yellow. Eddie, not sure he should have noticed, turned his head away for a moment. When he looked back Janet had drawn her sleeve down to her wrist again.

He noticed that her hands were shaking and knew she was uncomfortable with his being there.

'OK, well, I can't stop anyway, hope she's feeling better. Tell her to save me a dance on Saturday night. Her last night out as a single woman, eh?'

'I'll tell her Eddie, thank you.'

The door was closed behind him before he had turned the key in the ignition.

On return to the camp that evening, he sought out Bailey.

'Did you know your Iris is under the weather? Is she coming to the dance on Saturday d'you reckon?'

Bailey looked confused. 'I thought she was seeing the Minister today; he needs to be available along with the Registrar for the wedding. I've just written to my parents in Alabama. Jeez, I hope it's all going to be alright.'

'It's such a big step, Bailey, moving so far from home, but I guess that's your choice. Maybe stay in Ireland? It's not such a bad place.'

'Ed, I'm off to France after the wedding, once I've made an honest woman of her and she will stay here with her family. Once the war is over, who knows what will happen?'

Eddie felt even more uneasy about Iris's prospects after sensing there was something troubling her mother. He had to ask. 'Is her Ma OK, Bailey, have you seen much of her?'

'Her Mom is a real good stay at home Mom. She bakes and sews and cleans and cooks, she's a quiet woman. God-fearing and respectable.'

'And how's her Da, Bailey, is he a quiet man too?'

'Mr Grey is the boss in that house, no mistakin'. But although he's not too happy about me and Iris, he's goin' along with it far as I know. If he was to say no, then no it would have to be, she's only nineteen, not twenty-one.'

He didn't see Bailey for the rest of the week but as he was finishing his shift on Saturday, and planning a great night at the dance, he caught sight of him across the exercise yard, looking dejected and alone.

'Hey Bailey, lad, how're ye doin'?' Waiting on his side of the yard whilst Bailey, lifting his head, began to walk over to him, Eddie prepared for bad news.

'It's all off, she doesn't want me. She won't even see me.'

'What's the craic then, Bailey? Did her Ma give you any reason?'

'Yea, her Mom sent you this.' He handed Eddie a round parcel wrapped in brown paper. Looking inside he found a freshly baked fruit cake.

'Aw, come off it, Bailey, there must be more to it than this, man, have you tried everything?'

'I've asked to have my posting brought forward. I'm off to France, day after tomorrow. I've made a real fool of myself here and I can't wait to be away now.'

'Ye'll write to me Bailey, sure I have to know you're alright. Send to my home address, I'll leave it for you.

I'm not inclined to stay much longer myself, so I'm not. But believe in the Lord, Bailey, and you'll find another girl one day, maybe in easier circumstances. Then you'll look back on this an' be glad you didn't have to break away from your family and break her away from hers.'

Eddie decided against going to the dance that night, heading to the Mess Bar instead and hoping to bump into Michael and mend their friendship. He drank his way through several pints before giving up.

Retrieving his bicycle from the copse behind the camp he cycled over to stay at his cousin Harry's for what was left of the night.

The next day was Sunday, and he was free all day, once he'd been to early Mass.

Borrowing Harry's car, he drove over to the Grey's house in Ballymoney after church, his thoughts on the friends he was losing - both Bailey and Michael; he didn't think any amount of praying for them would change that.

Once again, the door opened even as he raised his hand to the knocker and Mrs Grey, her face looking even more pinched and anxious than it had a few days ago, motioned him inside with a nod of her head and the slightest wave of her hand.

'Thanks for the cake, Mrs Grey. I'll take it home to Mam tonight; we'll all enjoy it so we will. She's no' much of a baker herself. Now I came to say, missus, my friend Bailey's in a bad way, he really loves your girl. Is there nothing we can do?'

'Ye didn't come about the cake, I knew that anyway. There is nothing we can do, son, no. I'll tell you the whole of it an' then maybe you'll see it. The girl's disgraced, so she is, an' we are sending her away to Belfast to have her baby. She won't be bringing it back either.'

'Ah, dear God, does Bailey know?'

'He can't know Eddie; let him go to France and think of her as a good girl. He must never know. Promise me you won't tell him.'

'No, missus, I'm sorry to ask but if he is to be a father, he must know - he will want to stand by her and the child.'

Mrs Grey seemed to crumple as she lowered her thin frame onto a hard wooden kitchen chair and bent her head in her hands.

Still standing, he looked down to see bare patches in her head where the bun had been pulled over, as if in an attempt at concealing baldness.

Without waiting to be invited, he sat down opposite her, uncomfortable to be alone with this woman who was so clearly struggling; but he felt obliged to give the visit some time. How he wished he had not come, he hated confrontation, but it was too late now.

Janet Grey looked up at the big-boned, rugged farm boy, who, even now, on his day off, was still dressed in his American driver's uniform. His obvious concern for Iris encouraged her and so she said the words she had promised her daughter, and herself, would never need to be said. 'It's not his child.'

'An' suppose it comes out a black baby, might it be his child then?'

'It won't be black, son, she knows it's another soldier's baby, a white American and he doesn't believe her; he shrugged her off when she told him. And so, no one will want it, not us, not her, and certainly not Bailey. I hope some family will take it in, but it won't be us.

Her Da is ragin'. I had to beg him not to go to the camp; I think it's only the shame of it is keepin' him from going to see the Camp Commander himself.

'So, look'it, Eddie, she made a mistake and now she has to pay for it. And she's not the first girl in Ireland to fall either, the punishment is worse the more people know. So, she goes away and you say nothing.' Eddie sat for a minute in silence, slowly absorbing this new, unexpected information.

Then he rose, putting his hand gently on Janet's bony shoulder, surprised to feel her wince, and spoke quietly, 'I'll never tell a soul, that's my promise. Say to Iris I hope all goes well for her.

If I can ever help her, ever, please tell her I will.' Pulling his American issue memo pad from his pocket he scribbled his home address. Janet nodded her head and took the paper. Then he saw himself out.

Turning to close the door he looked back to see the pale worried woman still seated, her cheeks damp and her lips clenched in pain.

Once back at Harry's he collected his bicycle and returned to the camp. It was a long cycle ride but it gave him time to think and to work some of the anger out of his system. He went straight to the officer's station to tell them he was leaving, immediately.

Fortunately, he had just been paid and so he said he was needed at home.

'Not now, Driver.' The officer looked up from the rota he was rearranging with his colleague.

'More troops are arriving into Northern Ireland every day now and we are just getting to know the training grounds. Come on man, we are over here fighting your war and if you are not signing up yourself, then the very least you can do is give us a bit of support.'

Eddie was adamant. 'I didn't come here to listen to all this about blacks and whites and so on and anyway, I'm needed on the farm. And I am doing my bit. I'm a brickie, needed for rebuilding, essential skill so it is. Sorry, sir, I'm off.' Even as he made his excuses, he knew that the real reasons for leaving were not just that he felt let down by the Americans, but his visit to Ballymoney had upset him. He just wanted to go.

Walking away from the camp for the last time he kept his head down, feigning interest in his handlebars so as not to see any familiar faces; in particular he did not need to see Bailey.

Arriving home late afternoon, in better weather than his last visit, he crossed the brow of the hill before the evening sun had set and looked down on his homestead, once again relieved to find there was some constant in his now-troubled world. How differently he would tell the story of Iris and Bailey now, still keeping the details to himself but offering Mam the cake by way of explanation.

Chapter 6.

Iris. Ballymoney and Belfast, Northern Ireland, 1942

Iris leaned her forehead against the cool windowpane and watched Harry's motor receding down the middle of the street. As the car and Eddie became smaller and fainter so did her hopes of any future contact with that part of her life. Moving back from the window she let the blackout curtain fall, covering the room in darkness. She had loved Bailey, that tall, kind, strong, man. She had been scared, planning a life away from home and family, but she felt sure she was making a good choice, enjoying being loved and looked after. Her father's harsh approach to life meant there was never any laughter or loving in their house. Now this pregnancy had put a stop to all her hopes. Throwing herself down on her bed she moaned, 'Such a stupid fool. Such an idiot. Why did I let him near me? Why did I believe him? Why have I let one stupid event ruin my life?'

She thought back to that night at the dance. Bailey had not turned up, she didn't know why, and Bud was making a really nice fuss over her. Flattered, she allowed him to buy her a drink, then two. Not used to alcohol it wasn't long before her head began to spin and she felt the need for fresh air. She thought of how the good-looking, charming man that was Bud Willis really had looked after her.

He had even taken her to his own bed in the Nissen hut; luckily there were no other men in at the time, but still, he had taken a risk for her.

Once safely laid down, he had loosened her tight belt and opened the top buttons on her blouse. She had been so very grateful for his attention. She recalled how she had drifted into a comfortable sleepy daze, relaxed in his care and pleasantly aware of his kisses on her skin, then further down on her breasts as the buttons were unpicked. Sighing contentedly, she had let her legs drift apart as his hand began the inevitable journey up the inside of her thigh until she felt him unhitching her stocking from its suspender and slipping his hand beneath the silky fabric of her underwear. She remembered it all so clearly. She hadn't said 'no', he hadn't forced her, and he had promised her that he would be careful.

Even now, lying on her bed distraught by how her life had changed, she could still remember that pleasure and she had to bite into her pillow to stop herself crying. How different it had been with Bailey. He seemed almost as much a novice as she was and kept stopping to ask her if she was all right. Rushed, embarrassed, and sore, she was not 'all right,' but anyway, she loved him and thought she would never regret their time together. She didn't regret it now, but it had been really hard for her to face the fact that the baby wasn't Bailey's. For a while she had balanced the odds and thought she might take a gamble, but she couldn't do that and reckoned it would only make her situation worse.

'At least I did have that time with Bailey, and I made him happy.' She told her bedroom ceiling, the marks on its familiar stained surface resembled a friendly face, and that night she needed one badly. 'I never made Bud happy, he just shook me off when I told him I was late. He said he had been careful. I wish I'd never told him; he doesn't care about the baby, he shouldn't even have known.'

As the months passed, Iris's body began to change shape and she stayed indoors as much as possible. Eventually the move came, as she knew it must and one morning, shrouded in her roomy winter coat, she was bundled into the back of her parent's car and driven to St Gregory's Mother and Baby home in Belfast.

Into the bright, sparsely furnished hallway, her nostrils assailed by the smell of beeswax and dried out geraniums, Iris concentrated on holding back her tears.

'Bye, Mam, Dad, I'll be fine here. I'll write and let you know how I'm getting on and when my time comes...'

'When your time comes you be brave, Iris. Never let them see you hurting, and it will soon be over. Don't cry, don't make a fuss. It's the best way. Then once it's finished with we'll come and get you and say no more about it.' Janet hugged her daughter, ignoring her husband's impatience to be gone.

'They'll look after you here and you probably won't even need to go to the hospital but if you do, they have arrangements.'

'And so, I stay here until I sign this baby away. I have to watch them take my child and I never get a choice.'

'Now Iris, we've been through all this. You had a choice, you made it and now here you are. It's disgraceful.' It was her father who responded, his face and neck reddening as he shouted. 'You'll come home to us alone and people will never know. You have been very fortunate in getting a place here, and even more fortunate in no-one knowing about your bad behaviour and the shame you've brought on this family.' Iris stroked her swollen belly and felt a small foot kick against her hand. Tears swelled in her eyes as she looked up at her mother, ignoring her father's remarks.

'Is there really no way, Mam? Don't you know anyone who would let me work for them with my baby? Or couldn't we pretend it's our baby sister or brother and I could still see it growing up? Please Mam?'

'No Iris, we have to leave you now. Unpack and then go and get some tea. There's plenty of girls here in your situation, I won't say they are all bad girls; find some nice ones and forget about this baby, and then come home. Bye now, love.'

Janet leaned forward and kissed her daughter, hugging her carefully and turning quickly away before Iris could see her tears.

For a moment she thought her father was holding out his hand to her but as she moved towards him, he turned and pulled his wife away by the shoulder of her coat.

The heavy oak door gave a sigh as it glided into its frame, Iris felt it echo down the polished wooden floor and she wondered if this was how a prisoner might feel. She stood for a moment; a slight pale girl, wearing a heavy coat, allowing it to fall back as she never did at home, revealing her swollen outline. Around her she saw many other pregnant girls. There were also some who were probably not but, by the shape of their figures, looked as though they had recently been, pregnant. And through the groups of girls a few nuns glided, their smooth black habits elegantly moving across the polished floor, in silent criticism.

The girls congregated towards the refectory for supper and she heard an authoritative command, 'Grace before meals now, girls,'

'An' I'm not even a Catholic' she muttered. 'How I ever came to this I really don't know.'

Her days became a routine of prayers, which Iris soon managed to ignore and mealtimes, which she tolerated. Between prayers and meals, she was given chores, as were all the girls. Cleaning, preparing vegetables, washing dishes and attending sewing groups to make table linen to sell as a fundraiser for the home. Unlike some of the homes she had heard of, this one was not harsh or overly demanding.

The baby felt strong inside her and grew too quickly for her liking. She wanted to keep this child in her belly, knowing that once she gave birth the baby would no longer be hers.

She made friends with another girl, Carmel, who slept in her dormitory and had gone over to Iris's bed one night when she heard her sobbing. 'I know it's hard Iris, but we've all done it. You'll have your baby for a few days, probably ten, an' then the social worker will bring the new parents to see it.

You'll be allowed to bring the baby down in its pram; they have plenty of prams here, you don't need to worry. Then, if they like it, the hardest part is, you walk back with the empty pram and then you must tell yourself, 'Now I can go home.' If they don't like it, of course you bring it back until next time. An' you stay here until it's taken. Or for a bit anyway, I don't know how long. They're nearly always taken, as long as they're OK. But if they're not then I think they go to an orphanage and then you can go home.'

'Does it hurt, Carmel? Mam said not to cry, or it'll be the worse for you, she said never let them see it hurts.'

'Yes, it does bloody hurt, my friend, it rips you and you can cry all you like, makes no difference. I don't know why she said that.'

'I know why she said that. It's what she does when he gets at her.'

'Ah, for God's sake, yer Da, is it? He's not the only one. It's disgraceful how many women you see walking in the country on their own of an evening. They're feared to go home. So many of those men like to use their fists. Ever hit you, has he?'

'No, never, but it is so horrible at home sometimes. I was hoping to get away, and when I met this American soldier ...'

'Tell me no more, Iris, go back to sleep now. I'm staying here at the convent because I'm doing some work. Cleanin', and the like. My family's big with the church here and they don't want me back in a hurry. So, tell you what, if I can, I'll be with you or leastways as far as they let me.'

Reassured, Iris slept, with a hand over her belly, imagining the little body and wanting to soothe it if it woke in the night.

A week later she was woken by a rush of warm and wet fluid soaking her bed and her stomach gripped by what felt like a band of iron.

'Mam, where are you now?', she groaned as she heaved herself out of bed, stuffing a towel between her legs and pulling her small wash bag out from the dormitory cupboard. Disturbed by the noise, Carmel and another girl, Marie, the one who slept nearest the door, came out to find Iris on her knees trying to mop up the floor.

'Here Iris, come on, you need to get to the infirmary. I'll wake Sister Cecilia. Marie, can you go to Iris's locker, it should have a clean nightdress and her coat. She can't go over there like this and get some more towels, she's soaking.' Carmel took charge and helped Iris into a clean nightdress before swaddling another towel between her legs. Bringing a wheelchair, she helped the sobbing girl onto the seat and pushed her, wheels squeaking loudly along the quiet night-time corridor.

'It'll be alright now, Iris, so it will. They'll look after you and then you will stay for a few days, you know the rest.'

'And then you can go home, won't that be grand?'.

'An' your baby will be adopted, have a lovely home and want for nothing. You will make some poor, childless woman very happy.' Iris heard Marie and Carmel talking to her but did not have the strength to reply.

'Please hang on, baby, you are not ready yet and Mam isn't here to help me and anyway I don't want to be without you ...'

It took only moments to leave the house, cross the concrete yard to a grim granite building, just visible in the darkness and then a strong tug got the wheelchair through the infirmary door where Iris was handed over to a yawning, tired-looking young woman with Nurse Rogers engraved on her name badge.

They left her there being reassured that Sister Cecilia would meet Iris in the Labour Ward. Iris had never felt so isolated. It was even worse than those lonely nights when she had lain in bed listening to the angry shouts of her father before the inevitable thumping started. The room was cold and uncomfortable, but once Sister Cecilia arrived it seemed less impersonal. She was responsible for the girls' physical care whilst at St Gregory's, and one of the kinder nuns.

'Come on now, Iris, this will soon be over. Let's get you onto the bed and have a look at what Baby is doing.' Sister Cecilia was gentle and reassuring, helping Iris feel a little less frightened. Sometime during the night Sister Cecilia left the Infirmary, handing Iris over to a junior nurse, one who didn't look as tired as Nurse Rogers.

'Like most of our girls, this baby's for adoption, Nurse. If it's not chosen immediately it will be going to an English orphanage. So, make sure you take a sample of cord blood and get Dr Burns, when he comes in, to sign the birth register with father unknown. And Nurse, please do remember that young Iris is far from home and I'll expect you to be kind to her. Whatever she has done, we are not here to judge. I'll leave you now. Nurse Rogers is around if you need any help.'

'Hello Iris, I'm Dorothy Brady, Nurse Brady but you can call me Dorothy. It's hard on you too, having to do this on your own and I'll be with you all through, so I will. Now tell me about your labour so far.'

'I can't tell you anything, Nurse, I need to push an' he's not ready yet, he's not due for another month.'

'All right, all right, Iris, some babies come early, and some babies come late, we'll see when he arrives. Now let me have a look at you. Oh goodness, yes, push down for me. Nurse, I need a hand in here, please ...'

Over the sound of Nurse Rogers running to help she heard Dorothy exclaim, 'Good girl, your baby's head is coming.'

'Now we can see the head Iris, looks like baby has lots of hair, give me one more big push, there's a good girl.'

The child inside her ripped out, a strong healthy boy. Tightly curled black hair and a grey complexion caused the nurses to share a knowing glance as they wrapped him in a cotton blanket and gave him to his mother. As she looked down into her newborn baby's face she saw exactly who his father was and when the truth dawned, she realised what a terrible mistake she had made.

Chapter 7.

Eddie. London, England, 1943

Eddie heard there was plenty of work for builders in London - where they were also exempt from the army - and he decided to go. A few days before he left, he received a letter.

'Dear Eddie,

Please don't tear this letter up when you see who has written to you. Please help me. I don't know where to turn. I've got a beautiful baby boy, he's Bailey's son so I've called him Bailey although I had to register his father unknown. But I know he is Bailey's. He looks just like him and I can't get him adopted because he is what they are calling Mixed Race. Now there are plans for him to go to an orphanage in England, where there is more chance of an adoption or if not it's an orphanage where he will stay until he's grown up.

I can't bear it, Ed. He will never know his Mammy and Daddy, and Bailey won't even know he has a son. Please, please can you get in touch with Bailey and tell him, at least then he has a choice. But I have no choice, my family are taking me home next week, I can't stay here any longer. It's six weeks now so I have to sign him over for good and sign away my rights to ever see him again.

Please Eddie, I know you were Bailey's good friend, please do this for him if not for me.

You can always contact me in Ballymoney, I'll be kept at home now, my Da is really angry with me. He's said he won't be letting me out for a long time, at least until next year when I'm twenty-one. Once I reach the age when he can't stop me, I'll definitely be going away from here, but I'll always make sure Mam knows where I am.

Thanks Eddie.
Your faithful friend,
Iris'

Eddie had walked out across the fields to Scout Hill when he received the letter, it was his favourite place for quiet contemplation and sitting on the Mass Rock he read and re-read the contents, making sure he fully understood. Then he folded the letter into quarters and put it in his pocket. As he looked out over the familiar landscape, he wondered whether life had been easier in bygone days.

'Sure, those challenges between religions or armies, they were the easy ones. You knew which side you were on. Now I don't know whose side, if anyone's, I'm on and I've really no idea what to do.'

Looking up at the wide clouded sky, hoping for inspiration, he only found birds of prey, sparrowhawks and kestrels circling and screeching high above him.

They sounded angry and impatient, waiting, he supposed, for the rabbits and other small creatures to break cover at the end of the day. He felt angry and impatient too, put in a position where he didn't know what to do.

'Why ever did Iris go with another man, whoever it was? Probably that Bud Willis, an' I'm not too sure I want my friend to take up with her again. On the other hand, there's a child, I'll think on it a while so I will.' And so, unable to make a decision, the letter had gone into his wallet.

Then he had left for London, as planned. He had taken the ferry from Belfast to Liverpool, then the train down to London.

Once in London, he soon found work in the building trade and began to enjoy being his own master, no longer needing to feel subservient or uneasy with attitudes like he had done with the Americans.

The bombing made him anxious too, and sometimes he wondered whether he should have stayed in Ireland. But over the months he quelled his fears and settled into a steady round of work, football matches, occasional visits to the pub, regular attendances at the dances, and church on Sunday.

A couple of years passed, and the war ended. Eddie stayed on in London where he met and fell in love with Ellen West, then eighteen years old. One summer's evening, sitting together at a table outside an ice-cream parlour in the fashionable Maida Vale part of London, Ellen asked Eddie to tell her everything he could about his past life and his friends.

He looked up at his girl, clear skinned with a milky complexion and the dark hair from her Irish mother, Kitty, enhanced by strong features which sat more comfortably on her profile than they did on her English father, William. She wore a silky blouse with a bow at the neck and a pencil skirt, which showed off her slim hips. He thought he had never seen a woman as beautiful, and, just as William had with Kitty, he thought of her as virtuous and pure.

He wondered whether he should tell her about Bailey and Iris, the condoms and the camp, or whether she would be shocked. Deciding that parts of the story would interest her he began.

'Ellen, you do know I mixed with a lot of Yanks during the war? I drove their trucks and Jeeps an' sometimes, for work y'know, I even stayed in the camps.'

'Of course, I know, Eddie. The Yanks were over here too. They were lovely to us, gave us gum and nylons.

I didn't need to use my leg makeup, just the occasional pencil line down the back of my leg, an' we used to say, 'Got any gum, chum'...'

'Yes, Ellen I know all that', interrupted Eddie, impatient with the talk of nylons and gum when he knew his story was to be taken so much more seriously.

'I got very friendly with one soldier, a coloured man. Anyway, thing is, he got this girl in the family way, but she didn't tell him. An' now she has a baby and she wants him to know but I don't know if I should tell him or not.'

'Why would you be the one to tell, Eddie?'

'Here, see this letter she wrote me two years ago last August, soon after the baby was born, I've never done anything about it.'

Eagerly, Ellen reached across the table and snatched the letter from him, crying out in dismay, 'He'll be nearly three by now, that's such a long time for a baby. What were you thinking, Eddie?'

Unaware that she was attracting attention from tables nearby, she began to read the letter aloud.

'Can I get you anything, Madam?' a discreet enquiry from the waiter quietened Ellen.

'No thanks, just the bill. Ellen, you had enough?' Feeling unhappy with all the drama and attention Eddie wished he'd never told her. 'Quiet woman, be quiet, we don't need the world to know.'

'But Eddie, a little baby and no one wants him. Can we have him?'

Eddie groaned, 'No Ellen, we can't. He already belongs to Bailey and Iris unless he's been adopted, an' I really don't know what to do.'

'We'll find him.'

'Well, I think we might be able to find Bailey, and then he can find the child. It's not for us to get involved, Ellen. I know you'd love a family and we will have one soon. But not this one.'

Ellen looked up, admiring his confidence.

She really loved that, he had choices and he could make his own decisions. It made her determined not to let any time pass before becoming his wife. She'd be free, she felt, from other people's requirements and she would, at last, be able to lead her own life.

'You know Eddie, I've known other places and people in my life. I was captured by a soldier - a deserter - but it didn't scare me at all. I had a very exciting time in fact, in Wales.'

'Well you were twelve, Ellen, just a child.'

'You know I was allowed to go back there on my own. They trusted me to be sensible so why can't you trust my experience to guide you?'

'Ellen, you weren't captured but that poor deserter was. I know he did wrong to go AWOL but I do think it was a sad ending to his situation.'

'Yes, Ed and it was sad for the child also, not to have a father. So here we have the same thing again.'

'OK, Ellen, you win. I'll write to Bailey soon and fill him in. Now can you tell me more about your adventurous past life?'

Whilst Ellen recounted, in greater detail than was needed, her experiences of both wartime evacuation and her subsequent return visits to Llandeilo, she made it seem as though she was very well travelled and versed in another culture.

Eddie paid the bill but still they sat on. Ellen was happy to make it a long session and Eddie knew she'd endlessly embellish her wartime tales given the chance. He was only half-listening, giving himself time for his thoughts to keep returning to the problem of how he might locate Bailey.

Then, quite out of the blue, the problem was solved by a letter forwarded from his mother. This was fortunate, as during the intervening weeks he hadn't progressed at all with the challenge of where to find his friend.

'Holmworthy Camp
Dartmoor
Devon

Dear Eddie,
Hope this finds you well, man. I've been meaning to write but thought I'd wait until I came back from France. Then there was the Treaty and for a while I thought I was going to the Pacific. I'm not really supposed to say too much but anyway, now I'm back and I've been posted to a village in Devon until they send me back to the US or somewhere else. It's real pretty here and the people are so friendly, nearly as nice as you Irish. I'm staying well away from the ladies though and I haven't gotten over my time in Maydown. I often think about you, man, and hope life is treating you well.

I'm trying to settle myself into going home and thinking about what to do when I go back to Alabama, I was lucky to survive so I'll thank the Good Lord, as you always told me to, for whatever comes my way now.

You've got my address now Ed and I'd love to hear from you sometime. I don't suppose you ever see Iris? I expect she's forgotten about me years ago.

Your faithful friend,
Bailey'

Reading the letter twice, he knew he had landed a responsibility and he really shouldn't ignore it. After spending a sleepless night thinking about Bailey's letter, he paid a visit to Ellen's father. The quiet, reserved William, never given to impetuous action, seemed a safe bet to Eddie. And, he owned a car, had a store of petrol coupons and had shown himself to be a hero in the story of Ellen's rescue.

'Good to see you, Ed, come in for a cup of tea?'
Ellen's family still lived in the same modest three-roomed flat, which had been home since Kitty and William's wedding.

It was on the top floor of an ageing Victorian terrace in Kilburn. Climbing the stairs behind William he breathed in the faint but ever-present odour of boiled cabbage, mixed with a hint of Lifebuoy soap, and tobacco. He wished he could be out in the open air of his family's farm; the smells of animals, wet grass, and peat smoke were what he missed. This city never felt like home to him.

Seated at the spotless scrubbed wooden table taking tea and a rather dry type of fruitcake which Ellen's mother always baked, he shared his problem with William.

'I don't know what this American soldier is like, Eddie, but I do know that war makes soldiers do terrible things and I think you'd be surprised at some of the actions I've seen. A soldier needs to face up to his responsibility though. First he has to know and then he has to decide what to do.'

'Will you come with me, William? Ah, go on, I've a notion to go down to Dartmoor and tell Bailey face to face. I'm no good at letter writing, never was, an' I've an idea this isn't a job for a letter anyway. I don't want the women involved, too emotional, what with a child an' all.'

William agreed and the following afternoon he shut up the small basement cobbler's shop early. The men only brought a packet of sandwiches each and a flask of tea, hoping the tank of petrol would last the journey, although Eddie did have a few pound notes in his back pocket and Will had the coupons.

Of course, Ellen had wanted to come too but there was no question and she didn't object. Her future husband really did seem to have a way of stopping any objections.

Hour after hour they drove west. Wide, open roads, wide, open countryside and the familiar smells of animals and crops were a heady and familiar mix for Eddie. Stopping through the night to eat sandwiches and drink tea they talked mostly of their families. The topics drifted from the farm in Ireland to Ellen's childhood.

'You know she always tells the story of how she was captured by a deserter, and how I saved her life?'

'I've heard it many a time, William. It must have been very frightening for her.'

'Well yes, of course, but you know she wasn't captured. She decided to run away, and she just happened upon the hideout of this poor man. Now I'm not saying he was in the right. And, as a soldier myself I'd think very poorly of a deserter, but he had his reasons. Did she ever tell you about that son?

'See, the poor boy got his sweetheart in the family way, like your Bailey here. And he wanted to stay around just long enough to make an honest woman of her. I don't think he had decided what to do after the wedding. He might have given himself up and probably been sent back to the front, most of them were. Anyway, it all fell apart because he was discovered, due to the whole Ellen business.'

'French Leave' the Americans called it, though it never happened when I was at the camp'.

'Anyway, he was charged with kidnapping as well as desertion and he wasn't able to marry his girl after all. Straight to jail for him. Got to feel sorry for them all really. The girl, Betty I think they called her, left alone, expectin', an' without a husband, not a good start for a child. Talking about it with you here I maybe regret being so angry with him, but I thought he had hurt my girl, you know.'

'I will say for Ellen, she's made a right story out of it, Will. She's told everyone.'

'It brings to mind how the deserters in the first war, the war I served in, were court-marshalled and shot. Never shown any mercy or a second chance. I often think about that. What would be more natural for a human being than to take themselves out of the gravest danger. It's a wonder more didn't desert.'

'William, you never do speak about your time in the war. I'd often like to hear more about it; must have been very different from the experience I had.'

'You're right there. I don't talk about it and I won't. It was terrible and when I came back, I was so angry. I couldn't bear to see people out enjoying themselves, having fun.

It seemed as though all the effort was for nothing and no-one cared.'

'Yeah, well you men did have a really bad time, I can see how you must have felt, right enough.'

'As you get older, Eddie, you realise people just want to get on with their lives. Now I just want the best for my family. It will stay with me forever, that war, but as I get older, I understand better.' Ending the conversation, William rose stiffly to his feet and, gathering his coat and rug, returned to the car. Feeling humbled by the story, Eddie was reminded, not for the first time, that there was a lot more to William than most people assumed.

By early morning the car was struggling to climb Haldon Hill, just past Exeter, when William pointed out a rugged landscape set high on the horizon. Early dawn mists made the faint outlines, edged in purple and grey, look mysterious and moody. As Eddie looked across at his first sight of Dartmoor he realised that there were wild and beautiful places in England, which were so very much like the areas he was familiar with in Ireland.

'It reminds me of Donegal,' he said to William, who was concentrating hard on the road ahead, which was full of potholes and unexpected narrow turns.

'We stay on this road now and turn off when we get to Ivybridge. Then we head up to Harford - that's where the real Dartmoor starts. I guess we'll ask our way to the camp from there.'

'Reckon ye know the way that far then, Will?'

'Another couple of hours at least, so you get your head down, boy, and take a nap. I'll leave the talking to you when we get to Holmworthy camp, and I'll get a snooze then.'

Eddie slept, dreaming of Donegal and Bailey and his time in Maydown Camp, and in the dawn he experienced that strange phenomenon of dreams, the emotions remembered on waking even though the content has faded. He was ready to meet his friend again and offer his help.

Finding Holmworthy village easily, they arrived at the camp mid-morning. The US service tents and Nissen huts a familiar landscape to Eddie.

He left William in the car outside the perimeter fence to get some sleep and wandered quietly amongst the buildings unnoticed. Yawning and stretching, he leaned against the side of a lorry, and lazily pulled his pipe out of his trouser pocket.

'Man, are you still smoking that thing?' Eddie heard a familiar voice behind him and turning delightedly he found himself in the strong embrace of his friend.

'Great to see you, man, what are you doing here? Don't tell me, you're driving trucks again, eh?'

'Nah, Bailey, I came to see you. Got your letter and came straight down, my girl's old man brought me down from London, that's where I am now. Sure, he's right over there, asleep in that old Morris jalopy.'

The two men walked off to find some tea before Eddie brought the three-year old letter out of his wallet where he had kept it since Iris had asked for his help. He felt ashamed to have left it so long before making any attempt to find Bailey.

Consoling himself with having done the right thing at last, he was relieved to know that the next decision would have to be Bailey's.

Bailey was quiet. He seemed to have been reading the letter several times before he looked up from the paper, his usually relaxed face a mixture of amazement and sorrow.

'Eddie, I can't take it in, man. My girl, my lovely girl. What she has gone through? And a son! I'm a father but where is my child? Surely, it's not too late Ed, do you reckon? I need time to think but one thing I'm sure of is that I'll never rest until I find them both. I always loved her, Ed, you know that. I'm only sorry she didn't know it too.'

'Well, my friend, why not start with Ballymoney and see where ye can go from there? Sure, it's my fault too, so it is. I knew all along, but her ma made me promise...'

'That's it, Eddie, her ma! I'll go and see her, I've some leave to take before my next posting. Can I get a lift back to London now and then it'll be the boat and the train. Man, I could be there the day after tomorrow...' Bailey's eyes shone at the prospect.

'Sure Bailey, 'course we can. I'll be over there with William, get yersel' sorted out. We need a sleep before we head back anyway.'

Chapter 8.

Ellen and Eddie. Belfast, Northern Ireland, 1950

'Please Eddie, get home quick.'

Ellen hugged the new baby tightly, as she searched the street below, straining to see through the window of their tiny top-floor apartment before dragging her attention back to the sofa where her little boy was lying, pale and limp.

It was the end of January and although Ellen had left the two-bar electric fire on all afternoon, the room still felt cold. Despite the chilly temperature, the child, Toby, had kicked off his blanket. He had been listless all day and was now really difficult to rouse. Ellen didn't know what to do.

Married only three years, and so much had happened to them. Eddie had brought them to Northern Ireland just after the wedding, suggesting it would give them the opportunity 'to make their own way.'

The dream of a country life had been growing since Ellen's childhood evacuation to Wales and until they 'got on their feet' as Eddie would say, they had to make do with rented space in Belfast; really just two rooms, the kitchen and bathroom were shared with the owners of the greengrocer's shop below.

He didn't seem to mind about the bare surroundings, confident that they could work towards building a better future.

And they had both been delighted when Toby, a "honeymoon baby" was born. Two years later a daughter, Teresa, arrived and although Ellen was restless in Belfast, Eddie felt they were settling into family life.

Now she was anxious to see her husband home, desperate for reassurance from him that all would be well. Listening to her child's unusually rapid breathing, Ellen felt she had waited at the window for an eternity before she saw Eddie.

His canvas bag containing his precious bricklaying tools was weighing down his right shoulder, causing him to walk a bit lopsidedly up the street.

Ellen ran to open the door, calling down the stairs. 'Toby's ill, Eddie. He has a fever and been sleeping all day now.' Taking the stairs two at a time, he dropped his bag on the floor, and crouched down in front of the threadbare sofa which was providing a makeshift bed for his son.

Toby lay limp in Eddie's arms as he lifted him by the shoulders, the boy screwing up his eyes as though the light was too bright, before letting out a high-pitched cry.

'Toby, where does it hurt, son? Has he had anything to eat, Ellen?'
'Not a thing all day. Ed, please, what do you think, will he be all right? Or maybe it's an idea for you to take him to the surgery? He has been like this since morning and I'm worried he's getting worse.'

'Give me that blanket, I'll wrap him up. I think the surgery is open until eight and you can't go, stay here with the baby.'

'If they ask, tell them he hasn't eaten, but he has had some orange juice and some sugar and water. I'll get you your tea when you come back.'

Eddie knew his child's illness was serious as he carried him, wrapped up into a clumsy bundle down the stairs, along the road, and into the crowded surgery.

It was some time before he was seen. The surgery was filled with children and elderly people, most of whom seemed to be coughing and sneezing, some held bowls on their laps and were intermittently retching and dribbling globs of vomit. Eddie repeatedly carried Toby up to an irritable receptionist, asking for him to be seen urgently but it didn't seem to have any impact.

'Everyone here is urgent sir, you'll just have to wait your turn.'

Toby's breathing had become shallow and fast and whatever Eddie did to try and rouse him, there was no response, not even the high-pitched scream heard earlier. By the time the doctor called them through he was really worried.

'Lay him on the couch please, Mr McCann, and let me listen to his chest. There is a lot of pneumonia about at the minute. You did the right thing to bring him here.'

Eddie stood back, his heart beating wildly whilst Dr Gordon, a friendly man, who was not usually that short with anxious parents, examined the pale, limp little boy. He did not spend long, and his face was grave when he turned his attention to Eddie.

'This child is very ill and needs the hospital. I'll get him admitted to Musgrave Park. He may have an infectious disease. They have the Isolation Unit there.' Without the hoped-for reassurance, the doctor left the room.

Eddie's world turned upside down in that instant. He thought of Ellen at home with the baby, unaware of the seriousness of Toby's condition.

His thoughts flitted unbidden, from his future plans for the four of them to this awful situation in front of him.

He wondered how he had ever presumed he would have a perfect, secure family life. His son and daughter growing up together, maybe with more brothers and sisters in time. Now his main concern was on how he was going to get Toby to the hospital and let Ellen know what was happening.

'An ambulance will take you now, it's on the way.'

'We have no things with us Doctor, and I need to tell my wife, she's at home with the baby.'

'No time for that now Mr McCann, you should have brought him sooner.' Struggling to get Toby dressed and wrapped, his hands shaking with fear, he carried the child out to the waiting area where Dr Gordon was scrutinising the register.

'Mrs Barlow', Doctor Gordon was moving across the room, addressing the woman who owned the greengrocers and lived in the rooms downstairs. Although he did recognise her he had never spoken to her but thought Ellen had met her when they shared the kitchen.

'Please go to Mrs McCann, she lives upstairs from you, and tell her that her son Toby has been taken to Musgrave Park Hospital in an ambulance with his father.

She can visit him there, he will not need anything, no pyjamas or toys, but she needs to be told what's going on.'

Grateful for the doctor's intervention, Eddie moved forward to Mrs Barlow. 'Tell her I'll stay at the hospital until she gets there, tell her bring the baby.'

'You won't be allowed to bring a baby in, I'll mind your baby until you get back.' Mrs Barlow sounded confident as well as kind.

Eddie had no option but to agree. He needed his wife and Toby needed his mother. When the ambulance arrived, he heard the urgency in the crew's voices; his fears were confirmed when he saw them turn on their blue light.

Arriving at the hospital, Toby was taken from Eddie, who was given a handful of papers to fill in, and a nurse carried the boy into a curtained cubicle.

There was no sign of Ellen, although every time the door opened, he looked up expectantly, hoping it would be her, needing her there with him.

He kept reminding himself that she would have to catch two buses to reach the hospital and he tried to concentrate on completing the forms he'd been given.

An hour passed. To Eddie it felt much longer,before a crisply dressed nurse, whose calm, organised approach instilled some confidence told him he was allowed to see his son and led him to a small window set into a long green tiled corridor. It took him a moment to recognise Toby.

His shaven head had an intravenous drip on one side, his eyelids were purple and swollen. The rest of his face was covered by an oxygen mask and Eddie felt terrified, repeating the child's name over and over again. As he turned to the young nurse, hoping she might give some reassurance, he heard familiar footsteps hurrying towards him.

Ellen had arrived but Eddie couldn't turn around, dreading the emotions which were about to be released. Although he knew she was standing beside him, he could not move.
Looking sideways at her he saw that the shuddering running down her body mirrored what he was feeling inside. Breaking his frozen stance, he turned and reached out, drawing her towards him.

'It can't, it can't be, I won't let it,' Ellen was sobbing into Eddie's overcoat. He held her close, her body shaking against him, never taking his eyes from the window.

'He's alone, all alone, on a metal bed. He has no teddy bear or anything from us to comfort him. He needs us, I have to get in there to him, I have to. Please Eddie, tell them.'

'Mr and Mrs McCann, would you like to come and sit down?' The grave, cultured voice broke through their distress, shocking them into realising that life was still going on and giving them hope that there were people who might help, although the recently trusted nurse was now nowhere to be seen.

Reluctantly moving away from the window, they followed the brisk figure in white coat down the long cold corridor into an equally cold side room, painted a dull green, scruffy and bereft of any comfort.

Waving towards some hard-looking metal chairs, indicating them to sit, he spoke abruptly, seeming to be a man with no time to spare for niceties.

'I'm Dr Brady, I specialise in infectious diseases, and we are running tests on your son now to see if we can identify the cause of his infection.'

'But you will find out what it is, won't you, Doctor, then we can bring him home?' Ellen's dark worried eyes searched the doctor's face.

'We are doing all we can, Mother, but you should prepare yourselves for bad news. We suspect meningitis so we are treating him with penicillin now in the hope that it will increase his chances.'

'His chances of what exactly, Doctor?'

'Survival, I'm afraid. Meningitis is very serious indeed.' Eddie held her tight. He thought she was going to hit the doctor her body was shaking in anger.

'You liar, what do you know about it? He was perfectly all right yesterday; we're taking him home.'

'I'm afraid that is not possible. Mr McCann, can you take Mother home now? She's upset and we don't want her making a fuss in here. It won't help the child and it really distresses the other patients.'

Reluctantly Ellen allowed Eddie to raise her to her feet. 'Can we just see him one more time before we go, Doctor?' Eddie asked, feeling that he had never asked for anything more important in his life.

'One more brief visit, through the window, then I really must insist that you leave. You can read of his progress in the Belfast Telegraph. We post notices of the critically ill patients in the evening paper, that way you will know how he is.'

Ellen and Eddie looked through the window, imprinting every aspect of the medical equipment onto their minds whilst preparing the questions they would ask the next time they saw the doctor. They gazed greedily at his little body, trying to absorb the impression of his swollen eyes, his small pale face, and his strangely restricted limbs, before turning reluctantly away.

Each wrapped in their own thoughts, their hearts were breaking, and they were not able to offer each other any comfort. Two buses took them back to the Falls Road and walking home up the hill Eddie put his arm around Ellen and spoke gently.

'We will pray for him all night; we won't sleep and in the morning we'll go back to the hospital and demand to see him. He'll have had a good night's sleep and the medicine will help him get better. Remember Ellen, things are never as bad as they seem. Your Mum and Dad were frantic when you went missing in Wales, but they got you back.'

'Yes, and look at what Iris and Bailey went through, they never gave up. They got their little boy back. So will we.'

'Of course we won't give up, we'll all be together again before Easter.' Then added quickly, 'Long before Easter' as he felt Ellen's body stiffen at the thought that their little boy might be ill for so many weeks. Eddie spoke bravely but his heart was heavy. With sad slow steps they unlocked the side door and called in with Mrs Barlow to collect their baby girl.

They stayed awake all night praying and returned to the hospital at first light, but they were not allowed to see their son. They were told his condition was critical and that he had been moved to an intensive care ward.

They read of his death in the newspaper that evening.

Six weeks later …
'Is she sleeping, Ellen?' asked Eddie. It was late and he was tired, although anxious to help Ellen, who seemed to have lost enthusiasm for doing anything at all since Toby's death.
'Can we go to bed now and sleep a while ourselves? If she wakes can you lift her, I'm up again at five, not long.'
'Ed, this place isn't enough, I'm worried she will get the disease also, it's damp and small and I was so looking forward to open fields.'
'Shush now, Ellen, we'll talk about it in the morning, let's get some sleep, you need the rest for your milk. And whatever you want to do, we will do, that's a promise.' During the night, Eddie slept, but Ellen lay awake alternately wondering how she could keep her baby daughter safe and planning her next move.

She was homesick but too proud to admit it. Until she regained her strength after the trauma of Toby's death, so close on the heels of baby Teresa's birth, she couldn't or didn't want to make a move. She wasn't as close to Eddie as she had been. They had drawn apart, she felt, in their grief, and she was beginning to wonder whether she had married too young.

The following day, Ellen decided to visit the Botanical Gardens, she thought it was probably the nearest she would get to the green fields she believed she'd been promised.

She pushed the pram through the Falls Road area, where pale March sunlight made the doorknobs glint. The house-proud women who controlled the streets of the terraced rows were a force to be reckoned with, the doorknobs were just an indicator.

Continuing downhill to Shaftsbury Square Ellen considered that its busy metropolitan landscape, with the Grand Opera House, pubs, restaurants and commercial businesses, felt more like her home neighbourhood of Kilburn than the Ireland she had imagined. She liked to get out of the Falls Road area, which was almost exclusively Catholic and working class and move amongst a more mixed population.

Today she hoped the spring flowers of the gardens might cheer her up. And the grand Edwardian Palm House, a tropical conservatory in the centre of the garden was one of the most impressive and elegant buildings she had ever seen.

She loved the great glass dome and its sweepingly majestic design. Finding a bench at her favourite spot, in front of the palm house, she watched, through banks of daffodils and carefully managed borders of primulas, people coming and going. She thought they all seemed to have more purposeful lives than the one she was living.

Mostly it was women wearing headscarves and gabardine coats against the unpredictable weather who were visiting the gardens with their prams and small children.

Ellen felt sure they had never known a tragedy like hers.

There were also working men around, using the gardens as a shortcut through to the busier Ormeau Road.

Some wore knitted pullovers, there was an occasional more formal collar and tie, but most shirts were collarless, and an occasional hint of braces was visible.

Then there were the smartly dressed men in business suits and briefcases. What she noticed missing was the contrast.

'Here we are,' she said to Teresa, her unblinkingly wide-eyed baby. 'In the Botanic Gardens, just off the Malone Road, one of the most exclusive areas in Belfast and there is no evidence at all of 'other class', simply none.

'Where is all the big money? The nannies, the chauffeurs, the fur coats? It's like everyone's about the same here. Nice, though I never was part of the moneyed set and we wouldn't want a nanny for you anyway, would we, my darling?'
'Sure, are ye all alone here with this lovely wee we'an?'

Ellen's one-sided conversation was interrupted by the enquiry, the owner of the voice casting a shadow over them both. She looked up to see the rear view of a woman she didn't recognise, bent over and peering into the pram. Gripping the handlebars of the pram tightly she stood up.

'I was waiting for someone, but they appear to have been delayed, so I must get home now.'
'Ah, sure, no need to be disturbed, missus, it's just that I haven't seen you here before and I thought you might like some company. I'm going into the tearoom there, will you join me? The name's Jean.'
Ellen was reluctant to get involved with a stranger, but not sure how to refuse without seeming rude. She also wondered whether she might enjoy some company. Following the woman's determined stride across the path, she steered the pram between the stiff herbaceous borders to the tearooms.

Once seated in the steamy glass-roofed restaurant, at a table by the window, Ellen introduced herself.
'Ah, so you're new to Belfast, then? Thought you sounded English. What brings you here?'
'I'm over with my husband, Eddie. We've actually been living in Northern Ireland for nearly three years.

'Settling in then are ye, missus?'

'We are looking for a better place, what with the baby and everything. We need a garden, some fresh air and I thought, living in Ireland, there would at least be chickens. Well, you know, fresh eggs and sheep in the fields everywhere.'

'This is a city, a fine city it is too, but no chickens here. And what's the wee girl's name? Is she your first? I had four myself, but they've all up and gone now, one to America and three to Scotland.'

Ellen felt swept along by Jean's conversation and decided that she wouldn't say anything, assuming a response was not expected. Still, she was glad of the company and the newly arrived pot of hot tea. Teresa began to whimper. Lifting the baby from the pram, she pushed back the knitted pink bonnet and gently kissed the top of her downy head, before moving the small body onto her shoulder.

'Her name's Teresa, I lost her little brother two months ago, meningitis. So no, she's not my first but she is my only one now.' Ellen swallowed hard and felt her eyes pricking and a tickle in her nose.

'Ah, missus, sorry for your trouble. That's hard, so it is. Please God, you'll have another wee boy soon to take his place.'

'No, never. No little boy will ever take his place. He is our little angel and he's buried here in Belfast and wherever we go now he'll never leave, never.'

With tears running down her face, she wiped her nose and cheeks with her only spare hand and then put both arms protectively across Teresa's back, as though to melt the small body into her own warmth to keep her safe. Jean's earlier insensitivity disappeared and now she listened anxiously to Ellen's story, her eyes wide with sympathy.

'Let me take her for a minute while you drink your tea, missus. Ellen, did you say? And dry your eyes; we'll talk about something nice.'

Reluctantly handing Teresa over to Jean, watching closely until she could satisfy herself that she was being held correctly, Ellen drank her tea and wiped her face with a handkerchief.

'D'you get out much, Ellen? Wi' no family here it must be lonely. Ye could get a job easy enough.'

'Not really, not with Teresa, and I'd not leave her, and anyway my husband has a good job, thank you.'

'Well, I can set you up with a little cleaning job, offices and the like, and ye can work evenings. How's that sound? Most women are looking for a wee bit of a job in Belfast these days; you can take it or leave it, I say. It's no odds to me.'

'I was a secretary in London, Jean, I worked for a big jewellery company and I earned good money. I've never thought of doing a cleaning job in my life but thank you anyway.'

'Would you consider taking in another baby then? There's a great need for short stays. The girls in the Nazareth home, or St. Gregory's, go back to their families sometimes before their child can be placed for adoption. You could take a little one in for a while and get paid.'

'I'd love to do that, really I would, but we haven't the place, it's too small. What I really want to do is get out of the city, into the countryside, and bring my child up there. I really didn't leave London for a place like this.'

Jean's face flushed with the perceived insult.

'Look'it missus, I know it's been hard on you but that's not our fault. Belfast is a magnificent city, so it is, and your sort should be grateful to be here. We didn't ask you to come remember that. An' with your la-di-dah fancy ways, I was only trying to help.'

'I'm not la-di-dah, I'm just ordinary, but maybe I'll not stay and listen, if that's how you think of us. Here is a contribution towards the tea bill. I really must be going now.'

Ellen, face flushed with anger, put Teresa in the pram, leaving a sixpence on the table and elbowed her way out through the swing doors, across the park for home. She felt misunderstood and lonely as she manoeuvred the heavy pram up the hill. She didn't want to stay in Belfast any longer and hoped Eddie would take the decision for her.

Teresa was whimpering so she stopped and bent over the pram to comfort her. As she looked up, she was surprised to see a car parked outside the greengrocer's house, a small black Ford Anglia. Curiosity got the better of her and she walked faster, straining her eyes to pick out the details of the woman sitting in the driver's seat. She was smoking a cigarette, her greying blond hair was tucked under a violet felt hat, secured by a glittering black hatpin in the shape of a butterfly. And there was definitely something familiar about her. Still unable to place her, Ellen looked straight ahead, not wanting to be accused of staring.

'Ellen, is that you?' A soft Cork accent called through the wound down car window.
'It's me, Agnes, your Auntie Agnes, your Mammy's sister. We met in London at your wedding – remember?
'Of course! How lovely to see you!'
'I've been out here waiting for you since midday. I was hoping we could go and have a bite of dinner together somewhere but it's a bit late now. Will you invite me in, so?'
Settled in Ellen and Eddie's room, cold hands warming around cups of tea, Agnes, looking younger without the felt hat and cigarette, began to explain her reason for the visit.

'I'm going to be running a small hotel on the North coast, just outside Castlerock. It's a lovely place and a male friend offered me the lease, so I took it.

'Do you remember me telling you about my catering qualification? Well, I really enjoy the cooking and baking side of things. Oh, that reminds me, there's a cake for your tea in the tin in the back of the car, shall I go and get it now?'

'Well, how lovely, Agnes. Yes, please, I'm no use at all at that sort of thing.'

Whilst Agnes was downstairs getting the cake, Ellen began to wonder about the reason for the sudden visit. Maybe her mother, Kitty, had sent her? Looking down through the window she saw Agnes, wearing a bright red pair of sunglasses even though the day was overcast, looking rather glamorous and leaning against the side of the car, smoking another cigarette. A smile broke across Ellen's face. Her facial muscles felt stiff and unfamiliar, she realised that it was her first smile in a long time.

By the time Agnes returned with the cake tin, Ellen had fed and changed Teresa and opened a tin of corned beef for the evening meal which, she decided, would now feed three.

Slim and groomed, her guest looked out of place in the small sparsely furnished room, but Ellen was so pleased to have one of her own relatives in her home she didn't feel the need to deploy her usual defensive attitude.

'Agnes, it's so good to see you but do tell me why you are here. I had no idea you were in the north; Cork is such a long way away. Does Mam know?'

'Well, is there another cup of tea and we'll cut that cake, Ellen? Then I'll tell you, as I've a favour to ask and the favour should wait until Eddie's home, otherwise I'll have to ask twice. Let me hold this darling babby while you go down and make the tea.'

So the afternoon unfolded. Between cake, tea and admiring the baby, Agnes explained how she was struggling to cope with all the work involved in running the hotel.

'It's not really a hotel, Ellen, only eight guest bedrooms, but that can be sixteen breakfasts when we are full. And they all want their eggs cooked differently, especially the Americans.'

Reading between the lines, Ellen realised that when Eddie arrived Agnes might be asking for help to run the hotel. And with the offer of accommodation, real space and a garden. Fresh sea air for Teresa and maybe some green fields close by. Although that seemed a tempting prospect, she thought she should share her plans with Agnes before any more was said. 'We are leaving here. It has been decided. The people aren't what I'm used to, I don't understand them, and they don't understand me. And Ireland's really not like Eddie told me'.

Agnes looked surprised by the outburst but sipped her tea, raising her eyebrows as she considered the petulant young woman before her, saying no more about the hotel.

It was not long until Eddie swung in the door, filling the room and, dropping his canvas bag on the floor, wearily sat down and removed his heavy boots. He seemed really pleased to see Agnes and they were soon exchanging a gentle banter, seeming a lot more comfortable in each other's company than Ellen had expected.

'OK, out with it, Agnes, what's the story?'

'Straight up, I need your help. I've the lease on a lovely hotel facing the sea. Oceanview, it's called, and it really does have an ocean view across to Donegal. It's fully booked from April to September and I can't do it all on my own.
'I've plenty of accommodation, in what they used to call the staff quarters but I'll call it the family quarters and if you would consider coming out to Castlerock for the season I'd be very grateful. You are family after all, the only family I have in the north right now.'

'Well, Agnes, Ellen has been on about going back to London, so whatever you say, once she has her mind made up that's it. But thank you for the offer. It would have been great to have a decent place to live, so near the sea and not far from my family. But I dare say we'll have to pass that up and we'll be in back in London before ye' know it.'

Ellen realised that Eddie had now put her in the uncomfortable position of admitting she had been wrong.

'Oh yes. That's him alright, it'll be my fault now if we don't go to Castlerock but I can see he wants to, which means I have to change my mind. Well, I'll never do that, so he can take it or leave it.'

The atmosphere in the small flat was tense. Ellen excused herself, muttering Agnes an invitation to stay for the evening meal whilst she went down to the shared kitchen to cook and hope that somehow Eddie would devise a compromise without her having to lose face altogether.

Returning with a dish of corned beef hash and a handful of cutlery, she found Eddie and Agnes sharing a bottle of stout, she thought it was probably the one she had been keeping for Christmas, and studying the ground plans of what appeared to be the Oceanview Hotel, with Teresa snuggled comfortably on Agnes's lap.

Ellen sighed with relief as Eddie lifted the baby from Agnes asking, 'And how is my wee girl? Ready for a trip to the seaside?' The decision appeared to have been made.

Chapter 9.

Ellen. Castlerock, Northern Ireland,1951

The September sea was swelling with autumn tides, the clouds were lower in the sky and the bookings were slowing down. At Oceanview the team were also slowing down.

Agnes, a good cook and an even better baker, dealt competently with the breakfasts while Ellen's role as 'front of house' gave her the opportunity to meet a range of people and lifestyles; something she had missed since leaving London. For the first time in several years, she was feeling at home.

Never one to relish cooking or cleaning she focussed on the more decorative side of housekeeping, developing what she considered to be some quite impressive flower arranging skills. She stopped mentioning her plan of returning to London, or of Eddie and herself moving to a place of their own, although it was generally understood that that would be the next step.

Baby Teresa, now a year old, was a healthy child and Ellen's fear that she might contract the disease that killed her little brother was subsiding.

Ellen and Eddie saved most of their wages, they still hoped for a farm one day.

For now, they had managed to buy their own pram at last, a Silver Cross, as recommended by the style-conscious Kitty, and it turned the small rear kitchen-garden into a safe place for the child to sleep outside.

They listened anxiously when, during the last week of the season, Agnes began to discuss vague plans of what she would be doing during the winter.

'I'll probably close Oceanview up and go back to Drimoleague for a few months. See all my nephews and nieces. Then I think I'll take Roisin over to Cork or maybe even to Dublin for a few days. Since her husband doesn't like to travel any more, she lives a quiet life.'

'What will you do for Christmas then, Auntie Agnes?'

'Ah, for Christmas I'm invited to Birmingham, where Michael and Gina live now, so that will be a nice change. I'd have liked to spend some time with Kitty and Will, but it's unlikely. Of course, I'll see them next year at Daisy's wedding anyway.'

She never, Ellen noticed, included Eddie, Teresa or herself in any plans. This worried Ellen as she knew there was plenty of opportunity to tell them what was happening.

The afternoons were usually quiet, and the two women often went across the road to the beach with Teresa, but Ellen wouldn't ask, and Agnes didn't seem inclined to clarify.

'There is so much to do and see here. It's no wonder they call it Northern Ireland's favourite tourist destination', Ellen had written in one of her regular letters to Kitty. *'We took the train one day, from Castlerock to Derry City. It was worth it just for the ride. The train runs close along the coast all the way, then goes through a tunnel cut into the rock face. The scenery is stunning, Mum. The open fields and the wild spaces remind me of Wales and Teresa loves it here.'*

On the afternoon before the last guests left Ellen and Agnes prepared an elaborate picnic to celebrate their final day. Cold ham, homemade chutney, fresh wheaten bread – made by Agnes – treacle biscuits, and a flask of tea were all packed in a basket.

Woollen tartan rugs and a couple of cushions completed the requirements for an end of summer treat. They decided to picnic at nearby Mussenden Temple, an ancient disused small building, its dome majestically rising above the windswept headland around half a mile from the guesthouse.

It sat within the ruins of a bishop's palace and due to its stunning location was widely considered a go-to landmark by locals and by tourists.

The two women climbed the steep slope carefully, sharing Teresa between them. She was crawling now but couldn't be expected to navigate the rough ground on her hands and knees. As they walked over to the headland they speculated about the ancient bishop's community, how well they must have lived, in such luxury compared to those around them.

'Life would have been very hard two hundred years ago, wouldn't it, Agnes? I guess fishing and a bit of farming land coupled with high taxes made sure there was no energy for a revolution.'

'No change there then, the Church always did and always will have the best locations for its properties.'
'Don't say anything like that in front of Mum; she's very keen on the church.'

'I know Ellen, she always was. They'd turn in their graves now, those old bishops, if they could see us talking about them and picnicking on blankets right under their old broken-down temple.'
Ellen didn't respond. She was looking out over the Atlantic, past where the waves were crashing onto the rocks and across at the faint outlines of Magilligan Strand and then to the even fainter Donegal horizon.

'You don't know how lucky you are, Agnes, having all this. I'd give anything to have your luck.' With a sniff and a dramatic shake of her head she busied herself with laying out the picnic, hoping to be offered some consolation.

Agnes smiled sadly saying nothing, shrugging her shoulders. They had an afternoon ahead of them and it was the last of the season, and she responded sharply,
'Maybe it's you who don't know how lucky you are Ellen. Ever thought of that?'

She lit a cigarette and sat on the rug, propping herself on one elbow while watching Teresa pulling at the rough grass and squeezing the heads of any tiny yellow flowers embedded in the scrub.

They ate the picnic quietly, without much conversation, except the occasional 'This is nice, Agnes, you must teach me how to bake bread', or 'Here, wee girl, you'll mess your lovely dress if you dribble that biscuit. Mammy won't want that.'
There were long silences filled with unspoken words and Ellen was relieved when Agnes began to pack the blankets and baskets away. Handing Ellen the picnic paraphernalia to carry, Agnes lifted Teresa from the blanket and heaved the small body onto her hip, preparing for the walk down through the rough ground.

'I'll miss you, little girlie, I hope you remember that when I'm not here.'
Ellen didn't know what to make of Agnes's cool remarks but as she followed her down the rocky path, she began to think Agnes might have been right. Maybe she should count herself fortunate. Maybe life didn't owe her anything.

In bed that night, she turned to her husband.
'What'll we do Eddie, when she puts us out of here, where will we go?'
It seemed like Eddie had had his answer prepared for some time.

'Wherever you want to go, Ellen. I thought you were only staying here for the season. Then did you not want to go back to London? We can spend Christmas with your family in Kilburn and I'll look for work again.'

'I don't really want that anymore, Eddie, I love it here and Teresa does too. Maybe I can look for work in the village.'

'Naw, that wouldn't work at all, Ellen. There's no work for ye here, we'll go back, so we will.'

'Please ask her, Eddie, ask her for our Teresa's sake. We could have more children here too.'

'I'll think about it, now go to sleep.'

Eddie, she noticed, took no time at all to sleep whilst it evaded her, every time she closed her eyes her mind began whirling, a confetti of worries making her heart race.

After a couple of hours, she got up and walked across to the front window, gazing pensively out across the ocean. The noise of the seagulls could be deafening in daylight but at night all she could hear was the sea. She was not looking forward to whatever change was about to take place. She'd miss the sound of the sea, she'd miss Oceanview, with its setting high above the foreshore, and, she noted, surprised at the thought which appeared unbidden but clear, she would miss Agnes.

The poor night's sleep left her tired in the morning and when she checked out the last few remaining guests, closing the register, she felt sad. Not taking her usual care to wave her guests goodbye from the front door she simply shut the double entrance behind her.

Hearing Agnes call her, she feared what was coming. Usually at this time they discussed what needed to be done for the rest of the day but that wouldn't, of course, apply this morning.

Ellen, hoping at least to share a freshly brewed pot of tea with her aunt walked alongside Teresa who was speedily navigating the highly polished wooden floor on hands and knees.

In the front room, "the parlour", Agnes was standing by the window with her back to the door. She spoke without turning around. To Ellen, that felt ominous.

'Come in, Ellen and close the door, I don't want any interruptions now. I've important matters to discuss with you before Eddie comes home. It's you are family, remember, not him.' Ellen's heart was thudding and she pulled Teresa up onto her knee, moving to sit at the nearest smartly upholstered armchair. There didn't seem to be any tea.

Agnes turned round to face Ellen at last. In her smart calf length skirt and silky jacket she could have been preparing for a city visit and her attire looked incongruous in the seaside guesthouse. She walked slowly over to the window where her slim outline showed up dark against the mid-morning autumn sunshine, streaming in between the gap in the heavy velvet curtains.
Ellen felt sure that the smart clothes and dramatic setting had been designed specifically to make her feel uncomfortable.
'Let me say how much I have enjoyed your being here this summer, Ellen, and how fond I am of you all. Let me also say that I would never want to interfere with anyone's plans or lifestyle, and certainly not the plans of the people I love.'
'So I'll come straight to the point, and please don't look so worried, child, your face is white as a sheet. I am renewing the lease on Oceanview next year and having looked at the accounts, I can see it is making a good enough profit for me to employ a caretaker over the winter.
'I have made plans for myself too and I don't want to stay here without the business. So, a caretaker will move in.'

'What will he do, Auntie Agnes?'

'He will be required to redecorate where necessary, get the equipment serviced, and renewed or repaired, sort out the garden so there is little or no maintenance during our busy periods and keep the building safe, secured, and aired until I come back.'

'When are you coming back then?'

'In March, child. He will arrive at the end of October and stay until the middle of March. I will start the bookings again come April first. I have friends to meet and a social life to pick up, which I had no time for during the summer. In fact, I'll be out for lunch today.'

'Why are you telling me all this, Agnes? You know we wanted to stay and would have done anything if only we could have called this home. I'm a good worker, well, anyway I could be, you know that. I love the garden, the chickens... Have you even thought about the chickens, Agnes?'

'Yes Ellen, I have thought about the chickens.'

'And I expect I could decorate. Eddie would have worked on the guesthouse for us when he's not on the building site and together we would have had it spick and span for you when you came back.'

'Ellen, dry your eyes now, no need to upset yourself so.'

'Why do you want a stranger instead of your own family? I just don't understand. And where are we to go, Auntie Agnes, where are we to go next?'

Agnes moved to sit beside Ellen, who was rifling, unsuccessfully, in her pocket for something with which to blow her nose.

Passing her a clean handkerchief then putting her arm around her and stroking Teresa's head, with a fond smile she continued,

'Ellen, if you want the job it's yours. This winter and every winter while I have the lease. But I have to be sure it's what you want. No resentment, no what-ifs.'

'I do want the job, Agnes, I just told you.'

'Nothing would please me more than to keep your little family here with me in Castlerock, working with me in Oceanview for as long as you want to stay. But it's you has to want it, Ellen, not me.' Ellen couldn't believe her ears, or her luck.

She hugged Agnes tightly.

'Home at last!' she choked the words somewhat dramatically. Agnes raised an eyebrow as she smoothed her skirt over her knee .

Epilogue

Two months later

There were just a few days to go before Christmas and the dust sheets, so recently placed over the furniture, were coming off.

As agreed, Agnes had left Oceanview at the end of the season to spend some time back in her West Cork home.

She'd been to Dublin with Roisin and then promised to return for a few days before setting off for her Christmas visit to Birmingham.

Now Ellen and Eddie had a surprise for her. There were to be friends from England and a party, mostly, but not entirely, in Agnes's honour. In fact, for all of them it would be something of a family celebration.

The past two months had been taken up with deep cleaning and re-decorating, although they still managed some time to enjoy watching the early winter storms and take walks across the windswept beach.

They always looked towards Oceanview as a safe haven when they battled their way back across the strand.

All eight bedrooms were needed for the party and Ellen and Eddie shared the preparations. Beds had been made up and there had been much making of lists – plenty of lists – for festive food.

There were to be huge fresh bunches of winter greenery in vases in every room and Teresa, now walking, followed them as they worked their way through the empty house, seeming to be just as excited as her parents.

The kitchen cupboards had been filled and a ham ordered from the local butchers. A sack full of potatoes, fresh from the McCann farm, had been delivered. There was also a turkey, ready hung and plucked, and more eggs had been promised if needed to supplement Ellen's hens.

Before she left, Agnes had made a Christmas pudding and a rich dark fruitcake. Both were safely wrapped in the cool pantry, 'in case', Agnes had reasoned enigmatically, knowing how difficult Ellen found baking.

However, she had nearly mastered the art of pastry making. Only the evening before, Ellen had made two dozen mince pies, of irregular shape and size, and stored them in tins above the cake and pudding.

She had often heard her mother praising her grandmother, Deirdre, for her skills and wished now that she had inherited that talent. She felt sure she was becoming a reasonable cook though and confident that between them they could put on a decent spread.

Ellen knew she had filled out during the season in Castlerock. The sea air as well as the exercise had given her an increased appetite, which, she told whoever noticed, accounted for her increased girth, although she and Eddie knew that was not the real explanation.

She was certainly happier than she had ever been and now that they were more settled, she thought Eddie was too. He had been distraught when his mother Margaret had died earlier in the year but enjoyed visits from his brother James, with his young wife and family.

On the morning of the party, Eddie drove to the station in Castlerock to collect Agnes from the train. Normally he would have met her at the platform on foot. The station was less than a mile from Oceanview, but Agnes had asked him to bring the car as she had extra luggage.

Left behind in Oceanview, Ellen fed Teresa and helped her climb the stairs up to her cot for a sleep. Removing her pinafore and work dress she considered her reflection in the long mirror.

Pleased with her appearance, she no longer looked like a girl. She was sure she appeared more mature, a responsible mother and wife. She stood for a moment admiring her good pair of legs, neat calves and slim ankles before slipping a grey and white spotted cotton dress over her silky full-length petticoat, smoothing the skirt over her hips.

The fine narrow belt had become tight around her waist, soon she'd have to wear looser clothing, but, she hoped, not yet. 'Now you wouldn't want Agnes to notice anything, although by the time we open in April there'll be no hiding it.'

Pulling a soft pink lambswool cardigan over the dress she thought she looked as well dressed as the stylish Agnes. 'I think the polka dots will distract the eye for now.'

Smiling contentedly, she opened her vanity box and dusted talcum powder around her neckline before applying a fresh coat of red lipstick. Brushing her hair quickly she stood back for a final check before gently closing the door behind her.

Walking through the newly prepared rooms, she felt confident that her guests would enjoy a relaxing visit. She hoped they would also be impressed with her housekeeping skills. Marvelling at how her life had turned around, she paused by the front landing and looked out over the now familiar Atlantic shoreline, wondering whether this place, which she so loved, would appear magnificent or hostile to her guests.

Oceanview's old Ford Anglia drew up outside and Ellen gasped when she saw Roisin, her godmother and Agnes's friend, step slowly and carefully out of the back. Rushing down the broad staircase and flinging open the freshly painted entrance hall doors, she almost tripped as she hurried down the steps. 'Auntie Agnes, with Roisin, how marvellous, what a lovely surprise.'

Agnes helped the older woman up the steps while Ellen, on the other side, held on to an elbow.

Not having seen Roisin since her wedding five years ago she was surprised at how fragile the older woman had become and she stayed at her elbow until she was reminded, 'Maybe a cup of tea, Ellen?'

Agnes and Roisin settled into the nearest settee, watching as Eddie brought in ever more cases.

'I didn't want to let you know I was bringing Roisin, Ed. I thought it would be a surprise, but we did need the car as you can see. We're staying a few days now then I'm going over to England and Roisin will go back with her nephew, Seamus's son. He'll make sure she gets home safely.'

Ellen tore herself away at last, soon returning from the kitchen with a tray laden with tea and misshapen mince pies.

'Oh, Roisin, I'm so excited to see you here. You'll be at the party now.'

'What party, Ellen, whatever are ye talking about, girl?' Agnes asked, sounding confused.
'Secret, Agnes, it's supposed to be a secret.'

'Never could keep one to yourself could you, my darling wife?' laughed Eddie.

Ellen explained that she was preparing a surprise for Agnes and Agnes explained that hers for Ellen was Roisin. It was generally accepted that the surprises had worked out well all round.
Roisin's attention was on Ellen. She had so much to tell. Her new home was close to Hannah's house, where Deirdre, Ellen's grandmother, long since widowed, now lived. Deirdre was still her great friend and made Roisin and her husband Michael feel very much part of the family.

'I retired from teaching a long time ago, of course, Ellen, but it was a wonderful career for me. Moving up from teacher to headmistress, then more teachers and better education for the girls, Oh, I had it very well indeed.

I wasn't asked to leave when I married either, Father Daley put in a good case for me to stay. There was, you know, quite a scandal about him, the parish priest, many years later. He just couldn't stay away from the women and in the end someone, not me I assure you, reported him to the bishop and that was that.'

The following day, Roisin slept late whilst Agnes and Ellen prepared food for that evening's meal.

'It's meant to be a surprise, but can you make sure we have enough for ten now? And some children too...I don't want to say any more and as we've been told, I'm no good at keeping secrets.'

'Is that so, girl?' murmured Agnes, her eyes on Ellen's increased waistline.

Ellen's eyes were on the weather. She had seen Eddie off in the car mid-morning, giving him a packed lunch, hoping his journey to meet the ferry in Belfast would be uneventful. At midday, taking advantage of a break in the weather, Ellen and Agnes walked out together across the strand, leaving Roisin indoors with Teresa.

They gathered small pieces of driftwood and shells, which they used to decorate the long table, adding a splash of festive colour with some red berries amongst the holly branches. Ellen was delighted when the tall vases full of greenery, which she had arranged in all the bedrooms, were admired. She really hoped Agnes was beginning to see her as a valuable partner at Oceanview.

By dusk, the dining room looked impressive. The eight breakfast tables had all been pushed together and, covered in white sheets, it looked ready for a banquet.

A couple of hours before Eddie was due home the front doorbell was heard across the hallway, with such a loud insistent clamour, that Ellen, fearing it would disturb Roisin, who was having a lie down, moved quickly.

She was beaten to the door by Agnes and could only stand back and watch as the tall dark American stepped inside, telling her he had been invited for the party and introducing himself as, 'Herbert Bailey, one of Eddie McCann's greatest friends.'

Looking past him, she saw the tail lights of the taxi disappear in the late twilight leaving a small neat woman, who looked a few years her senior, gazing anxiously towards the front of the guesthouse. A little boy, about seven or eight years old, with tight curly hair and coffee coloured complexion was pulling her hand towards the door. There was also a smaller child, a little girl, who looked a bit older than Teresa but still not confident enough to step forward on her own, hugging the hem of her mother's coat.

The woman was shivering slightly, and as her maroon coat and hat were more than adequate for the early evening and the weather was only a little blustery, not particularly cold, Ellen thought she was probably anxious.

'Come in, please do. You must be Iris? I've heard so much about you. Bring the children in before they get cold.'

Quickly responding to Ellen's invitation, they all moved inside. Their arrival might have blown the cover on the surprise, but Agnes, as ever, looked calm and unflustered as she ushered Bailey, Iris, and the children in to join Roisin, who certainly wasn't going to stay upstairs resting when there were people to meet.

Ellen looked curiously towards Iris as she offered tea again and orange squash for the children.

Delighted to meet those friends of Eddie's at last, she had been intensely interested in their affairs since Eddie showed her the letter all those years ago.

Ellen had always credited herself with persuading Eddie to seek out Bailey and so she had been keen for them all to meet up. When they heard the family would be in the area a few days before Christmas, staying with Iris's mother in Ballymoney, she'd insisted they be included in the party.

Gathering up the used tea-tray from the lounge whilst the children warmed themselves by the fire she heard Bailey complimenting Roisin and Agnes on their hospitality and beautiful home and knew that she was going to like him very much.

Iris joined Ellen in the kitchen, where she held out a cardboard box, saying quietly,

'This is for Eddie, especially from my mother. It's a fruitcake.'

'Why how lovely Iris, thank you so much.'

'She said I was to give it directly to Eddie and tell him she is so grateful to him for everything. She said it all started when he brought her the eggs from his mother all those years ago. And now we are married, and she has two grandchildren, all thanks to Eddie.'

'And me too, Iris. It was me who told him to go and fetch Bailey.'

'Yes, of course, Ellen. Sorry I forgot that.'

'How is your mother, Iris? Eddie did speak fondly of her, but a bit anxiously also, I think.'

'Happier now she lives on her own. She left my father some years ago, he was a bully, Ellen. Sadly, many of her friends, and the neighbours too, blame her for how he was and so her life can be a bit lonely.'

While Ellen and Iris worked comfortably together, setting another tray of tea, deciding to use the mince pies Ellen had made rather than the fruitcake, agreeing that it should be left for Eddie.

Ellen hoped that the difficulties the couple had probably had to overcome would be shared at some stage but for now, she was pleased to have the company of this quiet, gentle woman.

Bailey and Iris were staying overnight so after tea they took the children up to the room they would all share whilst Agnes helped finalise the preparations for the evening meal.

Ellen had baked a ham, basted with honey and mustard, which was now gently caramelising in the oven. The McCann turkey had been cooked the day before and would be served cold. The rest of the dishes just needed to be accompanied by carrots, cabbage, potatoes, and a mustard sauce, all of which, Ellen decided, should now became the responsibility of Agnes and Roisin. She busied herself with laying the mince pies out prettily on plates with delicate paper doilies and felt that she had done all her organising already. Her intention for tonight was to be seen as the front of house hostess.

Halfway through the preparations, the sound of the motor was heard spluttering outside and, once again, Agnes beat Ellen to the door. This time her greeting was completely genuine in its surprise and delight.

There stood her beloved sister Kitty, with her husband Will, slightly older and more stooped than the last time she had seen him, helping Eddie get the suitcases out of the boot. Standing against the car, waiting for her mother to be greeted first, was a slender fair-haired young woman, wearing a powder blue coat and a fashionable pillbox hat.

There could be no mistaking Daisy, who had her mother's eye for style and always turned out looking elegant. At her side was her brother Billy, a lanky teenager, all wrists and ankles. The boy had no moustache quite yet but with his father's tousled hair and clear blue eyes it was easy to see the man he would become.

'Surprise!' shouted Ellen from the hallway, 'You never guessed, did you, Agnes? All these people we love have come to our home. Doesn't it make you happy to see us all together tonight? Everyone has had a long road to travel to get here. You could say there have been many turnings.'

Every journey has to end somewhere, for now, this one ends here.